Every Witch Way but Bitten

Magical Misfits Mysteries - book 3

K.E. O'Connor

K.E. O'Connor Books

Chapter 1

We're going on a ghoul hunt

I flexed my paw and winced. All this late-night walking was taxing on the toe beans, and we'd been doing nightly midnight rambles for two weeks, often for hours.

But I didn't mention my discomfort to Zandra, my wonderful witch and bonded magic user. She had enough on her mind, without having to figure out how to fit in a paw massage for me.

Ever since her mother, Adrienne the ghoul, had broken into Vorana Stowell's house and tried to bite her, we hadn't stopped searching. And if that meant my toe beans were tender, then so be it.

"This looks promising." Zandra crouched by the remains of a small, furred rodent. "This could have been one of her feeds."

I dutifully sniffed the decaying corpse, being careful not to wrinkle my adorable booping snooter. "It's possible. There aren't any holes in the flesh to suggest a carnivore got this one."

Zandra grimaced as she rubbed her eyes and yawned.

"Let's call it a night," I said. "You're exhausted."

She stood and placed her hands on her hips, her dark gaze flicking around the densely packed trees. "And I'll remain exhausted until I find Adrienne and bring her home."

Her tone suggested I shouldn't push unless I wanted an argument. We'd had a few of those recently. "Then take a rest and eat something. You've got granola bars in your pocket."

"I'm not hungry. Let's keep moving."

Ever since Zandra had learned I'd known about Adrienne's ghoulish situation and kept it from her, things had been tense between us. Before that gray-fleshed issue arose, we'd been a strong team, but it felt like I was on shifting sand, and I didn't know how to make things right between us.

"We could try the beach again." I walked behind Zandra, the moonlight overhead just breaking through the tree branches of Crimson Cove wood. "There have been reports of a figure lurking around there at night."

"We've tried the beach several times and found nothing, and there's barely any cover for her to hide over there. The angels have had recent reports of a shadowy figure in the woods, so it makes more sense she'd be here. Better coverage, more food, and more places to hide. The beach is too exposed."

"Your mother liked fish before she was a ghoul. Maybe her taste buds haven't altered that much." Most ghouls preferred their food on two legs and screaming, but they weren't picky when hungry.

Zandra shrugged. "True. Even though she was always trying to go vegetarian, she had a weakness for scales."

I understood that. It was my particular passion, too. Although the amount of fishy treats I'd received in the last two weeks had gone down, and I'd resisted the urge to do midnight raids on the treat jar, in case it annoyed my witch.

I needed to make things right between me and Zandra, and if that meant finding Adrienne, then I would. I'd walk through these woods for a hundred years to make things better.

"We should be careful about going much farther," I said. "We're heading into Cannibal Bill's territory."

Zandra huffed a breath out through her nose. "He's an urban legend. Vorana was messing with us when she said there's a real live cannibal in the woods."

"She seemed serious to me. And his hut is right around here." I lifted my booping snooter and sniffed. There was a faint tang of something half-dead in the air, and I didn't think it was ghoul.

"Vorana made up that story to get me to take a night off. I know you're all working against me." Zandra marched off, her arms swinging as if she was in a speed walking contest and the finish line was within sight.

I trotted in front of her and pressed a paw against her leg to stop her from getting away. "No one is working against you. We all want the same thing."

"Yet you hid important information from me. If I'd known Adrienne was back and changed, I could have helped her."

"What would you have done? I couldn't find her, and I can find anybody. She's keeping a low profile for a reason. Maybe she doesn't want you to find her." When Adrienne had burst into Vorana's home, the shame in her eyes had been clear. This ghoul still had some humanity, and seeing the stunned expression on her only daughter's face had been humiliating. No wonder she'd gone to ground to lick her wounds.

Zandra sighed. "Juno, we've talked about this. We're a team. Teams don't keep secrets from each other. That was a huge secret, and I should have known about it. You were wrong to hide it from me." She tugged on the ends of her dark hair, a sure sign she was stressed.

I risked hopping onto her shoulder and rubbed my face against hers. "I thought I was doing the right thing. I am sorry. I didn't want you worried until I knew exactly what was going on."

"I can handle worry. And I know you think I have a lot to learn, but I understand more than you realize. I was on my own for a long time before you showed up and started bossing me about."

"I never boss, simply gently steer when you go off-course." I slid her a glance out of the corner of my eye. Zandra thought she knew the ways of the world, but with her scattered upbringing and the use of an age-up spell, she'd missed important educational moments. It was one of the many reasons I was so protective of her.

She gently lifted me off her shoulder and placed me on the ground. "Let's keep looking. We'll stay out until midnight, and if we find nothing by then, we'll go home."

I wanted to keep debating with her, but we'd had this conversation many times over the last fourteen days. It made my toe beans tingle unpleasantly at the thought that I'd never make things right between us.

"Just watch out for Cannibal Bill's traps," I said. "I believed Vorana when she said he digs holes and sets them with spikes and hangs enchanted nets to catch the local wildlife."

"Sure. Keep moving."

We walked along the path in silence for ten minutes.

I slowed as I spotted large indentations on the ground. "This looks like more of those big cat tracks." I sniffed around them.

"Recent?"

"The scent is faded. Maybe a couple of days old."

"Some people have big cat familiars," Zandra said. "And there are plenty of wild animals living in the woods, too."

Which was another reason I didn't want Zandra out here in the dark. I took note of the print. I'd seen a few of these around since we'd been searching the woods, but I'd yet to meet who they belonged to. Whoever they were, they were large and possibly came with dangerous fangs I wanted nowhere near Zandra.

There was a rustle of branches up ahead. I froze to the spot, and my ears pricked.

"Did you see where that came from?" Zandra whispered, her gaze scanning the woods.

"Up ahead on our right." I carefully sniffed for a clue as to our sneaky lurker. Whatever it was, it was something large, since the branches that moved were seven feet above our heads.

Zandra cast a small light ball and held it in her palm.

For a second, a huge black shadow was illuminated, but then it vanished. There was a thud, a muttered curse, and then pounding footsteps heading away from us.

Before I could warn Zandra to be careful, she was racing after the ominous shadow. Or rather, whatever had caused that shadow. That very big shadow.

"Zandra, that's not Adrienne. It's way too big." Now the lurker was on the move, I caught a wet dog scent in the air. Possibly a werewolf?

Zandra didn't respond or slow down, leaving me with no choice but to chase her. As I loped along, I noticed enormous footprints in the soil. They were humanlike but too big to be your average human print.

"Slow down! It could be a werewolf." Although the footprints were the wrong shape, I was still panicked. Maybe it was a partially changed werewolf. Never a safe thing to be around. Werewolves always felt vulnerable when they were mid-change, and that vulnerability caused blood to spill.

"Werewolves don't run from anything," Zandra said over her shoulder. "And if this creature is living in the woods, it could have seen Adrienne."

Whatever the creature was, it had headed off the main path, and we had no choice but to slow as the undergrowth grew thicker. The moon was no longer visible, and only Zandra's light ball allowed us to see where we were going.

We came to a small clearing and paused. A faint path led off in two directions.

"You head around to the left. I'll go right. I can't hear movement, so it's hiding somewhere near here," Zandra said.

"Let's leave the creature alone. We probably startled it. It won't know anything about Adrienne. And it could be dangerous. I don't want you getting hurt."

She glared at me and then stalked away.

Reluctantly, I followed her order, keeping my booping snooter close to the ground. There was definitely the same wet dog scent around here.

There was a yelp and a grunt, followed by several curses from Zandra.

I charged across the clearing, my heart catching in my throat as I found her in a heap in the dirt, one hand on her head.

With a nimble bound, I landed on her lap and sniffed her face. "What happened? Did you fall?"

"Whatever we were tracking, it knows how to use tools. It used a tree branch to smack me in the head. It hid behind that tree." She pointed ahead of her. "Swung at me like I was a baseball."

Rage trickled from the tip of my tail through to my toe beans, and magic sparked around me. No one hurt my witch and got away with it.

Zandra tentatively touched the growing lump on her forehead. "I'm okay. There's no need to go into obliteration mode."

My magic didn't agree, and it continued to sparkle over me in pale red waves. My job as Zandra's familiar was to keep her safe, not let some monstrous shadow beast whack her in the head and leave her in the dirt.

Zandra hovered a hand over my head, her expression full of curiosity. "Your magic has felt different lately. It's like you've had a super charge. What have you done to make it so strong?"

I held in my rage to avoid my magic blasting out. This was another secret I kept from Zandra. "I'm the same as always. I'm just angry anyone dared hurt you. We should have stayed together."

She sighed and lowered her hand, gently stretching her neck from side to side. "I have to find Adrienne. She's here somewhere, and I must talk to her. I have to be certain she's still in control."

"All the evidence we're finding suggests she is. Your mother was always extraordinary, and even now she's a ghoul, she'll be just as unique." Most ghouls became mindless slaves with no ability to think for themselves, but my brief encounters with Adrienne after she'd been turned suggested she was different. She had some impulse control with her feeding urges, and she recognized people she had a bond with and did her best not to hurt them. It gave me hope there was something we could do for her when we finally found her.

Because if there wasn't, Angel Force had the power to destroy her. No questions asked. And that would devastate Zandra.

Zandra picked up a leaf and twirled it between her fingers. "I've been thinking about getting in touch with some of the Crypt witches. Maybe asking for help. Tempest keeps saying she's overdue a visit, and they've encountered just about every weird situation going."

My witch's relationship with her family was twisty. Her father had been under the influence of powerful magic when he'd met Adrienne, and Zandra resulted from their troubled union. There'd been plenty of sticky situations when the family reconnected, and I was certain there were more to come.

"They'd be happy to help you," I said. "Why don't you reach out to them? They could have advice about the ghoul situation."

She lifted her shoulders. "I have no clue how to tell my dad his former girlfriend is a ghoul. And... I don't want to look like a failure. I left Willow Tree Falls and set up home here partly to show them I was capable. They're so smothering."

"They smothered because they cared. And they missed out on a lot of your childhood."

"So did I," she muttered.

I bit my tongue. She'd made the decision to use an age-up spell on herself, and she had good reasons for it, but we couldn't turn back time - well, technically, I could - so there was no use dwelling.

"You do what you think best. And just so you know, you're not a failure. That would be impossible, because you never give up trying. The only time a person truly fails is when they raise their hands and admit defeat. And I've never seen you do that with anything."

She half-smiled. "Some call that stubborn or stupid."

"Then they know squat. Reach out for help if you need it."

Zandra raked her fingers through my fur, and I purred my appreciation. "We'll figure all this out. And I know you thought you were doing the right thing by keeping information from me, but I wish you hadn't. I feel like you don't trust me."

"I'm sorry about that, too. And I do trust you. I know we're a team."

"Then let's act like one, shall we?"

I was leaning in for more pets when a branch snapped.

My fur puffed up, and I whirled around, my magic sparking. "The creature's back." I raced off, ignoring Zandra's protests. I'd teach this monster a lesson. It hurt my witch, and that was unacceptable. I had a streak of benevolence in me when I chose to use it, but not when it came to anyone harming Zandra.

I lasered in on the shuffling sounds close by. The creature must have come back to see if Zandra was still alive. Perhaps it wanted to eat her.

I growled low in my chest at the thought of anyone damaging her.

As a high branch was pushed back and a shape revealed itself, I unfurled my ancient power, leaped into the air, latched onto a well-muscled arm, and shredded.

Chapter 2

Awkward!

"What the heck! Juno! Get off me. What are you doing to my wing?"

My rage haze had me so focused on destruction, it took me a few seconds to see I was ripping through Finn's white angel wing. Not only that, but there was blood trickling down his arm from where my murder mittens had latched on.

"I knew Juno would eventually see through your fake good guy act and give you a beating." Torrin Conner appeared behind Finn, grinning as he took in the scene. "Bad night, kitty?"

I removed my teeth from Finn's wing and dropped to the ground. "Greetings. And apologies. I thought you were back to attack Zandra."

"Um... Nope." Finn inspected his wounded wing. "Who wants to attack her?"

I smoothed my ruffled fur, dragging in my magic so no one would get injured. "We disturbed a creature in the woods and chased it. Zandra got whacked in the head."

"Is she hurt?" Torrin's eyes flashed amber for a second, revealing his part-dragon side.

"She's conscious and annoyed. I need to get her home. We've done enough searching for one night."

Torrin examined Finn's wing. "I'm impressed with your shredding skills. You're one powerful kitty."

I accepted the compliment with good grace. He didn't know the half of it.

"You wouldn't be saying that if she'd latched onto you and torn through your scales." Finn wore a rare scowl on his handsome face. "How will I explain this injury at work tomorrow? The boss will think I'm making excuses not to fly."

"No change there," Torrin said.

"You can say the most powerful cat you've ever encountered taught you a lesson." I licked a paw and ran it across the top of my head.

Torrin roared out a laugh. "The other angels would love that. Juno, you're something else." He reached down and tickled between my ears. "Should we go check on Zandra?"

"There's no need." Zandra stomped over, her steps wobbly. It was the first time we'd all been together since Adrienne's transformation had been revealed to her. "Are you two following me?"

Torrin raised his hands and took a step back, flashing a glance at Finn. "Not guilty. I'm just following orders."

Her disbelieving glare had a cut glass edge to it. "Then why are you in the same part of the woods as me?"

"That would be my fault." Finn finally stopped inspecting his wing.

"I'm not talking to you," Zandra said.

"You're talking to me, though, right?" Torrin said. "I did nothing wrong."

"You're almost as bad as Finn. You both knew about Adrienne, and you didn't tell me what was going on."

"To avoid upsetting you." Torrin glanced at me and waggled his eyebrows. "We figured it was for the best."

"I know what's best for me," Zandra said. "And it's my mother who's been turned into a ghoul. I've had to deal with her escapades all my life, so this is nothing new."

"Yeah, but turning into a ghoul is more than an escapade." Finn tucked his injured wing out of the way. "You need help with this."

Zandra huffed out a breath and crossed her arms over her chest. When my witch had a grudge, she could hold it for a long time.

"Blame me," I said. "Finn came to me after discovering Adrienne's purse at the ghoul factory, and I told him I wanted to investigate. And then when Torrin said he'd seen Adrienne on the beach, I needed to know how bad her condition was before giving you the news."

"And we know better than to ignore Juno when she makes a suggestion not to do something." Finn pointed at his torn wing. "We all know she's got a little somethin' somethin' in those adorable murder mittens."

Zandra sighed. "You've told me this already, but I'm not a child. I can't do anything useful if I don't know what's going on."

I kept my mouth closed. This wasn't the first time we'd bashed heads over the fact Zandra missed ten years of being a child and figuring out how the world worked. It meant she could be overly emotional and dove into things without giving them due consideration. But this was the wrong time to point that out, or if I did, I wouldn't get any supper and the treat jar would be banished to the trash.

"So, why are you here?" Zandra said.

"I'm on an Angel Force mission," Finn said.

I cocked my head. "At this time of night? Did a criminal escape?"

Torrin lifted his gaze to the sky. "It's even worse than that."

My hackles rose. Were there more dangers in these woods I needed to protect Zandra from?

Finn shoved his hands into his jeans pockets. "We're looking for winged, speckled scarabs. The dancing kind."

I swished my tail. "What do you want with them?"

"The boss has a VIP guest arriving, and she's obsessed with them. Cythera wants them to perform at tomorrow's welcome event."

"Has Cythera ever encountered winged, speckled scarabs?"

"Not that I know of. She told me to get some who'd agree to perform. She issued the order, so I got to work."

"With his trusty sidekick," Torrin said.

"Big mistake. They can't be trusted. Scarabs promise you everything and then deceive you. They're worse than genies. And if you don't use the exact phraseology when making a deal with them, you'll wind up wingless and powerless because they've taken everything."

"I've met a few," Torrin said. "They're an off-shoot of fairies, aren't they?"

"They are. Go back and tell your boss to find something more placid and reliable. Annoy a winged scarab, and Crimson Cove could be wiped out."

"Now I know you're exaggerating." Torrin rocked back on his heels, a grin on his face.

"If we don't find any soon, we'll need a backup plan, anyway." A wicked grin crossed Finn's face. "Juno, would you like to do a performance for us? You must have a few tricks up your fluffy sleeves. Just promise you won't shred our VIP's wings."

"I'm not a performing animal in the circus." I lifted my chin. "Besides, you couldn't handle all my power if I performed."

Finn chuckled. "It was worth a go. But if we don't come back with some winged scarabs, Cythera won't be happy. She's been on edge ever since she got the news she'd be entertaining Thomasina."

"What's so special about this Thomasina?" I said.

"She runs the Innovation and Evolution Committee. Cythera is worried her visit will mean changes for Angel Force."

Torrin and Zandra snorted at that comment.

"Hey, I'm just the messenger," Finn said. "I get my orders, and I follow them."

Finn mostly followed orders, but he was a half-angel, half-demon, so he had his darker moments. Although he'd been an ally since we'd moved to Crimson Cove, and I'd come to rely on his support when I needed the inside scoop into the latest mess happening at Angel Force.

"You're not with the angels," Zandra said to Torrin. "Why are you skulking about in the woods?"

"Helping a buddy. And getting free beer and burgers in return." Torrin slapped Finn on the shoulder.

"He got bored, so he tagged along," Finn said. "I never asked for his help."

"You practically begged me. You said you couldn't do this without me."

Finn shook his head, although there was a smile on his face. "So, are we wasting our time looking around the woods? I checked the habitat they prefer, and this sounded ideal for them."

Zandra twisted her mouth to the side. "I'll tell you what I know about winged scarabs, if you tell me if you've seen any sign of Adrienne recently."

The guys shared a look, although they already knew the reason we were out here so late. It wasn't for a moonlit picnic.

"We found signs of her feeding in this area," I said to encourage them to share. "Although we can't be certain it was Adrienne."

"It was," Zandra said. "She's still taking care of herself. I don't know how she's keeping hold of her humanity, but she hasn't let her ghoul desires overtake her. There's still a chance... a chance we can help her."

"That's great news." Finn's tone was overly enthusiastic. "I've left you messages to find out how things are going with your search, but you never got back to me, so I figured the worst."

"You didn't hear from me because I don't answer to you," Zandra said.

Finn winced. "I'll say sorry again if it'll help. I really am."

"It won't," Zandra said. "Have you seen her or not?"

Torrin rubbed the back of his neck. "We've seen a few track marks."

"Human or animal?" I said.

"Some of each. There's a big cat prowling the woods. We've found loads of fresh tracks. There were human-sized prints, too. Big ones. Some smaller."

"Adrienne's got small feet," I said.

"They could have been her prints, but there's no guarantee. Lots of people use these woods," Finn said.

Torrin nudged him. "Not exactly helping here, buddy."

He shrugged. "I don't want to get Zandra's hopes up. But it makes sense Adrienne could be here. I'd pick the woods if I needed to hide out and not be found."

"What about new reports coming into Angel Force?" I said. "You've had some about a shadowy figure lurking around late at night. Could that be her?"

He nodded. "We have, but most people describe a guy. Tall and dark. I guess some of the reports could be about Adrienne, but whoever is hanging about and looking in windows doesn't wait around when they're discovered."

"That sounds too sophisticated to be a ghoul," Zandra said. "Adrienne wasn't subtle when she blasted into Vorana's house and tried to eat her."

"She would never have eaten Vorana," I said.

"Ghouls eat people when they get the opportunity," Finn said.

Torrin shoved him. "Are you trying to start another fight with Zandra? She already hates you."

"No! I'm just laying it all out there. No more secrets. Isn't that right?"

Zandra pressed her lips together. "And while I appreciate that, it'll take more than a little cooperation and a few apologies to get things back on track. We may even be past that stage."

Finn and Torrin looked shamefaced and disappointed. They both crushed on my witch, which was understandable, since anyone would be lucky to spend time with her.

I shuffled back until my paws touched Zandra's boot. If she unfriended Finn and Torrin, I'd have to do the same. I'd always stand with her, even when she didn't make her decisions on sound logic and followed her heart. And right now, that heart was hurting, and it felt betrayed.

"So, the winged scarabs?" Torrin said after clearing his throat. "Any sightings?"

Zandra exhaled slowly. "I saw some in the woods about a month ago, but nothing since then. They're rare."

"They could be long gone by now," Finn said.

"Most likely. They tend not to stay in the same place for long," I said. "They usually cause too much trouble and get driven out when they're discovered.

Trouble follows them, which is why you should stay away from them."

"You really are overplaying how scary these critters are. They're tiny," Torrin said.

"Little can be lethal." I slashed my murder mittens through the air.

Finn grimaced and glanced at his wing. "I'm convinced by that argument."

"Try along the eastern edge of the woods," Zandra said. "That's where I last saw them. There were six of them. The purple variety."

"They're the worst. They give you a nasty nip if you get on their wrong side. They look cute until they unfurl their fangs. Then you need to run," I said.

"You're sure Cythera wanted us to look for these things? She didn't mean a cute pixie or a velvet imp?" Torrin said to Finn.

"That's what she said. Thomasina has been studying scarabs for decades, but their numbers are declining. Cythera thought it would be a good idea to host a performance during her visit to impress her."

"Does Cythera want to ruin Crimson Cove by agitating these flying nightmares?" I said. "I thought all angels were good."

"We are! Mostly." Finn grinned at me.

"If these things are as ruthless as Juno claims they are, we should give this a miss," Torrin said. "Let's go grab a late beer and forget about it."

"And risk losing my job? I'll find them myself." Finn turned away, but Torrin grabbed his elbow.

"Relax. I'll help. After all, I want that free burger."

"You should get going if you're to have any chance of seeing them," Zandra said. "They're most active at night."

"Yeah, we will." Finn hesitated. "I really am sorry about Adrienne. If there's anything I can do—"

"You've done enough."

"I want to help, too. If you need anyone," Torrin said, "you know where I am."

"I don't need help from either of you."

An awkward silence circled us like a witch about to dive bomb an enemy on her broomstick.

"You'd better go," I said. "Good luck with your search."

"And you," Finn said.

The guys trudged into the darkness.

Zandra pressed her fingers against her forehead again. "We should keep looking, too."

"Don't be so hard on Finn and Torrin." I trotted along beside her. I'd hoped Zandra would form a romantic connection with one of them, but she was barely talking to them, so that seemed unlikely.

"They deserve it. They kept information from me. Important information." She stomped along.

"And so did I, but we're still talking."

"We don't have a choice. We're bonded, and we live together."

"And we love each other," I said.

She slowed and then crouched. I placed my paws on her knee, and we touched foreheads.

"We do. But I need this time to be angry. And time to process what's going on with Adrienne. I still have no clue what I'll do if we find her. Should she be locked up? Is there any possibility she can live a normal life? Would the kindest thing be to destroy her?" That last sentence stuck in her throat.

I kept my forehead pressed against hers, sending out gentle, calming waves of magic. "We'll find her, and when we do, we'll do what's best for her. Adrienne is a different kind of ghoul, though. We've seen that for ourselves. That gives us options. And hope."

"I don't want her to suffer. She wasn't the greatest parent, but if she needs to be put out of her misery, that's what I'll do." A single tear trickled down Zandra's cheek.

I quickly licked it off and rubbed against her face. "We don't have to decide yet. But perhaps we'd be more effective if we let others into our lives. Finn and Torrin are sorry, and I know they'd do anything to help you. Maybe even take on some of the late-night searching so you get a decent night of sleep."

Zandra stood and shook her head. "I'm done with those guys. I don't need any guy in my life. They only cause trouble. Let's keep going."

I walked beside Zandra, hopeful we'd mended a small bridge back to normality. I didn't agree with her that she was done with guys. Maybe those particular guys. But she just needed to find the right one to make her smile again.

It wouldn't be Finn or Torrin, but there must be someone else suitable for my wonderful witch.

Before I tackled that thorny issue, we had a ghoul mother in hiding to deal with.

Chapter 3

A tricky conversation over bacon

"This bacon is delicious." I nodded my appreciation at Vorana across the breakfast table the next morning.

"It's got a honey glaze. I thought it might be a bit sweet." There was a warm smile on her pretty face, her cheeks rosy from standing over the hot griddle.

"It's perfection." I looked at Sage's untouched plate. "Don't you like it?"

"I'm too focused for food. I need to be on the alert at all times." Sage glared at me.

I returned my attention to the bacon. Usually, I had salmon for breakfast, but sometimes, a change was good. I continued eating, ignoring the death stare Sage sent me. She'd been like this since Adrienne had burst into the house and attacked Vorana. I understood her need to be protective, but she didn't have to take it out on me. It wasn't as if I invited a ghoul into the house.

"Do you need me to cut your bacon smaller, sweetie?" Vorana said to Sage.

"It's fine." She kept staring at me.

"I can hand feed it to you if you'd prefer."

Sage batted Vorana's hand away. "I'll eat later."

I chewed on my last piece of bacon and turned to her. "Let's get this out in the open. You don't want us living here anymore, do you?"

Sage wriggled around in her seat. "If you weren't living in the basement, the ghoul would never have come here. It was only here because of you and your witch."

"Sage, we've talked about this." There was a note of caution in Vorana's voice.

"We haven't talked to them. Your safety is my priority, and while they're still living here, you're vulnerable."

Zandra set down her fork. "I'm sorry about Adrienne showing up here. If I'd known she was a ghoul, I'd have been more proactive in finding her and making sure she wasn't a threat."

I ducked my head. That comment was aimed at me.

"I don't blame you," Vorana said. "And I'm happy Adrienne is back. When she showed up here as a ghoul, of course, I was shocked. But at least she's alive."

"Are ghouls alive?" Sage said. "Even if they are, they're dangerous and unpredictable. What's to say she won't keep coming back? The next time, I might not be fast enough to stop her from biting you."

"We'll move out," Zandra said. "I didn't mean to bring trouble here."

"You're staying." Vorana slapped her palms on the wooden table. "Sage is just being her usual adorable, overprotective self. And while I appreciate that, I have powers. And, after I got over the shock of being cornered by Adrienne, I could see she wasn't your typical ghoul."

"She tried to bite you!" Sage said.

"Because I scared her and she reacted. I shouldn't have run. If I'd stood my ground and talked to her, things would have been different."

"It's still not safe," Sage said. "Not while the ghoul is lurking about."

"My witch would never intentionally bring trouble to your door," I said. "If you're looking for someone to blame, focus on me."

"I am. Don't worry about that." Sage hissed at me.

"Settle down, you two," Vorana said. "This is my house, and I get to invite whoever I like to stay in the basement."

Sage grumbled under her breath.

Vorana petted Sage's head until she stopped grumbling. "I adore you for looking out for me, but I like having the company. It's been good for both of us to have Zandra and Juno stay."

"Not for me. I get no peace," Sage said.

"I rarely disturb you. And we're out at work most days," I said. "You're just looking for an excuse to get rid of us."

Sage's gaze went to the window. "I need to know what dangers are out there, so I can protect Vorana. You must understand."

I let out a gentle sigh. "I get that. We always want to protect those we're bonded to. I'd be just the same if the roles were reversed."

"Then you'll understand why I'm giving you your notice," Sage said.

Vorana stood from her chair. She walked to the counter and brought back a plate of blueberry muffins. "Zandra and Juno, you're staying. If Adrienne shows up again, I'll be prepared. I'll know not to run, and I'll have a conversation with her."

"Would that work?" Zandra said. "Did she talk when you saw her?"

"No, but it's possible she's kept the power of speech." Vorana passed around the muffins. "I keep going over our encounter in my head, and Adrienne displayed different emotions. She also had control over her urges."

"She cornered you in the room and drooled on the rug," Sage said.

"But she didn't attack me. I could see it on her face that she was battling with herself. There's still some of the old Adrienne left."

"I keep thinking that's possible, but then I lose hope," Zandra said. "I've never heard of a ghoul who can control themselves like that. It's not possible."

"We saw for ourselves, they don't always become violent when they're looked after," I said. "And I got Elijah stable after he'd been bitten by a ghoul. He didn't turn all bitey and mindless."

"Yeah, now he's only part ghoul, part jerk. Well done for that," Sage said.

"Adrienne's been turned for more than a month," Zandra said. "You worked your magic on Elijah as soon as he'd been bitten. What if Adrienne is too far gone?"

"And what if she shows up here again, even more vicious than the last time?" Sage said.

"She won't. But if she comes back, we'll welcome her in with open arms and help her," Vorana said. "I remember Adrienne before she was changed. She was fun and spontaneous. She lived in the moment and enjoyed her life fully. She'll still have some of that old spark left."

Zandra scowled at the muffin she'd taken.

Adrienne had always known how to enjoy her life, but that fun came with disorganization that meant Zandra went without when she was younger. Would the ghoul version of Adrienne be any less chaotic? Maybe she'd be worse. Combine Adrienne's frivolous side and the indecisive, chaotic thoughts of a ghoul, and you had an unpleasantly messy mix.

"I know this is a huge thing to worry about," Vorana said to Zandra, "but all we can do is look out for her. When you find her, we'll help her however she needs it."

Zandra kept her head lowered. "Even if that means putting her down?"

Vorana caught hold of Zandra's hand. "Even that. You'll do the best for your mother."

So would I. For all the trouble they'd had, Zandra loved Adrienne. And that meant I cared for her, too. If we had to make the tough decision of putting Adrienne out of her misery, I'd step up and make sure it happened with minimal distress.

Vorana checked the time and stuffed the rest of her muffin into her mouth. "I need to get a shift on. We're expecting more visitors than usual because of the Angel Force event. You going?"

"No plans to," Zandra said. "We'll be working."

"It's being held over lunchtime. You should drop by." Vorana placed her mug and plate in the sink.

"I don't even know what it's about," Zandra said. "I pay little attention to Angel Force events."

"Too many feathers for my liking," I said. "And if there are speeches, they can go on for hours. Angels never know how to get to the point."

"I'm looking forward to it," Vorana said. "Maybe not the talks so much, but Thomasina, that's the angel who's visiting, will update us on the framework for a voluntary service, so people can help with crime-fighting in their spare time."

"Sounds like the angels want people to do their jobs for them and not get paid for it," Sage said.

"I never see the angels do much work anyway when we visit," I said. "Unless you count sitting in a seat and drinking lots of coffee work."

Sage grumbled an agreement.

Angel Force did their best, but I was never certain they were the ideal supernaturals to maintain law and order. Of course, they were strong and hard to kill, but they liked everything to be done as a democracy, and that meant having far too many meetings, filling in forms, and never making a solid decision without having a dozen rounds of consultations, a referendum, and then the matters signed off by an elected committee.

"At least come for the free food after the talks," Vorana said. "The angels know how to lay on a good spread. And they've used local businesses to get the treats. There'll be pizza from the new place, and they put in a huge order at the bakery. And I'm setting out a bargain book stand, so you can pick up your favorite new read."

"We've had this discussion before about me and books. Not a massive fan," Zandra said.

Vorana chuckled. "I'm still working on converting you. Got to go." She lifted Sage down and settled her in her harness before strapping her in. Then they hurried out of the room, Sage giving me a stern backward glance.

"Maybe we should see what the angels have to say," I said.

"And listen to the boring talks? I'll pass. Let's get out of here and see what fun Barney has for us."

As soon as we entered the animal control office, the tension in the air made my whiskers twitch.

We entered Barney Hoffman's office and discovered him pacing. Sitting on the edge of his desk was my favorite fluffy friend, Sammy. Well, we were a bit more than friends.

"Is something up?" Zandra said by way of greeting.

Barney scrubbed a hand down his face. "I've just had a difficult conversation with Cythera. She's expecting me to find her some rare winged scarabs. I told her it wasn't that easy, but she insisted I'd know where they were. How? I'm not a scarab hunter. That's not what we do here."

"It sounds like Finn and Torrin weren't successful in their mission last night." I hopped onto the desk and rubbed my face against Sammy's.

"I've always had a solid relationship with the angels, but this is taking liberties. When I said I wouldn't do it, Cythera even threatened me!"

"What did she say she'd do to you?" Zandra said.

"Undertake a full review of animal control. She said the angels would take charge if things were slipping. I almost spit out my coffee when she said that. I run a tight ship. I'm here for the animals, not to fulfill the needs of some puffed up feathers."

I cocked my head. It was rare to hear Barney so angry.

Zandra's bottom lip jutted out. "I've heard several people mention not to get on the wrong side of Cythera."

Barney's eyebrows rose as he nodded. "I tried to convince her having winged scarabs at a public event wasn't sensible. They're often badly behaved."

"That's what I told Finn and Torrin." I settled beside Sammy. "How's it going?"

He shrugged. "Not too bad."

I glanced at Barney, who was still pacing the room. "Still struggling to form a bond?"

Sammy nodded, leaning close so his mouth was by my ear. "We're not ready. I'm planning on having a conversation with Barney. It's time to admit defeat."

I was disappointed my attempted bonding hadn't worked, but getting the right magic user was hard. It didn't mean I was giving up on Sammy finding a new magic user to bond with. The same for Barney. There was someone out there for him who'd be perfect.

"Knock, knock." Randal Nix rapped his knuckles on the door as he poked his head in. He had a baseball cap on backward and a lanyard around his neck full of USB sticks. "I'm about to start on the next network upgrade. It'll be down for an hour. If there's anything urgent you need, grab it now."

"Hey, Randal," Zandra said. "I need to get my list of jobs for the day, then I'm out of here."

He nodded, his forehead furrowing as he studied Barney. "What's wrong?"

"Rare winged scarabs," Zandra said. "The angels need some, and we can't locate them."

"It's not our job to do so," Barney said. "Those angels think they can push us around. It's not fair."

"I can help with that," Randal said.

Barney turned and stared at him. "Really! You've seen some in Crimson Cove?"

"No, but if you give me some stats about them, their size, habits, preferred habitation, and heat signature would be handy too, they'll be easy to locate."

Barney strode over and caught hold of Randal's shoulders. "You can work with Zandra and Juno. Take whatever equipment you need and track them."

"Track them? You mean like in the field?" Randal was shaking his head, an affable smile on his face. "This body is designed to sit in a chair and stare at the screen until the small hours. What I meant was, when I have those data points, I can track the scarabs online."

"Online. That doesn't sound like fun," Zandra said.

Randal grinned. "It's fun for those of us who hate traipsing around fields and woods, risking getting bitten by vampires, set on fire by angry dragons, or attacked by pixies. And it works for me. I'll show you, if you like. It'll blow your mind."

"A location spell might do a similar job," I said.

"Why exhaust your magic when we have gigawatts of power at our fingertips? Well, I'll exhaust a little of mine, but I don't mind." Randal grinned at Zandra then ducked his head.

"Yes! Work together. Zandra, give Randal all the information you can on the winged scarabs." Barney bounced on his toes.

"What about my jobs for today?"

"Leave those. If you get the chance, do some this afternoon, but none are urgent. Mainly home checks and ensuring licenses are up to date. The scarab situation is an emergency. The last thing we need is a review from Angel Force getting in the way of us helping the animals."

"You got it, boss." Randal turned to Zandra and bowed. "Let me introduce you to the wonderful world of online tracking. You'll never want to go out in the field again after this experience."

She shook her head, smiling as she did so. "I'm made for the field as much as you're made for the desk."

"Right this way." Randal left the room and headed along the corridor.

Zandra followed him, and after a quick nuzzle with Sammy, I followed her. I stopped at the entrance to an open door and looked in at a bank of screens. There were six screens placed around the room and several large snow globes.

"Welcome to my world." Randal spread out a hand.

"How do you keep all this going without magic interfering?" Zandra meandered around the room, inspecting everything.

He twirled a finger in the air. "Tech magic helps. I also ward this room to keep out the worst of the interference. Occasionally, something powerful creeps through and fries a circuit. It only happens about once a month, though."

"What does this all do?" I wandered in and sniffed a large snow globe that held a faint shimmer of gray, glittering mist.

"It's a global network linked into the snow globe system. I also use some of the non-magicals' technology. They have satellites that orbit the planet. I figured out how to connect our magic to the satellites. I get access to the same information they have, just faster."

"You can use this to search for the winged scarabs?" Zandra said.

"Sure can." Randal settled into a padded black seat with an angled headrest and wiggled his fingers over a keyboard. "I just need everything you've got on them."

Zandra pulled up a chair and sat beside him. "Let's get started."

Half an hour later, and after filling Randal's head with everything he needed to know about winged scarabs, a complicated looking program was running, scanning a five-hundred-mile radius around Crimson Cove for signs of the elusive scarabs.

"You sure know a lot about these little critters." Randal rocked back in his seat as his gaze swept across the bank of screens.

Zandra shrugged. "Not really. I mean, they're kind of interesting."

"You're pretty and smart," Randal said. "That's a great combination."

Zandra blushed, and so did Randal, neither of them making eye contact.

My eyes widened. They liked each other! I studied Randal. He wasn't the type I'd automatically pick for Zandra. He wasn't muscled or overly confident, but there was a quiet reassurance about him that was appealing. He was also smart and dedicated to his work. And he was cute in a tech geek kind of way. If they liked each other, I approved.

A toe bean curling silence grew as they fiddled around in their seats, neither of them seeming to know what to say next.

I was desperate to intervene and encourage this romance, but I was cautious about meddling. Zandra still hadn't fully forgiven me for keeping things from her, and I didn't want to give her another reason for being unhappy with me.

Randal reached for a pen at the same time as Zandra, and their hands bashed together.

"Sorry!" He pulled back, his gaze finally settling on Zandra.

"No, after you," she said. "This is your stuff."

"You take it. I've got plenty. Keep it. I want you to have it."

They stared at each other.

I didn't move. Were they about to kiss?

One of the screens pinged, and they jumped back in their seats.

"Hey! We got a hit on the winged scarabs," Randal said. "Look at this. Less than fifty miles away."

"Give me the information. We'll go grab them now."

I let out a gentle sigh. The romantic moment had passed, but we needed to make these winged scarabs a priority, so the smooching would have to wait.

Once Zandra had the information, she picked me up and settled me on her shoulder. "Let's do this the fast way. You ready?"

I nodded. "See you later, Randal." While we worked on getting the winged scarabs, I'd figure out a plan to get true love blossoming.

Chapter 4

Winged trouble

Zandra used a translocation spell to bring us to a densely forested part of the nearby town of Mindful Mallow.

We'd landed in the middle of the forest, so I had no idea what the town was like. The name made it sound quaint.

Zandra held a small mobile unit with several flickering lights. Randal had given it to her so we could track the winged scarabs. The faster the lights blinked, the closer we were.

"If this thing is working as it should, they're right up ahead," Zandra whispered.

"How will we convince them to come back with us to Crimson Cove?" I said.

"Winged scarabs love to make deals. We just have to find something they want."

"What will you offer them?"

"The angels are desperate to have them, so I'm guessing nearly everything is on the table. I'll ask them what they desire, and we'll take it from there." Zandra crept forward, staying as quiet as possible.

We didn't want to startle the winged scarabs and have them disappear.

I sat upright on her shoulder, looking for signs of them, but there was no evidence of anything winged or hooved in the forest. Not even much natural light filtered through the trees. It was creepy. Like the trees considered us trespassers and were waiting to see if we were a threat before making their move.

Zandra kept walking for a few minutes, then slowed. "I just caught a flash of something purple up ahead."

I narrowed my eyes, and after a few seconds of staring, I also saw movement. "It's them. I saw three. One big, two small."

"That'll do. It's enough scarabs to put on a performance and keep the angels happy." Zandra crept closer.

Zandra stepped onto the path and froze. In front of us were three purple scarabs. Their wings sparkled with what looked like glitter, but it was their magic keeping them afloat. Dark green striations ran across their heads, and they had hard looking bodies with a casing that was almost impossible to pierce. They also sported fanned antennae. The largest was the size of a fat mouse.

She cleared her throat and raised a hand. "Hey. Could I talk to you?"

The three winged scarabs fluttered in a circle for a few seconds then shot over to us.

The largest settled on Zandra's outstretched hand. "A witch. And her familiar. What do you want with us?"

"Greetings. I'm Juno, and this is Zandra Crypt. We need your help," I said.

"Help!" The scarab's tone shot up an octave. "We don't help for free."

"We know. We'd like to do a deal with you," Zandra said.

"Deals we like." The fanned antenna stroked Zandra's wrist.

"Then we can help each other. I'm here on behalf of Angel Force to ask if you'd do an exclusive performance in Crimson Cove today."

"Crimson Cove! One of my favorite places. Children gather around. Taking a trip, we are."

Zandra yelped as the world shifted around us. I clung to her shoulder, blinking as I discovered we were back in Crimson Cove woods. That tiny creature had translocated all of us. These winged scarabs had power. We needed to be careful around them.

Zandra staggered to the side, and the winged scarab on her hand shot into the air, giggling with her children.

"Creeping broomsticks! You could have given us some warning." She leaned against a tree and sucked in a few deep breaths.

"That was quite some magic you used on us," I said.

"I have great power." The largest scarab hovered by my face. "In my haste to return us to this delightful place, I didn't introduce my children. Saphic and Loris. My name is Amenia."

Her children fluttered away, playing with each other.

Zandra pulled herself upright, looking a little green. "It's nice to meet you all. Thank you for speaking with us and considering a deal."

"I was intrigued when you mentioned the angels. A fondness I have for those foolish creatures. I've seen so many of them come and go over the years. They are lovely to look at but as foolish as a love-struck teenager on a first date, to the point of being ridiculous and making serious errors in judgment."

Zandra grinned. "They have their moments. But they're having a special guest in Crimson Cove today, and she's fond of winged scarabs. She'd love to see you perform."

"I'm certain she would. Spectacular, we are. What particular performance would she like to see? Thousands, we have."

Zandra glanced at me. "I'm sure anything would be perfect."

"The essence of perfection we are. We could perform an enchantment dance or a dance of bedazzlement."

"Nothing too complicated," I said. "Something to entertain rather than beguile."

"Less interesting to me, that is. I'm not sure I want to take part if I cannot beguile my audience. Leave you, we shall."

"Wait! There must be something you want," Zandra said.

"Of course. There are always things we desire." Amenia's antenna quivered, and she shot into the air. "Children! Hide. Something is coming."

By the time I'd blinked, the winged scarabs were gone.

"Hey, who are you talking to?" A tousled looking guy with shoulder-length dark hair stumbled along the path. He shouldered a small backpack, and a camera was tucked against his side, supported on a thick strap.

I tilted my head as I inspected him, and my toe beans shivered. From his aura, he was a non-magical.

"Um... I was talking to my cat." Zandra looked at me and whispered the word *non-magical?*

I nodded. Non-magicals stood out to me because of their faint, pale auras. It was how I identified them, so I avoided ever blasting one with a spell and accidentally killing them or sending them insane. Magic did that to those who shouldn't be around it.

"You talk to your cat?" The guy scratched his stubbled chin. "Weird."

"Nothing weird about it," Zandra said. "What are you doing out here?"

"Camping. My tent isn't far from here." He cast a thumb over his shoulder.

"How long have you been camping in Crimson Cove?"

"A few days." He pulled a notebook from his windcheater. "What's your name?"

Zandra was silent for several seconds. "Why do you want to know?"

"Ha! So many people say that when I ask." He licked the end of a pencil. "I'm Bentley. You live here?"

"Sure. What brought you to Crimson Cove?"

"The weirdness. You?" He held the pencil poised above the pad.

"You think Crimson Cove is weird?"

"The weirdest."

"It's a boring little town. Nothing much happens here." Zandra sounded falsely breezy.

"You're kidding. I've been here three days and seen so much strange stuff. As soon as I set up camp, I knew this was the place to be. I'm planning on staying at least a month."

I held in an urge to hiss. If a non-magical was exposed to our powers for that length of time, it could kill them.

Zandra's tongue traced across her lips. "Why so long?"

"I travel around investigating weird towns. People love this kind of thing. I'm planning a special series of interviews and posts for my blog and podcast."

As much as I wanted to ask questions, I had to keep quiet. Bentley had already noticed a few strange things in town, but a talking cat would send him bananas.

"What have you seen that makes you think Crimson Cove is so weird?" Zandra gently rolled a loose stone under her shoe.

"It's the vibe. And I've seen odd colors and lights in the air at night. I wondered if it was an alien invasion." His gaze ran over Zandra. "You're not an alien in disguise, are you?"

A fake laugh burst from her lips. "I wasn't the last time I checked. There's nothing special about this place. You should move on and look elsewhere. I heard about some floating orbs a few towns over. Could be ghosts."

Bentley was shaking his head before Zandra finished speaking. "No way! I've been told that same story one too many times since I've been here. Nothing to see here. We're a dull town. Nothing happens in Crimson Cove. I've learned from experience that means I'm onto something juicy. People don't tell you to keep away unless there's a good reason. Go on, tell me what it is. If you're not aliens, is this some cult town? Or do you worship dark forces?"

"Um... Definitely neither of those things. It's your typical small town." Zandra stubbed the toe of her shoe into the dirt.

"I don't believe that. And I've been trying to get resident interviews ever since I arrived, but no one wants to talk. Well, they talk, but it's all surface level. How about you? Are you happy to give me an interview, Miss No Name? I can keep your name out of it and say you were an anonymous source who didn't want to be identified for fear of reprisal. The fans will love that."

I hopped down and weaved around her legs, sensing Zandra's prickly side rising. She needed to keep her cool, or this guy would only get more interested in our weird little magical town.

"Not long," she finally said. "I didn't grow up in Crimson Cove, so I can't tell you much about its history."

"Uh-huh. The history isn't so important. It's what's happening now." Bentley pointed his pencil at the ground. "These huge footprints I keep seeing.

And the big cat prints. I reckon you've got a yeti here."

"You don't say." Zandra glanced at me. "I thought those things were myths."

"They exist." Bentley puffed out his cheeks. "I'm excited to be here. And I have to get the inside scoop. It would be the making of my podcast."

"Doubtful, but good luck if you're into that sort of thing." Zandra looked around. "You probably don't want to camp in this part of the woods for too long, though. Since you've been digging around in our urban legends, you'll have heard about Cannibal Bill."

His eyebrows flashed up. "I haven't. But you've got to tell me about him now. Why that nickname?"

"You'll meet him if you're camping so close to his hut. You won't like it if you do. The guy isn't friendly. Some say he's certifiable. Even dangerous. Especially to people he doesn't know." Zandra slid me a smile and a wink.

"He's an actual cannibal?"

"Maybe. That's what people say. He's probably just an old guy who got jaded with the world. But he's fond of carrying a crossbow and using it rather than asking questions. You should move on before he accidentally shoots you."

Bentley laughed. "This is genius. I'm finding Cannibal Bill and interviewing him. If I take him some steak, I reckon he'll talk to me."

I repressed a groan, while Zandra scowled at the unwelcome stranger. The tracker she carried buzzed, and a message flashed in. I stood up her leg to read it.

It was from Randal. *No pressure, but Barney is breathing down my neck. Any sign of the winged scarabs?*

"That's an odd looking mobile." Bentley peered at the device. "Is that how you phone home?"

"Oh, yeah, it's an old model." Zandra shoved it in her pocket before he could snoop anymore. "Take care in these woods. If you're right about the big cat, you don't want to be trapped in a tent when one is stalking you."

"I can handle the local wildlife. I've camped for years. You sure I can't get your name and an interview?"

"Nope. I'm super boring."

"My instincts suggest otherwise."

"Then get them re-tuned. There's nothing around here for you."

He shrugged. "See you around for that interview."

"Maybe." Zandra lifted me, set me on her shoulder, and we hurried away.

I glanced back at Bentley. He shouldn't be here. Crimson Cove repelled those who had no magic. It was how we kept them away. Non-magicals were vulnerable if they encountered us because they had no natural defenses against our power.

"We need to find those winged scarabs," Zandra whispered. "We're running out of time, and the angels are getting testy. I don't want Cythera launching a review of animal control. It'll give Barney heart palpitations."

"Psst! Over here."

My ears swiveled. "They've found us."

Zandra headed off the path, and we discovered the winged scarabs lurking behind a tree. "Sorry about the interruption. Are you ready to do a deal?"

"Always. What can you offer us?" Amenia hovered with her children.

"Money?"

"Not interested."

"Magic?"

"Plenty I have."

"A special trip somewhere fun? A spa or a beach resort."

"We travel wherever we like."

Zandra looked at me and shrugged. "The angels have resources. Whatever you want, it's yours."

I tapped her cheek with my paw. "Is that wise?"

"The angels are paying, so it has nothing to do with us," Zandra said.

"Hmmm... Angels have deep pockets, so this'll be an entertaining deal. Agreed. Where do you need us to travel to?"

"The Angel Force office as soon as possible. The event has started, and the angels are stressed."

Amenia tsked. "Such a low tolerance level during difficult times angels have. Lead the way. Or would you like me to translocate us? My treat."

Zandra took a step back, her hand going to her stomach. "Once was enough."

She tinkled a laugh. "Then take us there. A performance of utter delight awaits your angel friends."

We dashed through the trees, closely followed by the winged scarabs.

"That was a risk, offering them anything they wanted," I whispered to Zandra.

"We didn't have time to negotiate. Cythera is desperate, and I don't want that desperation to ping back and hit us in the face."

I narrowed my eyes as I watched the scarabs from over Zandra's shoulder. I'd have to watch these winged troublemakers even more closely since we'd struck such a loose deal. They could decide to take over Angel Force or make the angels their slaves.

Amenia waggled her antenna at me and giggled. Her children joined in.

When we arrived back in town, it was full of locals and visitors, many of them angels, who must have flown in for the event. They were investigating the stalls the stores had set out and sampling the delicious treats from the bakery and cafe.

"This way." Zandra weaved us through the crowds.

"Hey, Zandra, Juno." Vorana stood beside a table piled high with books. "Come stand over here. I have a good view if you want to watch the show when things get started."

"Give me ten minutes," Zandra said.

As we approached the Angel Force building, I spotted Finn standing with his boss. They looked anxious. Barney was also beside them, along with Randal Nix, Glenda Ridgeback, and Oleander Yockley.

Finn dashed over the second he saw us, a grin on his face. "You got them! How did you do that?"

"Long story. Amenia, this is Finn. He'll look after you from here," Zandra said.

"It was a pleasure doing business with you, Zandra and Juno. Meet again, we will."

The scarabs fluttered off with Finn.

"We should get out of here," Zandra said. "Crowds of angels make me sweaty."

Barney walked over, relief plastered on his face. "You saved the day. Join us."

"You're good. We're busy." Zandra edged away but bumped into an angel.

"Stay for the celebrations. I've given everyone two hours off so we can enjoy ourselves."

Zandra wrinkled her nose. "Are you sure? I don't mind going back to work. There's always something that needs doing. I can catch up with the filing."

"I insist. We need to celebrate your victory. You and Randal came through for the department. No review for us."

Zandra's cheeks flushed as she allowed herself to be led over to the rest of the team.

My stomach growled so loudly, Zandra jerked her head back.

"My apologies. Chasing after the winged scarabs has worked up an appetite."

"Same here." Zandra looked around and pointed at the marquee. "That's where the food is being served. We should check it out."

There was a whine from a microphone, and an angel I didn't recognize appeared. She was a stunning giant with flowing blonde hair almost to her knees and teeth that sparkled.

"That's Thomasina," Barney said. "Angel Force's esteemed visitor."

"She's the one causing the hassle over the winged scarabs," I muttered. "She'd better be worth it."

"According to the angels, she's something special," Barney said. "And she has an educational speech she wishes to share with us all."

I groaned along with Zandra.

Finn reappeared and nudged her. "Hey, want to sneak into the food marquee early? I heard Thomasina rehearsing her speech. It's as dull as dishwater."

Zandra hesitated for a second before nodding. "You just saved the day. See you later, Barney."

He raised his eyebrows but said nothing as we snuck away. He must be letting us off for good behavior since we saved his bacon by locating the winged scarabs in the nick of time.

There was a round of applause, the mic whined again, and someone spoke. I couldn't see who it was, but it must be Thomasina.

As the low female voice droned on, Finn grabbed plates, and we piled them high with mini pastries, tiny hotdogs in rolls, and salmon crisp bakes.

"Good work on finding those scarabs. We didn't get a sniff last night."

"We had technology on our side," Zandra said. "It's amazing what Randal can do. He's so smart."

Finn narrowed his eyes. "He sounds it. I've met him a few times. Kind of quiet and geeky."

"He's a good guy," Zandra said. "Open and honest. Unlike some."

Finn frowned and drew in a breath.

"Let's not bicker," I said. "Let's enjoy the food and blot out the boring speech. What's Thomasina talking about, anyway?"

"Something about the reforms and some volunteer thing being set up," Finn said. "We're missing nothing."

We settled in seats in the corner and ate in a companionable silence. I was pleased the truce was holding, even if it was only while we stuffed down as much food as possible.

After about twenty minutes, eight prawn pastries, a tiny hotdog, three salmon crisp bakes, and a drink from Zandra's sparkling water, there was another round of applause, and the first few attendees entered the marquee.

I was considering a second plate of fishy treats when a gigantic shadow loomed behind me.

I stiffened and turned to discover Thomasina within touching distance. And she was staring at Zandra.

Chapter 5

A winged tragedy

I nudged Zandra's elbow with my booping snooter.

"Just a minute. I'll get you something else. I want to sample the desserts before all the greedy, sugar addicted angels get here."

Finn lowered his plate and cleared his throat. "Hey, Thomasina. I thought you'd be watching the winged scarabs for longer. Have they finished already?"

Zandra's shoulders rose, and she turned on her heel. "Err... hi."

"They're warming up for what I'm certain will be a magnificent performance. While I was waiting, I was informed you were involved in their recruitment. You're the witch who found these creatures?"

Zandra gulped and set down her plate. "Is there a problem with them? They're the right sort, aren't they? They said they know thousands of routines. One of them should work for you."

Thomasina's huge white wings fluttered behind her as she held up a hand to stop Zandra blabbering.

"No problem. And you're not in trouble. I wanted to thank you. For many decades, I've longed to see such a performance, but no one has ever achieved it. You must be something special to have arranged this for me."

"Not so much. And I had great help." Zandra rested a hand on my head.

"It's always our pleasure to assist the angels." I hopped onto Zandra's shoulder. "Greetings. I'm Juno, and this is my wonderful witch, Zandra Crypt. You must have heard great things about her."

Thomasina inclined her head. "I trust the winged scarabs weren't too demanding."

Zandra shifted from foot to foot. "No, they came willingly. They like Crimson Cove and are always happy to perform to an audience."

"Excellent. My extensive readings of them have shown them to be tricky creatures, but from the descriptions of their enchanting performances, I had to see them for myself. I adore anything that sparkles brighter than me. Few things do."

"Thomasina! There you are. I lost you in the crowd. The scarabs are almost ready to perform." Bertoli scurried over, not looking amused to find Thomasina standing with us.

"Perfect timing. I was just thanking Zandra and Juno for their help in bringing them here. I haven't been this excited since the last discount sale at All That Glitters," Thomasina said.

Bertoli scowled at me. "I'm sure it wasn't difficult. I could have gotten them for you."

Zandra smirked at him. "I didn't see you in the woods when we tracked them."

"The only wood Bertoli ever sees is the tree his desk is made of," I muttered.

"I... I was busy. We needed to make everything right for today's event. Only the best for Thomasina."

While Bertoli simpered and played up his involvement in recruiting the winged scarabs, I hopped off Zandra's shoulder and investigated the buffet again, not happy to discover I wasn't the only one who enjoyed a fishy feast. The salmon centerpiece had been picked clean.

While Thomasina engaged Zandra in uncomfortable small talk about the town, sparkles, and scarabs, I moseyed outside and looked around. There was an enormous crowd waiting for the scarabs to begin but no sign of our winged entertainers.

Several angels hurried past, heading toward Cythera. Anxiety rippled off them, and several feathers floated free from their wings. I batted one for a few seconds, stopping when more angels gathered around their boss. This didn't look like a fun chat over chicken wings and sparkling fruit juice. Something was up.

I trotted over to see what the impromptu meeting was about.

"We keep this quiet," Cythera said, her expression set to grim. "With Thomasina visiting, we can't afford any distractions, panic, or unpleasant rumors creeping through the town."

The angels nodded.

I hunkered down to make myself as small as possible and slid closer on my belly.

"If this is the same individual who's been prowling around recently, capture them quickly and quietly. This doesn't need to be a performance. No one must know what's going on."

Now I was intrigued. I was as close as I could get without being spotted or trodden on.

"Won't Thomasina notice us going missing?" one of the gathered angels said.

"I'll keep a few angels here, but the rest of you go into the woods right away. We need an immediate search conducted."

This was too much. I had to know who they were searching for. I stretched and barged past an angel, stopping when I was in the center of the group. "Greetings. What's going on?"

Cythera looked around, startled at the unexpected voice among her angels.

"Down here," I said. "Who's been seen in the woods? What did you find? Should we be worried? Is my witch in danger?"

Her head jerked back, and her large nostrils flared. "That's no concern of yours. This is an Angel Force matter."

"I'm a concerned resident of Crimson Cove. I should be told what's going on. Is this the same creature that's been hanging around late at night?"

"What do you know about that creature?"

"I know a lot about everything. And I can be useful in searches. I have an excellent booping snooter to sniff out trouble. You should make use of me. I don't always offer help to those who don't deserve it."

Cythera seemed puzzled by my words. Perhaps the sentences had been too complex. "We require no help from civilians. And this is a private matter."

"If it's so private, why are you having your meeting in a public place?"

"Could it be the ghoul? People have reported seeing it in several places," an angel said.

My tail swished, and my toe beans quivered. Were they after Adrienne? It was only a matter of time before someone spotted her and reported her to the angels. But she'd been discreet these past two weeks. What had changed to make her break cover?

If it was her, there must be a reason she'd chosen to show herself. Perhaps her ghoul urges were overtaking her senses, and she'd lost the ability to think rationally.

"Let's not get ahead of ourselves." Cythera glanced down at me, not happy I was still there, but I had no intention of leaving. "We don't know for certain it's a ghoul. We get all kinds of curious creatures in the woods."

"It's not a ghoul," I said.

Her gaze drifted down to me. "How can you be so certain, small fluffy beast?"

I lowered my ears. "It's Juno. You know my name. Ghouls wouldn't be able to stop themselves from coming into Crimson Cove and munching on the tasty walking food sources. You have no ghouls in town."

"There are plenty of smaller, easier to obtain food sources in the woods," Cythera said, a look of disgust on her face.

"True. But that implies this imaginary ghoul has rational thought. That's not how they operate. Ghouls go to where the most food is and attack. A ghoul in Crimson Cove would have been spotted by now. It's not a ghoul."

"We didn't know about all those ghouls the Shadow gang created," a pale, narrow-faced angel said. "Maybe one escaped and has been in hiding."

The angels stirred around me, wings fluttered, and feathers floated to the ground.

"Fenwick, spreading rumors like that is unhelpful," Cythera said. "We won't know what we're dealing with until we get out there and investigate. You three remain here." She pointed to three angels standing beside her. "The rest of you go to the woods. The sighting was reported in the southern area, close to the pet cemetery. Go."

The angels took off as one and blasted into the air, mussing my fur.

I dashed back to the marquee to find Zandra still being forced to make small talk with Thomasina.

"The variegated green winged scarab comes in three different sizes. The largest is bigger than my hand. Isn't that extraordinary?" Thomasina held out a large hand to be inspected.

"Um... it is." Zandra's gaze caught mine, and I saw mild panic in her eyes. She was never comfortable around the angels, after near misses of the mildly illegal kind when she was younger, so having to endure polite conversation with Thomasina would be painful for her.

I launched myself from the ground and landed on Zandra's shoulder. There was no time for discretion. We needed to get to the woods to make sure Adrienne wasn't caught.

"Angel Force just put out an alert about something dangerous lurking in the woods. Finn, you'd better go. Take Thomasina with you," I said.

His eyebrows shot up. "What are we talking? What kind of dangerous?"

"Cythera wasn't clear. Various creatures were mentioned. Maybe even a ghoul."

Zandra dropped her buttered scone. "Ghoul! They're certain?"

"No, but they're all taking a look. We should be there to lend support, don't you think?"

"Thomasina, would you like to be involved in this investigation?" Finn was already ushering her to the open marquee flap.

"No! Thomasina is our guest. We can't expect her to contribute to an investigation. She's here to relax, not chase villains." Bertoli ran along beside them.

"It's a wonderful idea," Thomasina said. "I spend so much time at committee meetings and poring over important paperwork, but it's good to get into the field now and again and remember how things are done. How exciting! Lead the way."

"What about the winged scarabs?" Bertoli bobbed along beside Thomasina. "I'm fascinated by your extensive knowledge of them. I'd love to know more. We could stay and watch them together. Then I could take you for a coffee. Or dinner, later?"

"Oh, no. I want an adventure. Let's go to the woods." Thomasina marched ahead of us.

Finn glanced back, and I nodded at him. We needed allies in the woods, and I was certain Finn would help if Adrienne was lurking about there. He could run diversions while we searched for her.

"We'll leave you to it." Zandra dashed past, with me on her shoulders.

"Catch up with you later," Finn called.

"Where did they see Adrienne?" Zandra whispered to me.

"At the pet cemetery. They're not certain it's Adrienne, but one angel mentioned a ghoul, and everyone got shifty. They know something dangerous is hanging about in the trees."

"Hold tight. I'll get us there as quickly as I can." Zandra cast a translocation spell, and a few seconds later, we stood beside a rough lump of rock that showed the entrance to the pet cemetery. Carved on it was a crude picture of a cat's face.

I tensed as voices reached us. "The angels are already here. We must hurry."

"If they catch Adrienne, they'll think she's rogue and put her down. Look for any signs of her. Footprints, recent feeds, anything that suggests Adrienne is out here."

"Of course. Shall we do a circuit of the pet cemetery?"

"Yes. We'll meet in the middle."

"Avoid the angels if you can," I said. "They'll think it strange we're out here looking, too."

"Zandra!" Finn landed angel style, with his wings outstretched and one hand fisted on the ground. He stood and shook out his wings. "I've handed Thomasina over to Cythera. Another team of angels has just arrived, and they're planning a sweep of the entire woods. Some will be in the air but the rest on the ground."

"Did Cythera tell you anything more about the sighting that got them so panicked?" I said.

"Only that Kismet Raynham contacted the office in a blind panic. She said this lumbering creature appeared from the shadows in the woods and grabbed her. It came at her from behind, so she had no idea what it was. It tried to scratch and bite her. She got free and came straight to us."

"Any idea of the size or height of her attacker?" Zandra said. "Adrienne isn't much taller than me."

Finn grasped Zandra's shoulder. "It may not be her. These woods are full of weird things. We've had loads of sightings of big cats and shadowy figures over the last few weeks. Something is drawing things that like to lurk in the shadows closer to Crimson Cove."

"It could be her. I need to keep Adrienne safe."

"We will. Let's get searching," Finn said. "If we find her first, we can get her out of here, and the other angels need know nothing about it."

Zandra closed her eyes for a second and pinched the bridge of her nose. "Thanks, Finn."

"Anytime. I'll always look out for you."

"We were about to start in the pet cemetery." I was glad to see their friendship was back on track but had little time to dwell on the bridges being mended.

"I'll cut through the center," Finn said.

We dashed away and hunted for signs of Adrienne. I kept my booping snooter to the ground, trying to pick up any hint of decay, but it was a battle to drown out the nasal noise coming from the cemetery.

This was an unofficial pet cemetery, created hundreds of years ago by Skye Dread, who'd run an abandoned familiar sanctuary similar to Finn. She'd visit this spot and lay the deceased familiars to rest. Pretty soon, the rest of the town used this area, too. There were hundreds of familiars of all shapes and sizes buried here. And some of their curious powers lingered.

Despite being laser focused on finding any clue, I picked up nothing to suggest Adrienne had been here. I met Zandra as she completed her part of the circuit, and Finn appeared a second later.

"Anything?" she said.

"Nothing in the cemetery," Finn said.

"I found nothing either." I took a second to get my bearings. "There are some small earth built huts around here. They're often used for dark sky camping. She could be hiding in one of those."

"Show us where they are," Zandra said.

I dashed ahead and within a few minutes discovered the five small, roughhewn huts made of compacted mud and clay with willow woven roofs.

We began a swift investigation of each one.

"There's something in here," Finn called out from the furthest hut. "Someone's been using it for camping."

We dashed over and discovered a rolled up sleeping bag and a few tins of food.

"It's doubtful any ghoul would have the sophistication to know how to open a tin of beans," I said. "Perhaps these belong to that non-magical we found camping in the woods. What was his name?"

"Bentley. Like the car." Zandra nodded. "This isn't Adrienne's space."

"I haven't heard any yells or alerts from the angels. They're not having luck finding her, either," Finn said. "That's good news. It means it might not be her."

"Or she's successfully evaded being captured," Zandra said. "I need to find her before they do."

Finn was silent for a second. "And then what?"

"I don't know! But I can't let her get captured. Not until I know... I know how bad things are for her."

"Let's keep looking," I said. "If Adrienne is out here, we'll find the evidence."

We hunted for another fruitless thirty minutes, and every minute that passed, I became more convinced Adrienne wasn't here. Ghouls weren't discreet and always left a mess. Whoever had grabbed Kismet wasn't a ghoul.

A white flare appeared over the top of the trees, spreading out before it sparkled down.

"What does that mean?" Zandra said to Finn.

"It means Cythera is recalling her angels."

"Because Adrienne has been found?"

"I couldn't tell you. Let's head over to the location of the flare. You two stay back, though. Cythera is funny about people interfering in her investigations."

"Don't we know it," I muttered.

We dashed in the direction the flare had come from and within a few minutes spotted other angels heading the same way.

Cythera stood in the center of a clearing, on top of a tree stump, as she waited for the remaining angels to gather.

I stayed back, hidden behind a tree with Zandra, so we could hear what she had to say. Encouragingly, there was no sign of any creature that had been captured, ghoul or not.

Cythera raised a hand to quiet everyone. "We've done an initial sweep of the woods. Our investigation found nothing suspicious. We're calling off the search."

Zandra tipped back her head and blew out a breath. "Adrienne stayed out of their way. Maybe she's no longer in town. If she was here, they'd have found her."

I doubted she'd gone anywhere. Adrienne was here for one thing. Or rather, one person. She wouldn't leave until she'd reconnected with Zandra.

"However, I still have concerns there's a dangerous creature in these woods. When we get back to the office, I'll arrange for a schedule of flybys. You'll all take turns to monitor the woods and ensure they're safe. We don't want to ban people from making use of them."

"That's worrying," Zandra muttered. "They usually give up faster than this. Whatever grabbed Kismet has them spooked." She winced as her mobile snow globe buzzed in her pocket. She silenced it as she pulled it out. "It's from Barney. We need to get to work. An emergency job has come in."

"We should go. Since the angels are calling off the search, Adrienne won't be caught now."

"Provided she keeps her head down." Zandra shoved her mobile snow globe back in her jacket pocket. "We'll catch up with Finn later. See what the plans are for the continued search."

We left the angels to their impromptu meeting and slipped away through the trees. As we hurried back along the path heading toward Crimson Cove, there were small piles of white feathers everywhere.

"These angels are so messy," I said.

"It must be molting season." Zandra chuckled. "They'll soon look like plucked chickens if they keep losing so many feathers."

I slowed as Zandra walked ahead of me. There was a surprising number of white feathers in the dirt. Angels were notorious shedders, but this was ridiculous. One of them had a problem if they were losing this many wing feathers. It would hamper their flying.

I batted a magnificent feather between my paws for a few seconds, marveling at its iridescent sparkle.

Zandra glanced over her shoulder. "Keep up. If we're quick, we can grab more food from the buffet, if there's any left."

I inspected another feather. It was freshly fallen and smelled strongly of sparkly angel. But there was something else in the mix. A scent that turned my stomach and prickled my fur.

"Is something wrong?" Zandra returned and crouched beside me.

"I think there might be." I turned my head from left to right, unease trickling down my spine like an unwelcome icy drop of water. My gaze narrowed on a big heap of white feathers on the ground.

Attached to those feathers was Thomasina.

Chapter 6

Did the ghoul do it?

I dashed over to where Thomasina lay. She was on her back, her arms and legs laid out straight in the dirt, and her wings flattened.

"Oh, crud! Is she hurt?" Zandra was right beside me.

"I'd say more than hurt." I took in the devastating scene of broken branches and scattered feathers. The visible parts of Thomasina's body were covered in bite marks. Bite marks that looked like a ghoul made them.

Zandra gasped and stumbled, landing heavily on her knees beside Thomasina. "Juno! Are you seeing this? All these marks. They... they look like ghoul bites, don't they?"

I weaved around her several times, pulsing out calming magic as Zandra's panic flooded over me. "Check for signs of life. Quickly. Angels are almost impossible to kill. We may be able to bring her back."

Zandra's trembling hand reached for Thomasina's neck, and she felt around for a pulse. "There's nothing."

"Keep searching. Her pulse could be faint." I sniffed around Thomasina. Although this must have recently happened, I detected no signs of life. Angels were bullet-proof though, and although Thomasina was covered in multiple bites, only a few had broken the skin. This death made no sense.

My paw landed in an icy puddle of water beside Thomasina, and I flicked my leg several times to disperse the water. I looked around for any footprints in the mud, but there were no distinct prints to show it was Adrienne who'd inflicted these bites.

"What should we do?" Zandra croaked out. "She's definitely dead. And these bites... it was Adrienne, wasn't it? Thomasina must have seen her and tried to stop her. Adrienne attacked."

I flooded out more calming magic, but a lump lodged in my throat, and I hiccupped. My fur puffed out as a wave of my recently acquired power pulsed out of me in an uncontrollable wave. It smacked into Zandra, causing her hair to fluff around her face as if she'd just been shocked.

Her eyes widened as she stared at me. "What was that for?"

"Sorry. I'm as panicked as you about this situation." I yanked back my magic, tugging on the slippery coil of power that wanted to unfurl and wrap around everything it touched. I was still learning to get comfortable with my recently reacquired power, and it didn't always behave the way I needed it to.

Zandra shuddered and shook off the spell I'd accidentally slammed into her. "Do you think... Was this Adrienne? Did she just murder an angel?"

I looked around, comforted to see we were alone. It gave us more time to figure this out. I sniffed around Thomasina again. "I'd suggest risking a reanimation spell, but I think she's been dead for too long. If we got her back and asked her who did this, it would be too dangerous."

"We don't need a reanimated angel corpse tearing Crimson Cove apart. We have enough problems with Adrienne being on the loose."

"We don't know it was her."

"We also don't know it wasn't her." Zandra pressed a hand briefly to Thomasina's cheek. "She's freezing. But this must have only just happened. We've been searching for Adrienne for less than an hour."

I pressed a paw on Thomasina's cheek. She felt like she'd been dipped in ice. I had no explanation for the intense cold. "From the amount of bite marks, this was a frenzied attack."

"No kidding. I count at least thirty bites. Ghouls get out of control and bite like that."

I wriggled my booping snooter. "Thomasina's still intact, though. If a ghoul did this, why not eat her? And there's no blood."

"Ghouls don't bite people for no reason." Zandra's gaze shot to me. "Does this mean it wasn't Adrienne? Something else bit Thomasina?"

My gaze ran over the body. "The bite marks were made with blunt teeth. And those scratch marks on her skin suggest they were done with blunt nails. It's possible it wasn't a ghoul, but…"

Zandra tugged on the end of her hair. "The only ghoul around here is Adrienne. It must have been her. We can't let the angels see this. If they figure out one of their own was killed by a ghoul, it'll be all out war on Adrienne. They won't stop searching until they find her. And when they find out my connection to the ghoul, I'll be public enemy number one with Angel Force. I'll have no way of helping Adrienne."

I cocked my head. "You want to hide the body?"

"It'll give us more time to find Adrienne. And as you said, although she attacked Thomasina, she didn't eat her. Adrienne's still in control. To some degree, anyway." Zandra stood and paced beside the body. "The angels will destroy Adrienne when they learn what she's done."

"If she even did it. It may not have been her."

Zandra shook her head. "Who else? I'm about to lose her."

Although her tone cracked my heart, I was tempted to suggest that would be the best thing if Adrienne was responsible for this attack, but Zandra was in no frame of mind to hear that.

I kept quiet, giving her time to process her panic and consider the options. Whatever she wanted to do, I'd support her. I'd even make an enormous angel corpse vanish.

Zandra looked down at Thomasina and groaned. "We can't conceal this. And as much as I want to protect Adrienne, if she did this, she has to pay. I'll defend her, though. She wasn't in control because she has no support. The angels might allow her to live. Do you think they'll do that? I could be her sponsor. A ghoul sponsor? It could work. I'll make it work."

"I've never heard of such a thing, but you could try. And the angels are usually benevolent with criminals." Although I doubted they would be when they discovered their esteemed Thomasina had been killed in this manner. This odd, unexplainable manner.

"They won't. And I'd be the same if anyone killed someone I worked with and respected. I'd want revenge." She tipped back her head. "We know what the punishment will be."

I nudged her calf. "You're doing the right thing. Summon the angels. They need to know what's going on. And they'll have noticed Thomasina didn't return to the group when the flare went up, so they'll be looking for her soon."

"And we don't want them to find us considering hiding her body," Zandra said. "I'll grab Finn and explain everything to him. He may help. Or at least slow down the angels before they go nuclear in their efforts to find Adrienne."

While Zandra dashed away through the trees, I looked around Thomasina's body again. A careful study of the bite marks revealed they were a strange shape. They weren't perfect semicircles, but more elongated. And they were big bites. That gave me hope, since Adrienne was a small woman.

Although ghouls had the disturbing ability to dislocate their jaws if they had a large meal to get through. But even if she'd done that, I wasn't certain the bite marks would fit her mouth.

Before I could investigate further, three angels slammed into the ground beside me, sending up plumes of dust. They stood and stared in silence at Thomasina.

Cythera appeared a second later with Bertoli and Finn flanking her. She strode over and stood by Thomasina's feet. A shimmer of emotions flashed across her beautiful face. "This is an outrage."

"It was the creature we were hunting." Bertoli's blue eyes were full of tears. "It must have attacked her."

"I should never have let her go off on her own." Cythera crouched beside the body, her wings drooping. "She'd seen a curious type of fungus and wished to study it. I didn't think there was any harm. What manner of monster could fell an angel?"

All the angels had appeared by now. So much for having more time to figure things out. The troop lowered their heads to pay their respects to their fallen comrade.

I did the same but also discreetly inclined my head at Zandra, showing I wished to speak to her without being overheard. We quietly dodged around the group after a respectful silence had passed and headed to a more private spot.

"Did you find something on Thomasina's body? Did you see Adrienne?" Zandra whispered as she watched the mourning angels.

"No, but I had another look at the bite marks. I'm not sure they're human. Well, ghoul. I don't think a ghoul did this." I also kept my voice low as the angels stirred from their silence.

Zandra glanced over her shoulder. "How can you be certain?"

"I can't, not without taking bite mark impressions from Adrienne. But the shape is odd and too big for your mother's mouth." I watched the angels as they stood around, not seeming to know what to do. "Some supernatural creatures bite each other as a form of greeting. It's a ritualistic thing. Maybe that is what we're looking at."

"What kind of creature are you thinking?"

"It could be a rogue yeti. And it fits with the reports of seeing a large lurking figure late at night. And when we've been in the woods, we've seen massive humanlike footprints. They'd tally with a yeti being in the area. Even that non-magical we found camping said he thought there was a Bigfoot around."

Zandra chewed on her bottom lip. "So this might not have been Adrienne, after all?"

"We must keep an open mind. We know Adrienne is different."

She didn't look convinced.

I continued to nudge and inspire hope. "Your sister investigated a case involving yeti bites. Now would be a good time to speak to her. Tempest could have useful insights."

Zandra didn't hesitate. She pulled out her mobile snow globe and made a connection.

"Hey, long time no hear. What's up?" Tempest Crypt's pale face appeared on the globe.

"I've got an interesting project I'm working on," Zandra said. "You know about yetis, don't you?"

"Yes." Tempest stretched out the word. "What are you mixed up in?"

I hopped onto Zandra's shoulder. "Greetings, Tempest. We have little time, so we'll keep the polite chat to a minimum."

She smirked. "Hey, Juno. Tried to kill anyone recently?"

"My obliteration days are mainly in my past, unless someone truly vexes me. We need to know about yetis. More specifically, the reasons they might bite an angel."

"Yetis biting angels?" Tempest's forehead furrowed. "Is that what's happening in Crimson Cove?"

"We're not sure," Zandra said. "An angel has been discovered with multiple bite marks on her body. I thought it was something else, but Juno reminded me about an old case you told her about."

"Yeah, sure. We had a case in Willow Tree Falls involving a yeti. He kept attacking people and biting them. Is that what's happening where you are?"

"Just one person, so far," I said. "The bite marks were extensive, though, and the angel died."

"Whoa! Yeti bites aren't toxic. Sure, they hurt, but they're more like crazy intense love bites. They suck and nibble their mates, and they're a display of affection and attraction. Those bites would never kill an angel."

"Have you ever heard of a yeti losing control and killing another supernatural using mating bites?" Zandra's tone verged on desperation.

"No. I suppose it's possible, though. But an angel! I don't know. Hey, quit doing that. I've put out enough fires for one day. Hang on a sec." Tempest disappeared, and when she came back into view, she held two adorable fluffy hellhound poodles in her arms. "Meet Trouble and Nightmare."

"Wiggles' offspring," I said.

Zandra grinned. "They're cute. I thought you'd found homes for all the pups."

"I did. But the owners who took them are realizing how much of a handful they are. These two have been re-homed twice, but they keep coming back. Honestly, I'm thinking about keeping them. Wiggles thinks it's a great idea, although he's insisting they don't share a bedroom with us."

"As charming as the fluffies are, could we focus on the killer yeti theory?" I said.

Tempest adjusted the squirming pups in her arms. "Sure. It's weird you say a yeti bit an angel. I can't imagine they'd be their type. Yetis have a thing about hair. The hairier their potential mate, the better. If it was a male yeti biting a female, they prefer females with dark hair. That was the case with the attacks in this area. I discovered a pattern with the victims."

"All the victims were dark haired?"

"Yep. And angels are blonde, white, and bubbly. I imagine yetis find them physically repulsive."

"Yeti love lust is a real thing, though, isn't it?" I said. "Could this yeti have been too out of control to realize who he was biting?"

"For a few seconds, but he'd have figured out what was going on. I can't imagine angels taste right to a yeti." Tempest got a slobbery lick from a pup and grimaced. "If you're having problems, I can find someone to look after the pups, and Wiggles and I can join you in Crimson Cove for a few days. Cloven Hoof is quiet. And, as usual, Merrie's doing an amazing job of managing things. Rhett's also away for a couple of weeks on business, so I'm kicking my heels, looking for something to do."

"No! You're good. Thanks for the information," Zandra said rapidly. "We've got this."

"I don't mind. And it's been ages since I've seen you. How's the magic practice going?"

"Perfect. No problems there. I'll catch up with you another time when I've got less on my plate."

Tempest scowled at her. "You can't keep making excuses not to have visitors. And there's an open dinner invitation waiting for you. The rest of the family keeps asking about you, too. You stay away too much longer, and they'll hunt you out and force you to be sociable."

"You're a one to lecture me on being sociable."

"I've mellowed." Tempest arched an eyebrow. "A bit."

"I'll get back for dinner soon. Gotta go."

"Don't get in too much trouble," Tempest said. "Juno, keep an eye on her for me."

"Always. Be well, Tempest."

One of the hellhound poodles let out a jet of flame, and the connection disconnected.

"That was helpful," I said. "It gives us another option."

Zandra blew out a breath. "Maybe you're right about it being a supernatural creature. Something strong that could destroy an angel. Maybe a yeti fits the bill. I'm not sure what we should do next, though."

"Find out how this biter attacked and killed an angel. Was it a targeted kill? Did they do it deliberately? And if so, why did they want Thomasina dead?"

"And make sure Adrienne had nothing to do with it," Zandra said.

I rested my head against the side of her face. "And if she did?"

Zandra gulped. "I have no clue. But we'll figure that out when the time comes."

Chapter 7

Once bitten...

Zandra paced in front of me across the length of our rented basement lodgings. She kept tapping her fingers on her thighs and muttering to herself.

"Try to relax." I was perched on the end of our bed, my tail tucked neatly around my front paws.

"I could barely concentrate at work today. I kept thinking about Thomasina and how Adrienne could be involved in her murder."

"We did everything we could to find Adrienne close to the scene of the crime. There was no evidence it was her. I don't think she was involved."

Zandra slid me a glare as she passed by again. "You don't know that for certain. And we can't go back and get a look at the scene again because Angel Force sealed it off. We could have missed something important. Something that points to Adrienne."

"We saw everything we needed to see when we discovered Thomasina's body." I grimaced as I recalled the unsettling sight of a downed angel covered in bite marks.

"But how did she die? Did we miss some fatal injury?"

"I don't believe so. There wasn't any blood. And it would have been obvious if someone had cut her down with an angel scythe. It was just the bite marks. Whoever bit her must have a toxic bite. And that rules out your mother."

"Does it? Everyone keeps saying she's not your typical ghoul. Maybe she evolved a poisonous bite since she's so different." Zandra threw up her hands and sighed.

"I don't think that's how it works with ghouls."

She glared at me again. "You're a ghoul expert?"

"No, but I have a wide knowledge base."

"Then you explain it. I don't think it's a coincidence Adrienne's still out there and this angel shows up dead. We knew it was only a matter of time before she lost control and killed. And Angel Force has had reports of a ghoul in the area. They'll be thinking the same thing."

"The statements we provided will persuade them otherwise. We suggested useful alternatives for them to investigate."

"You think they'll listen to us? Bertoli hates me, and Cythera looks at me as if she thinks I'm about to blast her with a dangerous spell."

"We have Finn on our side."

"Will that be enough? Not all the angels like him because he's different."

"Only Bertoli doesn't like him. Finn is competent in his job, and Cythera is aware of that. She'll listen when he suggests alternatives to a ghoul being the killer."

"It's not enough. We need to be in on this case. I have to make sure they don't focus on Adrienne or find out she's in Crimson Cove until I've figured out what to do with her." Zandra paced to the stairs but didn't go up.

"What you need to do is sit down and take deep breaths."

"I wouldn't need to be stressing and taking deep breaths if it wasn't for you."

I slow blinked at her. "And I understand you're angry with me, but it's not helping the situation."

"Sometimes, Juno, you talk to me as if I'm a child. I'm allowed to be angry."

I huffed out a soft breath and quelled my frustration. Zandra had no idea how old I was or how much of the world I'd experienced. And in my mind, I often saw her as a child. A young witch, growing into her powers. Although I worked hard not to talk down to her, I was failing in this moment.

"If I'd known Adrienne was out there having been changed into a ghoul, we'd have found her sooner. I could have gotten her off the streets and kept a close eye on her. This attack would never have happened." Zandra paced and turned, paced and turned, her hair wound around her fingers.

"Possibly, but I was looking out for any sign of her, as was Finn. And we still don't know she killed Thomasina."

"If I'd been involved, we'd have found her in time." Zandra stomped across the basement. "Now the angels will capture her and destroy her. When they get an idea in their heads that someone has committed a crime, they don't let it go. Even if she's innocent, which seems unlikely to me, they'll pin this murder on her. Then I'll lose her forever." The last sentence choked out of her.

I hopped off the bed and blocked Zandra's path. "I am sorry. I thought I was doing the right thing by keeping the information from you. I needed to know it was Adrienne and find out what had happened to her before worrying you. I insisted Finn and Torrin keep that information from you, too. This is all on me."

She raked a hand through her hair. "We're supposed to be a team. We shouldn't keep anything from each other."

"That's something I'm learning." I weaved around her legs. As hard as I tried not to let it, my past bonds with other magic users still affected me. I hadn't always been treated kindly, and as a result, I kept things to myself.

Zandra crouched and scratched between my ears. "I know how hard it is not to let our pasts mess with our present. Every day, I get annoyed when I think about what a lousy parent Adrienne was and wonder why I bother with her. But she's family, and family looks out for each other."

I could have debated that point with her for hours. Blood didn't have to mean obligation. The person who birthed you wasn't automatically a positive role model or even someone you should spend time with. But it felt like we were on the verge of reconciling, so I didn't want the arguing to continue.

"I'll always support you, whatever you do with Adrienne when we find her. I wasn't around when you were young, but I understand how difficult things were for you. If you want to walk away from this situation and never mention Adrienne again, I'll make that happen. I even know memory wipe spells if you want this taken away for good."

Zandra sighed and closed her eyes for several seconds. "No, I won't abandon her. I know how lousy that feels. She'd leave me alone for days sometimes when I was a kid. I used to get so scared and wonder if she was ever coming back."

I kept my anger in check. Every time I heard an example of her less than acceptable childhood, my hackles rose. But I was here now, and I'd ensure Zandra never felt like that again. "We'll find her before the angels and figure out if she had anything to do with what happened to Thomasina."

Zandra pressed her forehead against mine. "Let's make that happen. Although we still need to figure out how to get the inside scoop on what the angels are planning to do next."

I cocked my head. "The person who's arrived at the front door could help with that."

A minute later, the basement door leading into our cozy home opened. "Hey, is it okay if I come down?"

It was Finn.

"Sure. We're here." Zandra stood, a wary smile on her face as he appeared. "Any news?"

He tugged on his rumpled white shirt as he came down the stairs. "I just finished my shift. And we need to talk."

"Is it bad news?" I hopped back onto the bed.

"It's not great news."

"The angels still think a ghoul killed Thomasina?" Zandra perched beside me.

"It's one of their lines of investigation." Finn grabbed a wooden chair, flipped it around, and straddled it. "And an angel killer has everyone interested. Even the higher angels are prodding into this investigation and demanding results. When an angel dies, we act fast. This murder shows we're vulnerable, and it lets the world know we can be killed. There are bad guys out there who'd be thrilled to get this information."

"We were just figuring out how those bites killed Thomasina," I said.

"Were there any other injuries?" Zandra said. "Has an autopsy been done yet?"

"Nothing unusual was uncovered. There's been no full autopsy. It'll happen today. Thomasina was simply covered in bite wounds. Most of them didn't even break the skin."

"Are the bites still being considered the cause of death?" Zandra said.

"So far, the initial test results have come back with nothing toxic in her system. It seems like she was bitten to death." Finn shrugged. "I just don't get it. Thomasina was healthy, in her prime. This attack shouldn't have bothered her. She should have fought back."

"How is Cythera taking the news?" I said.

"She's alternating between sitting in silence at her desk, staring into space, and yelling at us. And she rarely yells, so it's a sure sign something is wrong." Finn rolled his shoulders. "No one knows what to do. Even I'm struggling with this one."

"The angels must still be looking for whoever did it," I said.

"Sure. There's been another sweep of the woods, but we came up empty-handed again. Cythera is considering expanding the search to the whole of Crimson Cove, but that'll take massive resources and external help from other branches of Angel Force. And we're still not even certain what, or who, we're looking for."

"You're looking for Adrienne," Zandra said glumly. "You have to."

Finn hesitated for a few seconds. "Not necessarily. One of the things I wanted to talk to you about was the bite marks. They're like a ghoul bite but not identical."

"I noticed that, too," I said. "I wondered if the ghoul, if it was a ghoul, dislocated their jaw to get in bigger bites."

Zandra grimaced. "Juno, you have some seriously disturbing thoughts."

"She does. But it's a possibility we need to consider," Finn said. "I've seen ghouls do freaky things when they find something they really want to eat. And there's something unusual about the bite marks. They're more wolf or dog shaped than ghoul."

"But the teeth impressions were blunt," I said. "If it was a wolf, you'd see fang marks."

"True. And nothing with blunt teeth should want to eat an angel," Finn said. "Blunt teeth usually mean we're dealing with a herbivore."

"Were there signs of missing teeth in the bite marks?" Zandra said.

"Nothing like that. Our killer has a fine set of gnashers. Why?"

"Adrienne always took great care of her teeth. She was proud that she didn't have a single filling."

"Ah, got you. All the teeth were present and correct."

"What about the yeti angle?" I said. "They have huge teeth, and they're mainly blunt. Yetis are herbivorous."

"I'm pressing that option whenever we talk about the case." Finn shifted in his seat. "But there's something else I need to speak to you about."

Zandra tensed, and I rested a paw on her thigh to keep her calm.

"We're not going to like this, are we?" I said.

"You're probably going to hate me, but I've got to tell Cythera about Adrienne and what happened to her. I'll get in trouble for concealing it this long, but Cythera needs to know all the information in case Adrienne is connected to this murder."

Zandra slumped forward. "But then Angel Force will only look at her as the killer."

"You should wait," I said to Finn. "We need to gather more information."

"I can't delay any longer. I've known Adrienne has been a ghoul and living in this area for a while, and I've kept it from everyone in Angel Force. If she killed Thomasina, she'll kill again. Once a ghoul attacks people, the hunt instinct gets out of control, and they can't manage the urge to gorge on fresh meat."

"Especially when that meat screams and runs away. Give us another day," I said. "We were planning to do our own search and try more locator magic to find Adrienne."

"We've already tried dozens of location spells," Zandra said. "They don't work. Now Adrienne's a ghoul, her magical essence has shifted. We don't know what we're looking for."

"We considered that option, too. Cythera called in a couple of powerful witches to find the killer, but they said the same thing. They need to know what they're looking for before they can locate it. Cast out a location spell, and it'll throw back dozens of anomalies that'll only complicate this case," Finn said. "I know you don't want me to reveal what happened to Adrienne, but I'm worried she could have a power we don't understand."

"You think Adrienne's a super ghoul?" Zandra arched an eyebrow. "You're really going with that angle?"

"If it was her, she's strong enough to kill an angel." Finn straightened in his seat, all signs of his usual casual demeanor gone. "I need to be clear on this. Everyone at Angel Force is scared. And when angels get panicky, they can get mean. They can also make poor judgment calls."

"You're jumping ahead too far. We don't even know it was Adrienne." I could sense Zandra's panic, and I needed to take the fear talk down a notch. "You must keep pressing on the yeti angle. We saw footprints in the woods that could belong to a yeti."

Finn raked his hands through his hair. "Sure. I'll do what I can. But time is running out."

I looked at Zandra, and the fear in her eyes made my heart skip a beat. "What about that non-magical guy we met? He was lurking around and asking questions. And he's not normal. He knows there's something special about Crimson Cove."

"Yeah, but he's a non-magical. He could barely hurt a fly, let alone bring down an almost omnipotent supernatural being. He's not involved with this murder," Zandra said.

"Or the big cat prints? When we've been looking for Adrienne, we've seen tracks in the woods. Maybe a rogue familiar got a lucky bite in on Thomasina."

"Big cats have teeth like you," Finn said. "And there was no sign of any fangs involved in this murder."

"I'm throwing out options," I said. "You should do the same. We need to find other avenues for the angels to look into."

Finn drew in a deep breath. "There is one piece of good news."

"Does the news mean Adrienne is innocent?" Zandra's expression grew hopeful.

"No, but unless she travels, it means this murder was less likely to be caused by her actions." He drummed his fingers on the back of the chair. "I need you to promise you won't spread this around. It's been a closely guarded secret at Angel Force, and we've been sworn to silence. I'll lose my job if Cythera learns I told you about this."

We both leaned forward.

"What is it?" I said.

"You must pinky swear silence." Finn held out his hand, smallest finger lifted.

Zandra glowered at him. "We're not in pre-school."

I dabbed his finger with a paw. "We won't say a word."

Zandra shrugged and did a brief pinky swear.

Finn nodded. "This isn't the first angel killed in this way."

Zandra's eyes widened. "There's a legit angel serial killer on the loose?"

"Yep. And Angel Force is scrambling to solve this mystery. Although I can't understand why anyone wouldn't like us." A little of Finn's usual confident swagger surfaced, but it seemed forced.

"They were all bitten to death like Thomasina?" I said.

"Exactly the same way. And all of them had multiple bite marks on their bodies. The tests run drew a blank as to the cause of death. Angel Force is seriously spooked. It's been a long time since they've had to deal with such a serious attack on the establishment." He pinched his chin together with his finger and thumb.

I curled around Zandra. Although this was bad news for the angels, it was positive news for Adrienne. "Where were these other murders?"

"All within a two-hundred-mile radius of here but getting closer with each kill. There have been four angels killed. Five including Thomasina."

"Is the killer looking for a specific angel, or taking advantage of lone angels and taking a bite when they get the chance?" I jumped down and prowled the basement, tossing this new information around to see how it fit.

"No one knows."

"I have no clue how mobile Adrienne is, but it seems unlikely she'd target angels or travel far to find a lone angel to bite. Ghouls aren't that smart, even if she is different from your average ghoul. They kill whatever prey they find. But to be certain she isn't involved, we must find her," Zandra said.

Finn tilted his head from side to side. "I have an idea."

"About how we can find the actual killer and rule out Adrienne?" I trotted over to him, my tail up.

"No, but I know you want to be involved in this investigation. I spoke to Cythera and pressed the case about the yeti. She agreed we need a specialist team to work with us." Finn grinned. "So, I bigged up your credentials. How about you temporarily join Angel Force as our resident animal experts?"

Chapter 8

The suspects line up

The next morning, I waited outside the animal control office with Zandra. She'd barely slept last night as we'd gone over the options regarding Adrienne's involvement in Thomasina's murder and the alarming discovery four other angels had been killed in the same way.

We'd pounced on Finn's proposal to be the specialist team working with Angel Force. All we had to do now was convince Barney to let us have the time off.

"You're here bright and early." He strolled toward us, the usual brown paper bag full of breakfast pastries in one hand and a large takeout mug of coffee from Sorcha's café in the other.

"I wanted to catch you before you got busy," Zandra said. "You've heard about what happened in the woods yesterday, right?"

He winced as he pulled out his keys and unlocked the office. "It's terrible what happened to that angel. I thought it was a sick joke when I heard the rumors. How did she die?"

We followed Barney into the office.

"That's what Angel Force needs help with," I said. "And they want experts on the case who know about dangerous animals who have the power to kill an angel."

Barney took the lid off his coffee, blew on it, and took a sip. "They think it was a rogue familiar who attacked this angel?"

"They're not certain." Zandra bounced on the balls of her feet. "Finn came to see us yesterday and asked if we'd help on the case."

"Oh! They're really that stuck? I assumed they'd have their own experts."

"They don't know which way to turn. And because the murder was so close to home, Finn's uncertain they can remain neutral when searching for suspects. We don't want them to target the wrong animal. Especially not if it needs help or has been abandoned and attacked out of desperation."

"Of course. It must be difficult for the angels when one of their own is slain." He shook his head. "I'm still in shock an angel was actually killed. There are few weapons or spells that do permanent damage to an angel."

"Which is why they need an impartial helping hand," I said. "I have extensive knowledge of all magical creatures, and you're always saying how well Zandra does in her role."

"I have no doubt as to your expertise, Juno. And you're right. Zandra is a model employee." Barney took out a pastry. He pulled it in half and handed one half to Zandra. "I could work something out with the others. How long will they need you?"

"They want this resolved fast. I can't imagine it'll be more than two or three days," Zandra said.

"Then you must go. This terrible crime has to be solved as soon as possible. Don't worry about your workload. I've got you covered. I may even do a few of the jobs myself. All this paperwork and the back-to-back meetings gets wearing." His gaze settled on a pile of papers that needed his attention.

"Thanks, Barney." Zandra blew out a breath and visibly relaxed. Mission accomplished.

I glanced around the office. "Is Sammy not with you?"

Barney cleared his throat. "We're taking a break from each other. We're... well, to be blunt, we're not enjoying each other's company. While I appreciate your attempt to bond us, it's not working. I feel so tense when Sammy is here, and he keeps trying to impress me and knocking things over. He means no harm, but..."

"He's not Izzie."

His gaze lowered. "Exactly. Some familiars can't be replaced. I shouldn't have bothered. Better off alone."

I nodded sagely. Sammy must have had the awkward conversation with Barney. "Better luck next time."

Barney glanced at the empty cardboard box in the corner of the office. A box made for a fluffy, plump cat to fill. "Indeed. If there is a next time. Well, off you go."

We hurried out of the office and headed to the Angel Force building.

"Play it cool when we get there," I said.

"No time for that. I'm gonna kick them in their feathery butts if they keep obsessing over Adrienne as the killer."

"Angels prefer sugar to spice."

Zandra snorted. "I'm intending to cayenne pepper their feathers and then dip them in hot sauce."

I gritted my teeth. I'd need to watch my wonderful witch. When her temper was up, her prickles came out, and that ended badly for anyone around her.

Finn was waiting for us at the reception desk. "All good?"

"Barney agreed you can have us on loan for a few days. Any updates overnight?" Zandra followed Finn into the open plan office, and I was right behind her.

"No, but we're having an overview meeting in a few minutes to talk over everything we know. And you're involved. I cleared it with Cythera, and she's happy for you to be here."

"Are you sure you know the meaning of the word happy?" I said.

He grinned. "She's tolerating outside help because of the seriousness of the situation. That's as good as I can get for you."

"That'll do. So long as we know everything that's going on."

"The second anyone gets a hit on Adrienne's location, I'm going after her," Zandra said.

"We're going after her," I said. "Carefully and with a plan in place, so no one gets injured."

Zandra simply nodded.

Hmmm... I still had some making up to do with my witch before we were back on the right track.

The usual easy-going buzz in the office was absent, and there were more angels here than I'd ever seen before. Not a single one was smiling. There was also a distinct lack of the usual pastries and coffee aroma in the air. These angels meant business.

Cythera stepped out of her office a few seconds later. Her gaze settled on me and Zandra for a second, and she gave a curt nod. "Now everyone's here, I'll review the information and lay out our next steps. As you'll all have noticed, we've called in assistance from animal control. There's the possibility a dangerous, powerful wild creature killed Thomasina, so we need expert guidance."

Bertoli, who was standing close to Cythera, sneered at us but made no comment.

Cythera strode to a large whiteboard on one wall. "This is the crucial information. Thomasina was killed between one and one-thirty yesterday afternoon. A thorough investigation of her body revealed no mortal wounds. Therefore, we must assume the multiple shallow bites covering her body were the cause of death."

There were several unhappy murmurs from the angels.

"Further tests have been requested, and a repeat magical scan will be undertaken. We must make sure we miss nothing. But for now, the cause of death is the bites."

Zandra raised a hand.

"There's no need for that," Cythera said the second she spotted her.

"Sorry, I don't know the protocol. Has there been any more tox screens run on the bites? Finn mentioned no poison was found, but it seems impossible such shallow bite wounds would cause an angel's death. Anyone's death."

"We repeated the tests to be sure, but nothing was discovered that caused us alarm," Cythera said.

"What about defensive wounds?" I said. "If a wild creature attacked Thomasina, you'd expect to see bite marks on her forearms where she was protecting herself or on her back if she was curled up."

"The bite wounds were concentrated on her shoulders. It appears she did nothing to ward off the attack," Cythera said.

"She lay there and let it happen?" I said. "Why didn't she defend herself?"

Cythera's forehead furrowed. "It's a question that needs answering. Moving on to the possible suspects—"

"I have another question," I said.

Cythera drew in a breath. "Go on."

"There was a puddle of icy water around Thomasina. I stepped in it and muddied my paws."

"How is that relevant to this investigation?"

"She's about to suggest we pay for her to go to the grooming parlor," Bertoli said.

I hissed at him. "It hasn't rained in Crimson Cove for weeks. Why was the water there?"

No one spoke as the angels exchanged perplexed glances.

"It can stay damp under the trees," Bertoli finally said. "Or there could be an underground well. I don't see how that has anything to do with how Thomasina was killed."

"It shouldn't have been there," I said.

"Thomasina didn't drown in a puddle," Cythera said. "A full autopsy will take place today. Everything will be checked. Moving on to the suspects in this murder."

"She's not listening to me," I muttered to Zandra.

"It doesn't help she's got Bertoli dripping poison in her ear. He's such a viper."

"I expect he's been telling Cythera not to trust us. We'll keep pressing until she listens, and the angels will have to get used to us being around. Now we're here, we're not going anywhere."

"My focus in this investigation is the reports of a ghoul roaming in Crimson Cove," Cythera said.

Zandra tensed beside me.

"I've had the reports reviewed again, and I have no doubt there's a ghoul in the area."

"I've seen no ghouls," I said. "And I'm in the woods all the time. It's practically my second home."

Cythera lifted her chin. "While I appreciate your input, you're only one small cat, and you cannot be everywhere. The woods are vast. The ghoul may have not been in the same area as you while you were out wandering."

"What about the big cat sightings?" Zandra said. "We've seen all kinds of footprints in the woods."

"A big cat with blunt teeth?" Bertoli said. "I thought you were supposed to be an animal expert."

"They could have a mutation." I sprang to my witch's defense. "Or it's an old cat. Sometimes, we lose our teeth, and they can get blunt with age."

"Some mangy old kitty wouldn't have done this to Thomasina," Bertoli said. "She was powerful and smart. She'd have been able to defeat a worn out old cat."

"Maybe Thomasina was attacked from behind, and she hit her head," I said. "If she was woozy, she wouldn't have fought so well."

"There were no significant head wounds," Cythera said. "And I agree with Bertoli. It's unlikely a big cat was involved in this killing. I want to focus on the ghoul. We find the creature and bring it in. We may not be able to question it, but we can check the bite mark patterns. That'll be enough to confirm guilt."

"That's not perfect evidence," I said.

Cythera glared at me. "Even if this ghoul wasn't involved in this heinous crime, it needs to be taken out of circulation."

"Ghouls are nothing but trouble," Bertoli said. "The sooner we destroy it, the better."

Zandra sucked in a breath, but I pressed a paw on her hand, and she didn't speak.

"I'm still in favor of it being a yeti attack," Finn said. "Zandra is an expert in yeti behavior, and she believes the bites were caused by a yeti."

Zandra's cheeks flushed slightly as she came under scrutiny from the angels. "I consulted with a specialist, and she confirmed yetis get mating lust. They bite their potential mate to show their interest."

"There haven't been yetis around here for some time," Cythera said.

"That doesn't mean there isn't one here now," I said. "They travel great distances in search of a perfect mate. Crimson Cove woods is a decent habitat for them."

"Why would a yeti target Thomasina?" Bertoli said. "Wouldn't he be more interested in another yeti if he's seeking a mate?"

"Yetis lose focus and make mistakes when their mating fever peaks," Zandra said. "There was a case in Willow Tree Falls where a yeti attacked women based on their appearance. And sometimes yetis pick other supernaturals as partners."

"And yetis have great physical strength," Finn said. "I'd find it a struggle to bring one down on my own."

"No surprise there," Bertoli muttered.

Cythera raised a hand. "It's a possibility. While we search for the ghoul, we'll look into sightings and evidence of a yeti visitor."

"There are fresh footprints in the woods," I said. "This yeti should be your prime suspect."

Cythera made a few notes on the whiteboard. "The number one suspect is the ghoul. I'm not discounting other possibilities, but this dangerous creature must be our target."

"They're not letting it go," Zandra whispered to me. "We need to find them a better suspect. Someone who's a perfect fit for the attack."

"Cannibal Bill!" I blurted out.

The angels looked at me.

I swiped a paw over one ear, feigning nonchalance. "Thomasina was killed in Cannibal Bill's territory."

"He's an urban legend." Bertoli did a slow, deliberate eye roll that was impossible to miss. "He doesn't eat people."

"I'm not familiar with this individual," Cythera said. "Should he be a cause for concern?"

Zandra nudged Finn. "You must have tangled with Bill. Tell the others about him."

He pulled himself upright. "He's real enough."

"Could Cannibal Bill have killed one of us?" Cythera said. "What kind of magical creature is he?"

Finn glanced at us, indecision on his face. "He's a mid-level warlock. There's nothing special about his magic, although he's good with stealth spells."

"Why does the small white cat think he's an angel killer?" Cythera said.

"Because she's amusing herself by wasting our time," Bertoli said.

I ignored the slights and pawed at Finn, so he'd continue to conjure our ideal suspect.

Finn pursed his lips. "Cannibal Bill has a troubled past. He lost the plot five or six years ago. He was your typical out-of-condition, middle-aged guy, but he got dumped by his long-term girlfriend. She went vegetarian and wanted him to do the same. They argued about it and split up."

"So he started eating people because his girlfriend said he couldn't eat a steak anymore?" Bertoli shook his head. "This really is pointless."

"Let me finish. After that, Bill got obsessed with the keto diet. It's that meat and fat heavy diet that excludes fiber. Something also happened to his sister around the same time. I can't remember if they fell out, and she moved away, but she hasn't been seen around here for a long time."

"Oh, please. Next, you'll be saying this keto diet turned Bill into a supernatural monster who kills angels." Bertoli's derision was clear.

A flicker of red sparks shimmered across Finn's neatly tucked in wings. "No, I'm not saying that. But the guy has some weird beliefs. And... well, I've had to speak to him about illegal hunting practices in the woods. He's staked his claim on an area, and he hates anyone going near it. And Juno is right. Thomasina was killed on what Cannibal Bill believes is his land."

"And I expect he knows plenty about hunting dangerous animals," I said. "He'd know how to bring down an angel. And if he has advanced stealth spells, he could have crept up on Thomasina and gotten her when she wasn't expecting it."

"He uses inventive traps to catch his meat," Finn said. "He hunts all his food and never buys from the local stores."

"If he was hunting and discovered Thomasina, why bite her and then leave the body?" Doubt was written all over Cythera's face. "Wouldn't he have taken her if he intended to feast on her?"

Finn headed to a filing cabinet. "I'm not sure, but there have been reports filed recently on Cannibal Bill. Let me get the details. I didn't deal with the case."

"Meat heavy diets are dreadful for the colon. They negatively affect the brain and make people do all kinds of strange things," I said. "People who exclude yummy fibrous goodness always run into problems. I've heard of many cases of spells backfiring because people only ate meat and fat. It's bad for your magic. My advice, if you wish to eat a flesh-based diet, stick to fish. It's much lighter on the digestion."

"Thanks for that, Juno," Zandra muttered.

I inclined my head. Always happy to share useful information.

Finn walked back with a file in his hand. "Here we are. Cannibal Bill confronted a couple who'd gone into the woods to have some private fun together. Huh! I didn't know this. He tried to bite them."

"There you go! I told you too much red meat was bad for you," I said.

Most of the angels looked cautious, but a few seemed angry. They were finally paying attention to this new suspect.

"Cannibal Bill sounds unwell," Cythera said. "Everyone should have plenty of fiber in their diet. It keeps you regular."

"He'd have blunt teeth to match the bite marks," Zandra said. "He's a great fit as a suspect."

"I don't disagree," Cythera said. "But there are enough of us to cover all the suspects. Finn and Bertoli, you interview Cannibal Bill."

"I'll take Zandra and Juno with me, too," Finn said.

"As you wish. The rest of us will continue to search the area. Anyone with information, report back to me immediately. Look for evidence of ghouls and yetis. Be cautious when approaching any suspects. We can't afford any more fatalities."

I jumped onto Zandra's shoulder. "What do you think? Could Cannibal Bill have done it?"

"Not a clue, but I'm glad you threw his name into the mix."

"I had to do something. The angels were circling the ghoul possibility too closely."

"Finn, let's go chat to Cannibal Bill. See what he has to say," Zandra said.

He grimaced. "Sure, but it might not be as simple as you think."

Chapter 9

How to catch an angel

"I'm still amazed Cythera agreed to us helping like this," Zandra said as we headed out of Angel Force with Finn and a grumbling Bertoli.

Finn shrugged. "It's a sign she's panicking."

"Cythera never panics. She has full control of this situation." Bertoli's scowl revealed what he thought about having to work with me and Zandra.

"Considering an angel has just been ruthlessly slaughtered on her watch, she was eerily calm," I said.

Bertoli grimaced. "She's a professional and has hundreds of years of experience leading successful troops of angels. Of course, she'll be calm. Although..."

I glanced up at him. "You've noticed her struggling?"

"No! Never. But perhaps she is stressed. After all, I can't understand why she's allowing amateurs to be involved in such an important case."

"Zandra and Juno aren't amateurs," Finn said. "They're professionals trained by animal control.

And since there's the possibility of a dangerous animal involved in this crime, we need their skills. You should thank them for helping. They don't have to. It's not like they're getting paid."

"Although a few nice fish dinners wouldn't go amiss," I said. "But we're always willing to lend our expertise to the angels in their time of need."

Bertoli grunted and stomped ahead of us.

"Ignore him. Everyone's rattled because of what happened to Thomasina and the other angels," Finn said.

"It's no surprise," Zandra said. "It wasn't a fun ride to discover her in the woods."

"Are you okay?" Finn said. "Dumb question. Of course, you aren't. It would freak anyone out to discover a body."

"Yeah, but it's not my first since moving to Crimson Cove," Zandra said. "It's as if Death has started following me."

I glanced up at her as we reached the edge of the woods. I didn't want Death becoming a close friend. It got everyone eventually, but Death had no place in my young witch's life.

"It'll be easier if I fly in from here," Finn said. "Cannibal Bill has weird magical mojo around his hut. And it's deep in the woods. It'll take a while to get there if we go on foot."

"No flying for me," I said. "We'll make our own way there."

"Sure thing. His hut is three miles north of the pet cemetery. When you get there, you'll sense the magic."

"What's he using?" I said.

"Mainly wards. They discourage people from lingering. You'll know you're in the right place when you feel chills and paranoia. It's nothing to worry about, but it's how Bill operates. He hates anyone bothering him."

"He'll have to get used to it, since he's a suspect in a murder investigation," I said. "We'll see you there in a moment."

Finn's white angel wings flared red as he shot into the sky and disappeared.

"Shall we?" Zandra patted her shoulder.

I leaped onto it and clung on while she cast a translocation spell, bringing us deep into the woods. The second her feet hit solid ground, a wave of anxiety rippled along my spine.

Zandra shuddered. "I'm glad Finn warned us about Cannibal Bill's horrible magic. This place gives me the heebie jeebies."

I rubbed my face against hers. "I'm here to protect you."

She patted my side. "Right back at you."

Finn landed a few feet away and tucked his wings behind him. He looked around and grimaced. "I'm not sure where his house is, and he keeps it concealed. It's basically a massive mound of compacted earth. It's got a flat moss roof, so it blends into the environment. He rarely leaves this part of the woods, other than to hunt."

"He'd better not hunt us," I said, as we made our way slowly through the thick foliage.

"Be on the lookout for him. Cannibal Bill startles easy and has a quick trigger finger. He always shoots first."

"I've heard he prefers crossbows to conversation," Zandra said.

"The guy has issues."

"Where's Bertoli?" I said.

"I'm here." Bertoli appeared from behind a tree. "I was scouting the perimeter." His wings trembled, as did his hands. Cannibal Bill's magic was doing a number on him.

"Let's make this fast," Finn said, "before the paranoia gets too intense and we end up attacking each other."

We walked as quietly as we could along a non-existent path. There were plenty of dry leaves and crunchy twigs underfoot, so if Cannibal Bill was on the lookout for trespassers, he'd know we were coming. That was no bad thing. If he knew we were out here, he may be less likely to let loose with his crossbow. I looked around. Or he could be lining up his crossbow sight, ready to let an arrow fly.

I shook out my fur, happy to stay on Zandra's shoulder for now. I'd have to watch this paranoia magic. It was powerful stuff.

"We need to hurry this up," Bertoli said. "Cythera wants a quick result."

"Don't go too fast," Finn cautioned as Bertoli surged ahead of us. "Cannibal Bill loves his animal traps."

"They won't affect us."

"You could miss a trip wire. Who knows what it'll be rigged with," Finn said.

"We're angels. We're indestructible."

"Try telling that to Thomasina," I muttered.

Bertoli must have overheard, because he glared at me. "We should split up. We'll cover more ground and won't get under each other's feet."

"I vote for sticking together," Finn said. "No one wants to be cornered on their own by Cannibal Bill if he's hungry."

"You're being ridiculous. Cannibal Bill is an absurd urban legend dreamed up by sad loners who have too much time on their hands." Bertoli diverted off to the right. "I'll yell if I see anything useful."

"He's his usual ray of joyful sunshine," I said as Bertoli vanished from sight.

"Well, it's complicated. Bertoli had a thing for Thomasina. I overheard him talking to someone before she arrived. He was thinking about asking her on a date."

"Bertoli gets crushes on a lot of people, doesn't he?" I said.

"The guy's lonely. And he's a jerk, so he struggles to get dates the regular way."

"I heard that," Bertoli yelled.

Finn chuckled. "I'm only speaking the truth, my friend."

"Hey, look at this." Zandra stopped by a tree with three lines gouged into it. "Cannibal Bill's work?"

"Could be." Finn looked around. "It makes sense he'd mark the places he'd rigged traps to make sure he didn't set them off and get knocked out by a flying boulder."

There was a high-pitched yelp that was cut off abruptly, and something crashed to the ground.

We dashed through the trees and discovered Bertoli strung up between two solid pines in a huge net. He was squirming around, his wing feathers sticking through the netting.

"Get me down from here!"

"I told you to be careful." Finn was grinning as he walked beneath Bertoli.

"I can't get out. There's magic attached to this net." Bertoli continued to squirm.

"It couldn't have happened to a nicer guy," I muttered.

"Cut me down," Bertoli said.

"Give me a few minutes. I need to figure out how this works. If I drop you on your head and give you a concussion, you'll complain about it for weeks." Finn walked away to investigate the trap mechanism.

I waited with Zandra, enjoying watching Bertoli swinging gently in the breeze. "The more I find out about Cannibal Bill, the more I think it's possible he could be the killer. And the guy has powerful magic. I've got the creeping chills running all the way along my spine."

"And whatever he's wrapped around the net to trap Bertoli, it shows he knows what he's doing." Zandra tilted her head as she watched Bertoli. "But why bite Thomasina so many times?"

"Perhaps he wasn't sure he liked the way she tasted. Angels probably taste of sugary candy floss."

"We do not taste like candy floss," Bertoli snapped. "Where is Finn? Why isn't he getting me down?"

"He's working on it. Relax. It's not as if you can go anywhere." Zandra crouched and turned her head so her mouth was by my ear. "I can't figure out why Thomasina lay there and let someone bite her so often."

"If Cannibal Bill's as shady as I think he is, he could have gotten into the dark stuff. Maybe he's using illegal spells that damage angels. He could have cast one on Thomasina and then got to work. Munch, munch, munch."

Zandra grimaced. "But why bite and not eat? Is angel skin abnormally tough?"

"Of course it's tough," Bertoli said, still ear wigging into our private conversation. "And our hearing is also excellent. You can't hide anything from me."

Finn returned a moment later. "Bad news, Bertoli. There's serious magic tying up this trap. It'll take me time to break through it. It might be easier if we get Cannibal Bill to help get you down. I don't want to blow your head off by accident."

"Then hurry up and find him," Bertoli said.

"You hang tight up there. We'll hunt him out."

Bertoli stopped struggling, and his face paled. "Wait! What if he comes for me?"

"You don't think he's the killer, so why are you worried?" I said.

"I didn't say I was."

"Then stay where you are. If he shows up, you're more than a match for Cannibal Bill," Finn said. "And as you said, Cythera wants fast results. Or are you happy to explain we spent a couple of hours getting you out of a mess you landed yourself in because you wouldn't listen to sense?"

Bertoli glowered at Finn. "Don't leave me behind when you're done. And keep this between us. No one needs to know about this situation. It could have happened to anyone."

"Anyone with half the intellect he was born with," Zandra whispered.

"Whatever you say, buddy." Finn inclined his head at us. "I found storage sheds close to here. They most likely belong to Bill. That suggests we're close to his home."

I flicked my tail at Bertoli as we left him swinging. That would teach him to be so grumpy and unwelcoming of our assistance.

Finn led us toward two large wooden sheds. I hadn't even gotten close to the first one when a wave of unpleasantly fetid magic whacked into me. I hopped off Zandra's shoulder, wrinkled my booping snooter, and stopped to assess the situation.

"It's not just me feeling that, is it?" Zandra had also slowed, her hands curling into fists.

"It's more of Cannibal Bill's diversion tactics," Finn said. "He doesn't want anyone to see what's inside these sheds."

I forced myself to move closer and sniffed around. There was a gruesome tang of old blood and sweat.

"They've got protection spells around them," Finn said. "But this one feels weaker. I can break through this magic."

"I almost wish you wouldn't. But go on, let's see what disturbing things he's hiding," Zandra said.

I kept sniffing around the first shed. I wasn't certain, but I thought I'd heard a faint scratch of movement inside. I pressed a paw against the magic shielding the shed, and it stung me.

"Hey, Juno. Finn's got the door open. Wanna look?" Zandra said.

I trotted over and sat beside her as Finn pulled open the door to reveal dozens of metal cages and traps. Some were equipped with vicious spikes. There were also nets, plenty of rope, and bottles of foul looking liquid.

"Who wants to go first?" Finn said.

Neither of us volunteered.

"We go together. Let's get this over with." Zandra pulled open the second door, and I stood in between her and Finn to take in more of the unpleasant sights.

She flared a light ball and hovered it in the air.

I stepped inside and almost retched at the overwhelming smell of dank fur. There was a pile of mangy pelts in one corner, along with several small bones.

"I know everyone needs a hobby, but this is the wrong hobby." Finn poked around the bottles of unpleasant looking liquid. "I think there's blood in these."

"There must be over fifty animal skins over here." I reluctantly inspected the pelts.

"I've got something here, too." Zandra was crouched on the floor.

I walked over to see what she'd discovered and found a primitive cold store made of stone with a faint whiff of magic about it. Inside were piles of neatly butchered carcasses.

"At least he's doing something with the animals he kills," Zandra said.

Finn looked over. "It's better to kill them and eat them than just kill them for sport. Sort of."

"But who needs this much meat?" I said. "This would keep me going for over a year, and I have a big appetite."

"If this is all he eats, he'll go through it fast enough." Zandra pulled a face. "It's enough to make me turn vegetarian."

I tilted my head to the side. "Consider becoming a pescatarian. All those Omega three oils will make your hair glossy."

Finn headed back toward the door. "Look at these tools. He's got dozens of knives. Even a couple of scythes." He brushed his fingers over them. "Nothing with powerful magic, though."

I looked around the shed, and my gaze settled on a pile of something white in one corner. "Zandra, take a look at this." I trotted over to what looked like angel feathers.

"That's not good," Zandra said. "Has Cannibal Bill been hunting other angels, or did he take these from Thomasina?"

"They smell like angel to me," I said.

"Finn, get over here," Zandra said. "You need to bag these feathers as evidence."

"Um... that might be difficult."

I turned to see a man in the doorway with a crossbow aimed at Finn's head.

Chapter 10

An unwelcome arrival

I remained still, not wanting to take a step closer to the skinny, nut brown man with a bald head and deep lines around his eyes and mouth. There was something about him that made my skin crawl.

"Greetings. I'm Juno, and this is Zandra Crypt. If you're Cannibal Bill, we have questions for you."

"I don't care who you are." His voice had a smoker's rasp to it. "All I care about is that you've broken into my property. That gives me rights."

"What rights would you be talking about?" I said as breezily as I could. "And in case it's slipped your notice, you're holding a crossbow up to an angel. That'll get you in a heap of trouble, no matter what rights you desire to uphold."

"This is my shed, and you're on my land. That means I can do whatever I like." Cannibal Bill sniffed, the crossbow remaining pointed at Finn.

"No, it doesn't," Zandra said. "And we're here investigating on behalf of Angel Force."

"You ain't no stinkin' angel." Cannibal Bill's eyes narrowed. "And I don't want any of you here." He shot Finn with the crossbow.

There was a dull thud as the bolt hit home. Finn flew back and slammed onto the ground, sending up a cloud of dust and feathers.

Zandra yelped and ran toward him, but Cannibal Bill was so fast, he had another bolt notched and was pointing it at her. "Uh-uh, witch. Keep moving, and you're next. Unless you want one of these stuck in your stomach, you stay where you are. Both of you." He stepped into the shed, the crossbow focused on Zandra but also waving in my direction.

A hot wave of rage flickered through me, and I growled. "Get that crossbow off my witch before I obliterate you."

"I'll be the one doing the killin' around here." Cannibal Bill moved closer to us, his back to the door. "Before I kill you both, skin you, and put you in my freezer, tell me what you're doing here. Are you alone? What do you want?"

"No one skins me," I said. "This fur is priceless."

"Yeah, I don't want to be skinned either," Zandra said. "And I've already told you, we're from Angel Force, and you just landed yourself in a heap of trouble by shooting an angel."

Cannibal Bill's crossbow didn't move. "I'll only get in trouble if someone finds out what I've done. And since neither of you are leaving here alive, that won't be a problem. I love it when free food comes a-knockin'."

"Now, you see, that's where you're wrong," I said. "Angel Force knows where we are. And when we don't return promptly, they'll send an enormous party of angels to your door. You can't kill them all."

"And there's another angel in the woods." Zandra nodded at the door. "Bertoli will be here any second."

"Hah! If you mean the dumb blond squealer trapped in my deer net, he won't be getting free anytime soon. His power is being drained through that net. The more he fights to get out, the weaker he'll become, and the stronger the net will be."

That was unfortunate news. Although I didn't reckon Bertoli would be much good in a fight. He'd probably pull out a rule book and start listing restrictions.

I glared at the crossbow. If I was certain I could be fast enough, I'd kick it from Cannibal Bill's hands, but he hadn't paused when downing Finn, so I couldn't take that risk with Zandra.

It was time to attempt a distraction. Get Cannibal Bill doubting himself. "You may be able to fell one angel and incapacitate another, but you won't bring down an entire troop."

He opened his mouth to argue back, when a skull splitting roar had me flattening my ears.

Finn reared up, the crossbow arrow sticking out of his right shoulder. Gone were his fabulous white wings. They were coated with a reddish hue that dripped black liquid onto the ground. His eyes were hazed black, and red flames flickered from his fingertips.

"Finn! Calm it down a few thousand notches," Zandra yelled.

Finn growled, thrust out his hands, and the barn exploded.

I barely had time to throw out a protection spell around Zandra as the demon blast hit. We flew back, surrounded by exploding wood, metal, and dirt. Huge chunks of salted meat flew through the air and plopped down around us.

I spun around and landed on Zandra's chest as we hit the dirt, making her grunt. I lay flat on her stomach, strengthening the protection spell as debris slammed down around us.

She clasped me against her chest with one hand, her gaze shooting around. "You good?"

"Surviving, no thanks to Finn. Where was the warning before he went full demon and hit the explode button?"

"Being shot with a crossbow must have made him forget his manners." Zandra lifted her head and peered around. "Cannibal Bill's not far from us. And he's still moving."

I wriggled around and took in the scene. The barn was flattened, the contents either evaporated or blasted apart by Finn's demon energy. Impressive. He was almost as strong as I used to be. "You check on the cannibal. I'll deal with the angry demon."

"You sure you want to handle Finn when he's like that?" Zandra kept a tight grip on me.

My gaze was fixed on Finn, who hovered ten feet above our heads, flickering different shades of red across his wings. "He just needs to calm down. Get the crossbow before Cannibal Bill tries to shoot anyone else."

We waited another thirty seconds until the fallout had died down, then Zandra rolled to her feet, taking me with her and settling me on her shoulder.

I propelled myself up and latched onto Finn's leg. I scrambled up his torso until I was at eye level. "Greetings. I've yet to meet your full demon side. It's an intense combination. You're scarily handsome when you turn dark."

Finn growled again, little recognition in his eyes.

"As interested as I am in meeting powerful supernaturals who can blow things up with a click of their fingers, if you don't get control of your demon side, I'll take you out." I stuck my booping snooter in his ear. "You're a threat to my witch, and that's unacceptable."

"You can't destroy me," he rumbled out.

"I believe I could. And even if I failed to destroy you, I'll inflict severe damage. Enough that Zandra could safely get away."

His dark gaze slid my way, and the waves of red energy pouring off him slowed. "You have such a strange power. It tastes of heat, sand, and destruction. You're like me, but older."

"In another life, I wielded my power in a way that caused the occasional tickle of destruction. But we all learn and grow. And that includes you. Finn, get control of your demon side. You won't get another warning." My magic was nowhere near full strength, and I knew, if I fought Finn, my survival odds were grim. But my witch came first. Whatever it took, she'd remain safe and would escape.

"My barn!" Cannibal Bill was struggling to his feet. "It's gone. My supplies." He looked up and shook his fist at Finn. "There was three months' worth of food in there, and you've blown it apart. You dumb demon cretin."

Finn snarled, revealing impressively sharp teeth.

I hopped onto his other shoulder, pressed my paws around the spot where the crossbow bolt was lodged, and pulsed out healing magic. "Take deep breaths, think happy thoughts, and count to five."

"Why?" Finn howled as I yanked the bolt free. "You irritating fuzz bucket."

It was a touch stronger than fuzz bucket, but I don't want to offend by repeating expletives. I spat out the crossbow bolt and continued healing his injury. "Sometimes, it's better not to know what's about to happen. You don't have time to imagine the worst."

"Get down here! You need to pay for this," Cannibal Bill yelled. "And I'm suing Angel Force. It took me weeks to get those supplies."

"You must hunt non-stop to get so many carcasses," I said. "Have you ever thought about adding fiber to your diet? Plants don't run when you want to eat them."

Finn's demon coloring slowly faded, and white rippled across his wings. He shook his head and blinked. "Urgh! I do not feel good."

"Hardly a surprise, since you're recovering from being shot and going super demon."

He looked around and grimaced. "I did all that?"

"You did. Everything went boom. Congratulations."

Finn blinked sweat from his eyes. "I got so angry. When that crossbow slammed into me, all I could think about was getting revenge. No, I wasn't thinking. I just felt pain, and then..."

"I'd be the same. I'd have obliterated Cannibal Bill with a snap of my paw. Not that I can snap. I have no opposable thumbs. But we know we can be better. And we want to protect the ones we love, don't we? That means reining in our destructive tendencies when Zandra is around."

Finn reached up and gently touched the wound on his shoulder. "Thanks for this. I'm feeling more like myself. Sorry for going raging demon on you. I'd never hurt you or Zandra."

"You're welcome. Perhaps, one day, I'll ask you to return the favor."

He gave me an odd look. "Sure. And thanks for the pep talk. My demon side has been causing me trouble recently. He sometimes gets twitchy if I don't let him out occasionally."

"Interesting. I know a witch who had the same problem. Zandra's half-sister. Sometimes, it's not so bad to let the dark side peek out. Although I only do it when I'm on my own, to minimize harm to others."

"You'll have to take me with you the next time you do that," Finn said. "We can lose control together."

"Consider it a date." I gestured to the ground. "Shall we? I don't want to leave my witch with the crossbow cannibal any longer than necessary."

Finn descended from the air. He landed and walked over to Cannibal Bill and Zandra.

"Everything good?" Caution flickered in Zandra's eyes as they traced over Finn.

"We have the situation under control," I said. "Our angel friend is back."

"You have nothing under control, idiots. What about my food? What am I supposed to eat?" Cannibal Bill grabbed up pieces of dirt covered meat.

"Don't you like charred barbecue? Add some hot sauce, and it could still be edible." Zandra nudged a lump of something gross with the toe of her boot.

"Edible! Nothing here is edible."

I paced around Cannibal Bill. "What about the animals you have in the other shed?"

He slid a glare toward the shed. "That's none of your business. This is an invasion of privacy. You won't get away with it."

"You brought this on yourself. If you hadn't shot Finn, we'd have been gone by now," Zandra said. "And since you were so keen on shooting an angel, perhaps you also did something to Thomasina."

"I don't know no-one by that name." Cannibal Bill shuffled back slowly.

"I doubt you asked her name before you bit her to death," I said.

That made him stop moving. "I didn't bite no one. You got the wrong man."

"You must have heard about the attack on the angel in these woods." Zandra held the loaded crossbow at hip height, a bolt loaded and ready to launch.

Cannibal Bill kept glaring at Finn. "It's no business of mine. All I care about is my barn. You're paying for a new one."

Red shimmered across Finn's wings again, and his hands clenched into fists.

"Take a time out," I said to him. "We've got this."

He didn't argue, simply turned on his heel and strode away.

"You must have seen all the angels in the woods after the murder happened." I kept a close eye on Finn as he stalked about, looking like a caged panther waiting for an excuse to attack.

"What if I did? I keep out of their way, and they keep out of mine. And I don't care about any dead angel. I care about my damaged stock. That was prime meat."

"Stop focusing on the carcasses and consider the corpse found near your home," I said. "Especially since you have a motive for killing that angel."

"I do?" Cannibal Bill rubbed the back of his neck. "What is it?"

"Your meat fetish. You're happy to stalk anything that moves. I saw rabbit, stoat, cat, possibly some kind of large wolf pelt in that barn. And angel feathers."

"Are angels a new target for you?" Zandra said. "You upped the stakes and planned on bringing down supernatural prey?"

"You people are crazy. I have standards. Angels require too much plucking. And they're all muscle. There's no fat on them. Look at that one." He jabbed a finger at Finn.

"It's true. Making biscuits on his flat belly is never a joy." I was glad Finn wasn't close enough to grab Cannibal Bill, because from the glare he gave him, it suggested he wanted to gut him like a fish.

"Where were you yesterday lunchtime?" Zandra said. "Thomasina died around one o'clock."

"Here. Same as always."

"Were you with anyone?" I said.

"Never! I hate people. You can't rely on them, so I stay out of their way. I keep this place warded to discourage anyone poking about." His nose snitched, and he looked around. "That magic needs to be strengthened."

"Your creepy wards are effective enough," I said. "But you must have heard the angels searching for Thomasina's killer."

He shrugged. "What if I did? I wasn't gonna ask them what they were doing. I got no time for gossip."

"This looks bad for you," Zandra said after a short pause. "You have no alibi for the time of the killing, you have an obsession with hunting, and Thomasina died close to where you live."

"And you have weapons that could hurt an angel," I said. "And there were angel feathers in your barn."

"I didn't even know angels could be killed. I wouldn't mind trying it, though." He grunted. "I enjoy it when the prey fights back."

"You're not helping yourself by saying dumb things like that," Zandra said.

"It wasn't me! I keep my head down and mind my business. And I'm right. Look at the trouble that's come to my door since that dumb angel got herself whacked. I want nothing to do with this. Leave me alone."

"We can't do that." Zandra sounded hesitant. Was she doubting Cannibal Bill's guilt?

I'd only thrown his name out as a distraction to take the angels' focus from Adrienne. Seeing his crossbow happy actions, I considered him a suspect, but perhaps I'd missed something.

"So, if it wasn't you, who killed the angel?" I said.

Cannibal Bill was quiet for several seconds. "I've seen footprints. They could belong to your killer."

"What kind of footprints?"

"All different kinds. I've even seen big cat prints. That's my next hunt. I'm bringing down that kitty and eating it. And I need to do it soon, since you've destroyed my store."

I wrinkled my booping snooter, and my claws extended from my murder mittens. I should have permitted Finn to finish what he started with this scumbag.

"I reckon you've got a madman out there," Cannibal Bill said. "Someone going around bringing down angels. It's unnatural."

"Perhaps that madman is you," I said.

He shook his head. "Nope. I have my hunting patches, and I stick to them. I never hunt too close to home. You should look for the fella who's been leaving all those prints around recently."

Since no confession seemed likely, the least we could do was gather useful information. Cannibal Bill lived and breathed these woods, so he could have seen something relevant to the case.

"You're sure it was a male?" I said.

"I know my prints. Course, you get some girls with enormous hooves, but I'd bet my best crossbow it was a guy. Same print, tracking all through the woods. Also heading into Crimson Cove. Whoever it is, they're looking for something specific. Maybe they found it when they met the angel."

I glanced at Zandra, and she raised her eyebrows. Cannibal Bill had a lousy alibi. In my mind, he was still a suspect, despite his attempt at deflecting with the footprints.

My gaze went to the other locked shed. "You still haven't said what you've got in there."

His expression soured. "Old tools. Nothing special."

"Then you won't mind us taking a look," Zandra said. "You've got some tasty magic around it. Anyone would think you don't want people to look inside. What are you hiding?"

"You're not looking in there. It's my private property. And keep that monster away from it. He'll only blow it up like the other one." Cannibal Bill hurried to the shed and stood in front of it.

I was done pussyfooting around this monster. "Hey, look at me."

His gaze went to me, and I shoved my magic at him. "You'll do exactly as I say."

"I... I will?"

"Focus on me. Love me and obey me. Follow my orders."

"Sure. I... I can do that." Cannibal Bill's eyes glazed over.

"Juno, be careful." Zandra joined me. "Beguiling magic is tricky to control."

"I know what I'm doing."

"Are you sure? You just told Cannibal Bill to love and obey you. It sounds like you're about to get married."

I smirked. It was the commands of the old days, a time I remembered so fondly. "Cannibal Bill, unlock the shed and let us look inside."

He turned and wavered toward the barn. He raised his hand and brought down the magic.

"Now, open the door."

His movements were robotic and jerky as he yanked open one of the large wooden doors to reveal the contents.

My mouth dropped open, and Zandra gasped.

Chapter 11

A cage of nightmares

Finn dashed over and caught hold of Zandra's shoulder. His gaze lifted to take in what was inside the barn. "What the..."

I stepped closer to the entrance, not wanting to step over the threshold and accept what I saw. My toe beans tingled, and my heart raced. There were cages everywhere. And they were full of terrified animals.

Finn wheeled around and stalked toward Cannibal Bill, flickers of demon power cascading over his wings. "You did this? Why keep them like this? In the dark. Scared and alone."

Cannibal Bill raised his fists, but Finn slapped them down. "It's my right. I must feed myself."

"What's wrong with you?" Finn grabbed Cannibal Bill by the front of his grubby T-shirt and lifted him off his feet.

I settled in to watch Finn destroy this monster. It was no less than he deserved. It also gave me a moment of respite from all the sad, desperate faces in those cages. It was too much to witness.

"Juno, do something," Zandra said.

"I could get popcorn. Salted or sweet?"

"I'm as angry as you about this." She waved her hand at the shed. "But Cannibal Bill is a suspect in Thomasina's murder. We need his confession, so the angels stop looking for Adrienne."

"I still vote for letting Finn obliterate him. Or I could do it."

Zandra's gaze went back to the inside of the shed, and she recoiled. "I'm tempted to help, but if he dies before we get answers, it solves nothing. Please, stop Finn."

I snorted my disgust and then stomped over to where Finn was shaking Cannibal Bill and growling in his face. I hopped onto Finn's shoulder and clamped my teeth around his ear, drawing blood. "Calm your demon self. As much as I approve of your actions, my witch has made me see sense. Obliteration is the wrong course of action."

"Get this creature away from me," Cannibal Bill howled. "If this is the angels' idea of law enforcement, it's a joke. Do they even know what kind of creature they've employed to keep the peace around here?"

"You shouldn't irritate a half-demon when he's not in control of himself." I cocked my head. "Or carry on and see how long you survive when your head's been separated from your body."

Cannibal Bill gurgled out his panic, his legs kicking in the air and his fingers ineffectively clawing at Finn's hands.

"Or maybe he'll put you in a too small cage and see how long you survive without being properly treated. It's what you've done to those animals. An eye for an eye, perhaps?" I hissed in Cannibal Bill's face, while Finn rumbled out his approval.

"That's my food! They won't be alive for long. I was planning on dealing with them all this week."

"Even a food source deserves kindness," I growled at him. "You'll never see me punishing the small rodents I catch for my wonderful witch. And I never go after the young ones. That's unfair. What you've done is cruel."

"I'll destroy him," Finn hissed out in a voice I'd never heard come from him before. It sounded like he'd smoked a cigar and downed several throat burning whiskeys while singing karaoke all night.

I went back to chewing on his ear to give him something else to focus on. "Sadly not. We need a confession from Cannibal Bill to ensure Zandra's mother is out of the frame for Thomasina's murder."

"Please, put me down," Cannibal Bill stuttered. "You can shake me all you like, but I won't confess to something I ain't done."

"There are so many things we seek a confession for," I said. "But for now, you're a murder suspect, and we need your confession to prove you killed Thomasina."

"I already said that wasn't me."

"You have no soul. You could easily have done it. It's clear from your treatment of these animals and the way you callously shot my demon friend that you have no hesitation in taking life. How long have you been planning an angel hunt?"

"I'm still intending on destroying him," Finn said. "So he'd better talk fast."

I dug my claws into Finn's shoulder and shot out my most powerful calming magic. "Don't let the demon side win. You're a much better angel than you are a demon. If you fail to contain your dark side, Zandra won't want to hang out with you, especially if you sprout horns and your breath smells like brimstone."

"Stop figuring out ways to gut the suspect. I need your help with these animals." Zandra had edged closer to the shed and was looking inside.

"Yes! You love animals. And these desperately need your attention. You can look after them at your sanctuary. But you won't be able to do that if you obliterate this repulsive individual." I gently hissed into his ear. Finn had to settle back into his angel power, or this could get complicated. I didn't want to destroy him, but he might leave me with no choice.

After a sweat inducing, heart pounding moment, where Finn growled and shook Cannibal Bill, the waves of demon energy faded. Finn groaned, his body convulsing as he dropped Cannibal Bill into the dirt.

"Good demon." I petted Finn's head. "Cannibal Bill, stay there. If you move, it gives me permission to take you down for good. Don't think I won't. I have too much to lose, and you're a threat."

He gulped, his face dripping with sweat. "I won't move a muscle."

"Finn, you're with me. Let's go see what we're dealing with in the shed." I nipped his ear one last time. "Are you sure you're back with me?"

He winced as he pried his little finger into my mouth to dislodge my teeth. "I'm right here. And I don't need an ear piercing. Those fangs are sharp."

Zandra stood at the entrance to the shed. Her face was pale as she glanced at me, still perched on Finn's shoulder, and nodded a thanks. "We all good?"

"I've got a handle on things." Finn's voice still sounded rough but more like the regular angel Finn than the kill-everything-on-my-path Finn. "When I saw all these caged animals, I lost control again."

"We'll make things right," I said. "Let's check them, get them healed if they need it, then fix transport and get them out of here."

"They belong to me." Cannibal Bill was wisely still in the dirt.

I glanced over my shoulder and hissed at him. "They're not yours. They were never yours. You're a despicable creature. It's no surprise to me you'd happily destroy an angel to fit your twisted desires."

Cannibal Bill's mouth dropped open, and he stared at me. "I... no! Not an angel."

"I have your number. Keep your foolish opinions to yourself while we deal with this caged misery." I drew in a fortifying breath, all too aware of the stench that would greet my sensitive booping snooter once I was inside the shed.

We stepped inside together, united in the horror we were about to encounter.

There were five cages, containing twenty miserable looking fluffies. While I worked along them with Zandra, administering healing and calming spells as needed, Finn kept watch over Cannibal Bill.

Luckily for Cannibal Bill, the animals weren't injured, and they had water in their cages. But they reeked of terror and despair. They'd resigned themselves to a miserable end at the bottom of a cold store.

"I should get transport," Finn said. "It might be too much of a shock to magic these animals to the sanctuary."

"What about Cannibal Bill?" Zandra looked up, her mouth set in a grim line.

"I'll hog tie him before I leave. He's going nowhere."

As much as I longed to watch that encounter, my focus remained on the animals, feeding them more calming magic and words of reassurance that their nightmare was over.

"This strengthens the case against Cannibal Bill." I rested a paw on the head of a skinny, one-eyed rabbit. "Anyone who cages animals like this could easily move on to harming supernaturals."

"Agreed. I'll take pictures on my globe," Zandra said. "We can show them to Cythera so she knows what a monster Cannibal Bill is."

"One day animal trapper, the next day angel killer."

"I ain't either of those things," he said, his tone plaintive. "I must be able to take care of myself. And I never hurt them. They got water. I feed them, too, and make sure the shed isn't too cold."

"If you'll excuse me for one moment." I bounded over to Cannibal Bill, who Finn had tied so his hands and feet were bound behind his back, and jumped on his head. "Change your ways. Add vegetables to your diet and stop thinking it's fun to trap and terrify."

"I don't terrify. It's nature. I've always done this."

"Just because something has been done for a long time doesn't mean it's automatically the right thing to do."

He grunted. "I'm independent. I look after myself."

I stomped a paw on his mouth. "You won't get the chance to kill anything else from behind bars. And you won't have a choice over what you eat. Maybe the angels will put you on a fruit smoothie only diet as punishment."

He mumbled under my paw.

I stepped back. "Only speak if you have something useful to say."

"How many times! I didn't kill that angel."

"You killed plenty of other creatures, though. Why not an angel, too?"

Finn zoomed down from the sky. "He causing you problems, Juno?"

"No, I'm just giving him valuable life advice." I hopped off Cannibal Bill, digging in my claws as I leaped.

"I couldn't get the van too close, but we can manage." Finn grimaced as he shook out his wings. "Sorry for going all demon on you."

"No apology needed. It's a part of your nature, so it has to come out from time to time, especially when you encounter such unpleasantness." I kicked my back legs, showering Cannibal Bill with dirt.

"Yeah, don't get me started on him." Finn's glare was on Cannibal Bill as he headed to the shed. "How are the animals?"

"They're all alive and in better condition than I first thought." Zandra stood from her crouched position as we entered. "Have you got room for them at your sanctuary?"

"I'll make room. And I contacted the vet I use. She's meeting me there in an hour to administer any treatment."

Cannibal Bill wriggled until he faced us. "I was never unkind. I looked out for them."

We all ignored him.

Finn looked around the shed, a scowl on his face. "I'll be busy dealing with this lot. They won't be a simple fix up and foster out intake. They're traumatized."

"At least they'll be in safe hands with you," I said. "They won't have anything to fear."

"Perhaps you and Zandra could volunteer at the sanctuary so we can get them dealt with quickly."

Zandra pursed her lips. "Sure. I've been meaning to drop by and help, but with everything going on at work and Adrienne, I have little free time."

"It wouldn't have to be for long. Even a few hours a week would be great. And I'll need all the help I can get to rehabilitate and re-home these animals. I may get a few of them back into the wild, but I doubt many would survive long."

She glanced away. "Do you mind if I bring someone else with me?"

"Every willing pair of hands is welcome," Finn said.

"You're thinking about bringing Vorana?" I administered another spell of calm to a sad looking cat.

"No, not Vorana." Zandra was focused on a cage containing three dogs.

"Sorcha? We know she loves animals. She takes in all the stray cat familiars."

"She's busy with the café."

"Then who?"

Zandra glanced at Finn. "It's someone new to our team at work. I figured this would be a good way for them to get to know people."

I cocked my head. Was Zandra thinking about inviting Randal? He wasn't all that practical, so I was uncertain how he'd feel about a first date getting down and dirty with the unwanted animals of Crimson Cove. It would be a good test, though. If he could deal with that, he'd go up in my estimation.

Zandra joined Finn after she'd finished administering the last spell. "They're good to go. I just need to contact Barney. I'd planned to drop by animal control to give him an update about the case. He'll be wondering what's going on."

"Sure. You do that, and I'll move them. I parked the van as close as I could, so it won't take long."

"I can help with some translocation magic to speed things up," I said.

"Perfect. Let's get these animals out of here."

The next twenty minutes were focused on transporting the terrified animals from shed to van quickly and calmly.

When we got back to the shed after depositing the last cage, Zandra stood next to Cannibal Bill, glaring down at him.

"He's not been misbehaving, has he?" I stalked over, more than happy to evoke some last-minute smiting.

"He's been pleading his case and is still claiming he's innocent. I've not been listening. Did you get all the animals in the van without a problem?"

"All packed away and already calmer." Finn landed beside us. "Now it's time to make an arrest."

"No! Not for that angel's murder. Why would I kill an angel?" Cannibal Bill rolled from side to side in a pathetic attempt to escape. All he succeeded in doing was covering himself in dirt.

"For the same reason you shot one," I said.

Finn crossed his arms over his chest. "Perhaps we don't have enough evidence to charge you with Thomasina's murder yet, but we throw the book at people who make animals suffer."

"I can't be charged with collecting my food. Is that what this world is like now? A man can't work to feed himself, and—"

I stomped on his chest as he flailed about. "The animals were terrified. You should be ashamed of yourself." I looked up at Zandra. "I still want to obliterate him. Give me permission to do so."

"Yeah. Go on, Zandra. You turn your back, and we'll deal with this." Finn cracked his knuckles, a wicked smirk on his face.

She arched an eyebrow as she looked at Cannibal Bill. "It's tempting."

"Please! I didn't realize I was doing anything wrong. You saw they weren't hurt. I wasn't just gonna leave them there. I had plans."

"Hmmm... as much as I wish he was no longer breathing, we should let him plead his case. And we still need to figure out how he murdered Thomasina," Zandra said.

"If you're sure we can't obliterate him, then he needs to come with me." Finn hauled Cannibal Bill to his feet, and he wobbled in his tight bindings. "Cythera will want to talk to you."

"Will she hold him while we look for more evidence?" I said.

Finn pressed his lips together. "The fact he shot me will be enough to keep him overnight."

"I was defending my property from trespassers. I didn't know who you were. You could have been about to rob me."

"I'm a freaking huge angel. We're the good guys."

Cannibal Bill's gaze flickered across Finn. "You didn't seem good when you shook me so hard my teeth rattled. If you take me in, I'll report this. You're not supposed to use intimidation tactics."

"It wasn't an intimidation tactic," I said. "Finn planned on destroying you. You're fortunate to be breathing."

Cannibal Bill muttered under his breath, loathing shining in his beady eyes.

"You can tell my boss what you like, but you're still coming with me, and we're throwing the book at you," Finn said. "Zandra, I hate to ask, but can you and Juno take the animals to my sanctuary?"

"No problem. Give me the keys. You get this guy behind bars where he belongs."

Finn tossed her the keys then shot into the air, while Cannibal Bill wailed and flailed in his grip.

"If he keeps kicking like that, Finn will drop him," I said.

"Let's hope he keeps kicking, then."

We headed along the path in search of the van.

Zandra spun the keys around her finger. "What do you think about Cannibal Bill? Is he really our killer? It almost seems too simple."

"The guy's unstable. Maybe he lost control and killed Thomasina."

"By biting her?" Zandra shook her head. "We're missing something, but I have no idea what."

"We'll figure it out. For now, we focus on the animals, let Finn get Cannibal Bill processed and in a cell so he can't harm anyone else, then we need downtime."

"No downtime."

I hopped onto her shoulder. "You've just helped calm twenty animals. Your magic needs to rest. So does mine. Shower, food, then bed. That's an order."

"What about Adrienne?"

"Later. We'll find your ghoul mother later."

Chapter 12

An angel intervention

"I thought you'd better know about this." Finn's unusually surly face loomed in the mobile snow globe in Vorana's living room.

I swished my tail, irritation making my fur crackle. "Why would Cythera think it was a good idea to let Cannibal Bill go?"

Finn sighed. "It's a long story. Sadly, not an uncommon one."

I'd been awoken by Zandra's mobile snow globe buzzing a few moments ago. I'd checked the caller, silenced it, and then headed up the stairs and into Vorana's living room to return the call. I had a bad feeling, if Finn was making contact this late, it wouldn't be to give us good news, so I wanted to find out what it was before sharing it with Zandra.

"Give me the condensed version," I said.

His mouth twisted to the side. "Cannibal Bill had information about some criminals the angels are interested in."

I made a noise like I needed to hack up a fur ball. "They cut a deal with him?"

"You got it. He'll not serve any time for what he did to me or those animals. And there's more."

"Go on."

"Cannibal Bill made a formal complaint against me."

"Annoying but no surprise. Because you went a smidge demon on him?"

Finn was silent for several seconds. "Juno, I lost control. If it hadn't been for you biting on my ear and bringing me back to my senses, I'd have killed that guy."

"I hope you didn't tell Cythera that."

"Cannibal Bill did. He kept shouting about it to any angel who'd listen to him. My boss doesn't ignore complaints about angels overstepping their boundaries."

"Even though Cannibal Bill has a mildly legitimate complaint, he must still be locked away. He tried to kill you, and he's a suspect in Thomasina's murder. And don't get me started on the animals we found in his shed of horrors."

"I know, I know. But Cythera is a stickler for ensuring protocols are followed."

"You'd never have killed him."

"Are you sure? I'm not. I had this red rage in front of me and no control over what I was doing. I wanted to destroy. Maybe Cannibal Bill is right, and I shouldn't work at Angel Force. Angels keep the peace. They don't incite fear."

"You're the best, most effective angel I've ever dealt with."

"And while I appreciate those words, I know your low opinion of the angels," Finn said.

"It's increased since I've gotten to know you. I'll visit Cythera and speak on your behalf. She can't lose sight of how important this case is."

"Cythera is still reeling from Thomasina's murder. She said the higher angels are hassling her hourly, so she wants a positive result ASAP."

"All the more reason for her to focus on Cannibal Bill and not open an investigation into an angel who knows how to do his job." I flicked my tail. Angels always focused on the wrong thing.

"I'm doing what I can, but for now, Cannibal Bill has been released. He's been told to stay in the area and stay home as much as possible. He's also been told not to hunt. That was the thing he was the least happy about."

"If the angels refuse to do anything about him, I will."

"It's kind of why I got in touch. I don't trust that guy not to make a run for it. He needs watching."

I nodded. "I'll put a plan together. Cannibal Bill's hunting days are over. No more angels will die on my watch. And no more cute fluffies, either."

"Your plan doesn't involve obliteration, does it?"

"Only as a last resort. I'll be in touch." I ended the communication. I wouldn't disturb Zandra with this news, but I knew the perfect individuals to help with this crucial mission.

Twenty minutes later, I was outside Sorcha's café, tapping on the glass.

Sage sat beside me, yawning. "I don't know why I agreed to come on another of your harebrained missions."

"Because you're a decent cat who usually does the right thing." I gestured at Sammy as his sleepy, adorable face appeared in the window.

Sage huffed out a breath. "Maybe my life could do with a little shaking up. It's easy to get coddled living with Vorana."

"I wouldn't mind all that coddling you receive."

"Then speak to your witch. Even though you two are having difficulties, she still adores you."

"We're working through a few things."

"She's figured out you've got weird magic?"

I sniffed. "Perhaps you should go back to bed if you plan on asking inappropriate questions."

Sage chuckled darkly. "I'm here now. And I'm no fan of Cannibal Bill's. I don't mind keeping an eye on him and making sure he doesn't go out with that crossbow and his nets."

"Hey, what's going on?" Sammy appeared around the side of the building. He had Elijah with him.

"It's another one of her kitten impossible missions," Sage said. "We're tracking a madman."

Elijah yawned. "Sounds dull." He raised a paw as I drew in a breath to tell him to get lost. "But I'm bored. And someone needs to watch Sammy's back."

Sammy bristled under the insult, but I gently soothed him by rubbing my face against his.

"Cannibal Bill needs monitoring. He's a suspect in a murder investigation, but he's weaseled his way out of being locked up until the angels can find evidence to charge him," I said.

Elijah grimaced. "That nightmare of an individual."

"You've had dealings with him?" I said.

"No, fortunately not. But I've heard plenty about him. A friend of mine disappeared, and the evidence pointed to Cannibal Bill hunting him and eating him."

"He eats us?" Sammy whispered, a quiver in his voice.

"Cannibal Bill is a disturbed individual with a love of all things meat-based," I said. "We found rabbit, cat, dog, and even a couple of young deer in his shed. And that was the animals still alive. The angels were foolish enough to let him go, so I decided we'd watch him. If he puts one foot out of line, we'll stamp on him."

"I'm all for stamping on a creep like that," Sage said. "Let's go. I'll take us to the woods."

"Hey, don't leave without me." Archie bounded into view. His fur looked silken and gleamed in the moonlight, and he had an impressive dark purple collar around his neck, speckled with silver moons and stars.

"I wasn't sure you got my message," I said. "The vampire I spoke to said you were too busy to play."

Archie attempted to greet us all with huge slobbery licks. I dodged his giant pink tongue, Elijah was knocked off his feet, and Sammy got a face full of drool.

"I was in the middle of one of their legendary hog roasts. They put it on in my honor because I'm such an awesome hound, and I didn't want to leave early and upset anyone. Vampires are surprisingly sensitive. I explained everything to Remus, and he realized I had an important mission to complete. He's an understanding partner."

"You're getting on well," I said. "I'm happy things are working out for you."

"Vampires are the best. No offence to your witch, Juno. Zandra is cool, too. Just not vampire cool. So, who are we hunting?"

"Perhaps not the best choice of words," I said. "Sage was about to translocate us. I'll explain everything once we're there."

Sage cast a group translocation spell to take us deep into the woods, and a moment later, we were secluded behind a bush close to Cannibal Bill's hut. It had taken a few minutes of sniffing and checking, but we'd discovered the mossy roofed building behind a huge row of ancient oak trees.

"Watch every paw step if you have to move. Cannibal Bill has traps everywhere," I whispered.

"I've heard this bozo eats his meat raw," Sammy said.

"And he enjoys offal," Elijah said.

"Oh, yuck! I know who we're after. We're chasing Cannibal Bill. That guy massively sucks." Archie lowered himself to the ground.

"He does. And he's a flight risk in a murder investigation," I said. "If he's crazy enough to murder an angel and shoot Finn, he won't think twice about attempting to escape Crimson Cove during this investigation. We're here to make sure that doesn't happen."

"Will we get to chase him?" Archie said. "I won't hurt him, just rough him up a bit."

"We should do to him what he does to the animals he hunts," Sage said.

I shook my head. "The thought has also crossed my mind, but for now, we simply watch him."

"What are these?" Archie had his nose to the ground. "They smell fresh."

I left Sage, Sammy, and Elijah watching Cannibal Bill's home and headed over to where Archie was sniffing. "Be careful. We don't want to alert Cannibal Bill that we're here by setting off a trap." I glanced at the ground. There were freshly made big cat prints in the dirt.

"Do you think this creature belongs to Cannibal Bill?"

"I've seen these prints before. I thought it might be a wild big cat roaming around. But wild animals have territories they protect, and these prints have been showing up all over the woods."

"You think, whatever it is, it's looking for someone?"

"Possibly. Or it could be a rogue familiar. Maybe they've lost their bonded magic user and they're struggling to manage on their own."

Archie nodded wisely. "That almost happened to me, didn't it? You saved me, and now I'm a happy vampire dog. I even got gifted gold eating bowls a week ago. I don't want to use them because they're so pretty. And Remus keeps showing me off to everyone. I'm the luckiest hound alive."

"I'm glad we could help find you your forever home."

"And it will be. Vamps live almost forever. Just like me."

I sniffed the prints again. "If it is a rogue familiar, we should help them."

"Oh, yeah. We have to. It makes my heart hurt to think someone's out there and they have no one to turn to. We must make them happy again. As happy as I am."

"Give me a moment." I trotted back to Sage, Sammy, and Elijah. "Any movement in the hut?"

"All quiet," Elijah said.

"Good. I'm taking Archie to investigate some prints. We won't be long."

They nodded, their attention on the faint light flickering out of a tiny window.

I went back and joined Archie. "Let's see if these lead anywhere. These prints are fresh, so whoever they belong to could be close by."

"And when we find them, we'll fix them up and get them a home."

"Let's not get ahead of ourselves. We need to find the animal first. It may not even be a familiar. And they may not want help."

"It is a familiar. I can feel it in my bones."

"Make sure your bones are careful when tracking. One false move, and you'll find yourself in Cannibal Bill's net. He digs deep holes in the ground, too. Some of them have spikes."

Archie growled. "I do not like Cannibal Bill one bit."

"Same here."

We tracked the indentations for half a mile, when another set of prints distracted me. Huge, flat-footed prints.

"They're different from the tracks we're following." Archie sniffed around them. "Kind of dog smelling, too. What creature made these? A part changed werewolf?"

"I'd say yeti. And there are more here. Different size. Smaller."

"Cannibal Bill's wife?"

"You can safely assume no one wants him as a husband. If a woman was foolish enough to entertain a relationship with him, she'd never sleep, thinking he was creeping into the bedroom with an axe and a pelt knife to add her to his collection." I tilted my head as I inspected the marks. "They could be female, since they're smaller."

Could Adrienne have passed this way? If these smaller prints belonged to her, would a yeti be stalking her? Or would a yeti and a ghoul find something in common and hang out together?

"What you thinking, Juno?" Archie said. "Did I do good? Did I find a clue?"

"You always do good, Archie. You're a good boy."

He bounded around until I gestured for calm, mainly to avoid him setting off any traps. Archie may be a good boy, but he was also a hulking great clumpy foot.

"Hey, what kind of fur is this?" Archie lifted his head. He held a mouthful of coarse, dark fur.

I wandered over and had a sniff. "You're sure it's not yours?"

"I smell of flowers these days. This smells funky."

"Some sort of rodent?"

Archie went still, and his ears lowered. A tickle of a growl echoed in his throat. "Don't turn around. Something is watching us."

"Where?" I whispered.

"Behind you. It's hiding behind a tree. And it's big. Much bigger than me, and that's saying something."

"Two legs or four?"

"Two."

I whirled around, and my gaze met two shining dark eyes. There was a grunt of surprise as the creature realized it had been spotted, and then the shadowy figure vanished.

"Quick! After it." I raced away, the ground shaking reassuringly to let me know Archie was my backup. I blasted past trees, the wind whipping my fur back. I knew exactly what we were chasing.

"What is it?" Archie said. "Did I find more clues?"

I bared my teeth in a triumphant snarl. "Much more than that, you clever hound. This could be another murder suspect."

Chapter 13

What's furry, fast, and furious?

The yeti was fast. Given it was the size of a rhino tipped sideways, its speed impressed me. And the pace it set suggested it had something to hide.

"You want me to blast it with flames?" Archie said. "I've gotten real good with my fire. Remus lets me practice on the grounds."

The yeti roared its anger. It must have overheard Archie's suggestion.

"Not yet. I'm enjoying this run, and I'm not even at full speed."

Archie's tongue lolled out of his mouth. "Same here. I love to run. But I also love to catch things."

With fleet of foot, we continued after the yeti. I could see it was tiring. Its pace had slowed as we leaped over fallen trees and avoided holes. I'd almost forgotten about Cannibal Bill's traps, but we were out of his territory by now, so we were safe from nets, holes, draining magic, and spikes.

My underfur grew unpleasantly warm. "That's enough fun. Archie, if you'd do the honors and stop our two-footed friend from going any farther."

Archie belched a jet of flames that scorched the ground around the yeti.

It howled and leaped the flames, stumbling as it did so and tumbling into a forward roll.

I dodged the fire and landed on the yeti's back. I slammed a powerful restraining spell through all four paws, pinning the creature to the ground. It took considerable effort as it bucked and writhed, continuing to howl.

"A little help," I grunted to Archie, who stood with his tongue hanging out and his tail wagging.

"Oh, sure." He launched through the air and landed on the yeti, almost squashing me flat.

I yanked my tail out from under Archie's enormous head and positioned my face so I wouldn't get any unwelcome licks.

"Let me go," the yeti grumbled, his deep voice rumbling through my paws.

"Why were you watching us?" I said. "And stop fighting, unless you want this to go badly for you."

"I wanted to know what you were doing in the woods. Most creatures aren't out at this time of night unless they're up to no good."

"Which suggests you're also up to no good," I said. "What nefarious activities were you plotting?"

"Nothing! It's just quieter in the woods at night. It's been full of angels recently, and I hate crowds. They make me anxious."

"More likely, you hated the idea they may find you and charge you with Thomasina's murder."

"Oh, boy! Did you kill that big angel?" Archie said.

The yeti squirmed some more. "No! I'm a peace-loving creature. I'm just passing through Crimson Cove. I know nothing about any angel dying. Let me go. I want no trouble."

A heady tang of fear sweat and anxiety poured off the yeti, mingling with his dark fur.

He was hiding something from me. "You're not passing through. We've seen your prints in these woods for two weeks. Why stay so long?"

"I like to slow travel. And I thought Crimson Cove was a friendly place for all magic creatures. Not so much now, given you two have pinned me to the ground. What are you planning on doing to me?"

I eased back my magic a fraction, showing the yeti I had no cause to obliterate just yet. "Forgive my lack of manners. Greetings, I'm Juno, and this is Archie. We're hunting for an angel killer. Know anything about that?"

"I already said no. I'm not here for angels."

"I like your purple neck ruff," Archie said. "Maybe I should get Remus to dye me like that, too. It's pretty."

"It's not dye," the yeti said. "It's just me. It's how I am."

I nodded. "Changes to yeti ruff color shows their mating desire. How long have you been seeking a mate?"

"I'm ... I'm not. Everyone tells me I'm too young to find a mate."

"There's no use lying. Your desire is written all over your fur. You're pursuing a female through Crimson Cove?"

The yeti grumbled some more. "What if I am? It's not a crime to find love."

"Should I do that?" Archie said. "I wouldn't mind someone cute to hang out with. Perhaps the single hellhounds around here don't know I'm interested because I don't change color. Would I look good in yellow? Or maybe pink? I'm manly enough to handle any color."

"I'm sure they're all aware of your marvelous presence." I sat upright and gestured Archie to ease off on the pressure, so the yeti could move. "What's your name?"

His gaze flashed from Archie and then to me. "Forzi. And I don't want trouble. Let me go, and I'll leave Crimson Cove right away."

"That's not happening. Yetis get lust drunk when seeking a mate. And you have huge, blunt teeth that could be a fit for the marks on Thomasina."

He trembled beneath my paws. "I'd never bite an angel."

"You're coming with us. There's a group of angry angels who have questions for you."

Forzi shrunk against the dirt. "It wasn't me. Maybe I've spent more than a few days in Crimson Cove but not because of the angels. They're so flappy and bright and shiny. They make my eyes hurt. I could never love an angel, let alone bite one. Gross."

"You need to explain that to them, although leave out the flappy part. Now, do I need to use stronger restraining magic on you, or will you come with us peacefully?"

Forzi huffed a breath through his broad nostrils. "I suppose you'll try to set me alight again if I run?"

"That would be a last resort. I expect charred yeti doesn't smell good."

He seemed to consider this point. "Fine, I'll come with you. But this is a mistake. I'm only being helpful, so I can clear my name."

I stepped off Forzi, and a second later, Archie did the same. I tensed, waiting to see if the yeti would run, but his air of defeat suggested he knew when he'd been bested.

As we led him through the woods back to collect the others and return to Angel Force, there was a flash of cat's eyes watching us from the shadows.

I hesitated for a second then shrugged. I had little interest in a single large cat roaming the woods, although I'd check on them and ensure they weren't having any problems, but they were irrelevant to this mystery.

A smile flickered across my face, and I shared it with Archie. Case solved. Adrienne wasn't our killer. The angels hadn't found her. Zandra no longer needed to worry, and Crimson Cove wasn't under threat.

We'd just found our angel killer.

***

I carefully placed the freshly dead mouse on the edge of Zandra's pillow. I'd been so pleased with myself after discovering who murdered Thomasina that I decided we needed a celebratory treat, and I always found a brief bout of hunting invigorating.

It also gave me an opportunity to give Zandra a wonderful gift.

She cracked open one eye. For a second, it was unfocused, then her gaze sharpened, and it settled on the mouse. She made a noise partway between a scream and a grunt and shot back in the bed. She went so far, she pitched off the edge of her mattress and thudded to the floor.

I shuffled to the edge of the bed and looked down at her. "Anything broken?"

"Juno! How many times do we need to talk about this? No dead rodents as gifts. Definitely no dead rodents on my pillow."

"But flowers and candy are boring. And I have wonderful news."

She stayed on the floor. "I'm not talking to you until you get that thing off my pillow and outside."

"Don't you want to hear my news?"

"Dead mouse removal. Now!"

I shuffled around on my belly and picked up the mouse. Zandra never appreciated my gifts.

After I'd deposited the sad little creature in a small hole in the ground and covered it up, I returned to find Zandra in the kitchen, rubbing the back of her head and holding a large mug of coffee.

"I got whiplash from that fall. Why the unwelcome corpse gift wake-up?" she said. "It's still early. And you were the one whining about getting rest last night."

I turned in a circle, dancing on my paws. "I found the angel killer. With a little help from some friends."

Zandra's mouth dropped open. "How? When? Why wasn't I involved?"

"I didn't want to disturb you after you'd had such a stressful day." I settled on the countertop. "But late last night, I learned from Finn the unhappy news that Cannibal Bill got released."

"Why do something so stupid? We saw what a monster he is."

"Apparently, he had useful information about some unpleasant criminals the angels have been failing to arrest."

Zandra tipped back her head and groaned. "He did a deal with them, didn't he? Does that mean he won't get charged with anything? He shot Finn!"

"He's not getting away with it completely, but it's unlikely he'll serve time behind bars."

"Those angels are useless. The information he gave them had better be worth it." She sipped her coffee, spilling some on her hand and issuing colorful cuss words as she wiped it off. "How does this link to you finding the killer, though? It wasn't Cannibal Bill?"

"I took some friends out last night, and we watched him to see if he'd do anything he shouldn't. I was looking around with Archie, and we discovered a yeti hiding in the woods."

Zandra set her mug down with a thud, causing more of it to slop over the edge. "I knew it! That's amazing news. So our theory was right? A yeti killed Thomasina."

"I think so, although he protested his innocence. His markings reveal he's seeking a mate, so it's legitimate to claim he bit someone while in mating lust."

She paused. "Even an angel?"

"I reckon so. He has huge teeth."

Zandra's bottom lip jutted out. "What are the angels doing about it?"

"It's why I needed to wake you early. They have Forzi, the yeti, but they've requested a yeti expert sit in on his interview."

"Makes sense. Who are they getting?"

I tilted my head. "You need more coffee if you can't figure that out."

She pointed at her chest, her eyebrows raised. "Juno! I'm no yeti expert. I got my information from Tempest, who got her information from I don't know who."

"You know plenty about yetis. You pretend you hate to study, but you know stuff."

Zandra edged away from the kitchen counter. "I can't do it."

"Are you no longer interested in this case? You're not concerned the angels may still want to find Adrienne and charge her with this crime? Or trap her and study her to see if she's a danger."

"Of course I'm still interested." Zandra's mouth twisted to the side. "What if the angels figure out I'm not this all amazing yeti expert, though?"

"You're better than you realize. And if we get stuck, Finn will back us."

Vorana strolled into the kitchen with a still sleeping Sage tucked into a cozy papoose on the front of her chest. "I thought I heard voices. What's with the early start? Have we got rampaging animals in town that need dealing with? If so, tell them not to visit my bookstore."

"Juno found Thomasina's killer last night," Zandra said. "We're just figuring out what to do next."

"Oh! Does that explain why this little one is still sound asleep?" Vorana kissed the top of Sage's head. "I heard her come in late and asked what she'd been up to. She said you'd been on some kitten impossible adventure. She was tired though, so I didn't press for information. The second her head hit the pillow, she started snoring."

"Sage is a worthy hero in this mission to find the angel killer," I said.

"I'll let her sleep longer as a treat," Vorana said. "Breakfast?"

"Only if you can make it to go," I said. "We need to get to Angel Force and question the killer."

"Give me five minutes." Vorana bustled about the kitchen, making fresh coffee and putting muffins into a plastic box. "So, who killed Thomasina?"

"A visiting yeti called Forzi," I said. "A young buck of a guy in full mating mode. We caught him watching us in the woods and gave chase."

"You felled a yeti?" Vorana turned and stared at me. "They're incredibly strong."

"As am I. And I had a hellhound as backup, as well as Sage, Sammy, and Elijah, keeping watch on another unsavory character."

Vorana shared a smile with Zandra. "This yeti confessed to you?"

"Not as such. But he will this morning. It's just a loose end to tie up."

Vorana handed over our food, and after giving Zandra a few minutes to make herself decent, we were out of the house and soon walking through the doors of Angel Force, looking like we knew how to handle a panicked yeti and make him confess to murder.

There was no sign of Finn when we arrived, but Bertoli marched over, looking like he'd been chewing on a cactus. "Where have you been?"

"What's it to you?" Zandra said.

"Cythera won't start the interview with Forzi until you're here. I told her she was wasting time waiting. You're not to be relied upon."

"Then you should show respect," I said. "We're the experts who solved a murder while you were flapping around like a headless chicken at a barn dance."

He rolled his eyes. "This way."

"Where's Finn?" Zandra reluctantly followed Bertoli toward a closed door.

"He's not around. I'm interviewing Forzi along with Cythera."

I winced. Bertoli was a prickly character, and Cythera was odd. This wouldn't be an enjoyable experience.

We entered the room and discovered Forzi on one side of the table, his hands gripped together and the stench of anxiety pouring off him. Cythera sat on the other side, a picture of angel calm.

She nodded at us. "Now we're all here, we can begin the interview."

Bertoli took the seat next to her, leaving us to grab a foldout chair and pull it up to the table. Zandra placed it at the end of the table. A sign of neutrality I approved of.

Cythera ran through the formalities before spearing Forzi with an icy glare. "Did you know the angel, Thomasina?"

He shook his head. "I don't spend any time with angels. We move in different social circles. You always look so clean, and I... well, I'm more of an outdoorsy type."

"Where were you on the afternoon of March twenty-eighth, between twelve forty-five and one-thirty?"

He twirled his thumbs around each other. "Most likely in the woods. It's where I've been spending my time since I've been in Crimson Cove. I was doing nothing wrong, though."

"What were you doing there?"

Forzi lowered his gaze. "Hanging about."

"Who were you with?"

"I know no one in Crimson Cove. As I said to Juno when she pinned me down, I'm passing through. I can leave. I'll go now if you like." Forzi went to stand from his seat, but Cythera gestured for him to remain seated, so he slumped back down.

"Forzi said to me he's been slow traveling in the area," I said.

"Slow traveling to where?" Bertoli said.

"Anywhere. I'm ... I'm just looking for a place to call home. It's not easy to find somewhere to put down roots."

Zandra leaned forward in her seat. "That's an attractive ruff. How long have you been looking for a suitable mate?"

"I'm not! I don't want a mate."

"So why has your fur changed color?" Zandra said. "That only happens when a yeti is seeking someone to bond with."

"Forzi, be honest. You told me you were looking for someone," I said.

"Maybe I'm different to other yetis, and it just does this whenever it likes." Forzi brushed his fingers through his colored fur. "Like I said, I'm on my own. I've been using the woods as a base."

"Did you encounter any angels while you were in the woods?" Cythera said.

"I saw them all there for a while, but I kept out of the way. They meant business, and I didn't want to get in trouble if I wasn't supposed to be there."

"Which proves you were close to the sight of Thomasina's murder," Cythera said.

"Close enough to commit the crime," Bertoli said. "We'll need to take a bite mark impression to match the wounds on Thomasina's body."

Forzi's tongue darted across his plump lips. "Hold on now. Just because I was in the area didn't mean I killed anyone. I don't know this angel. I've got no fancy connections like that or reasons to hang out with angels. I just want to be left alone."

"Does that mean you refuse to have a bite impression taken?" Bertoli's voice held a surprising edge of menace.

"I didn't say that!"

"If you don't cooperate, it suggests you're guilty," Bertoli said.

"Let's ease off from the mild threats," Zandra said coolly. "Everyone here believes in innocent until proven otherwise, don't they? Or has Angel Force changed its rules again?"

Bertoli looked distinctly unimpressed about being reprimanded by Zandra.

Cythera issued a brief nod. "No changes. You are correct."

"Do you mind if I ask questions?" Zandra gestured at Forzi.

"Go ahead. You're here as our expert. I expect questions."

Bertoli looked like he wanted to argue, but a brief glance at Cythera kept him silent.

"Has your mating lust been troubling you?" Zandra said to Forzi.

"No. I barely notice it." He shifted around in his seat.

"Perhaps you're not aware when the urges hit," I said. "It can get you like that. The primal part of the brain takes over, and everything else goes into standby mode. Have you ever found yourself in places you don't remember going to? Or woken in a strange environment and wondered how you got there?"

He shuffled around some more. "Maybe. Even if I've been experiencing a few side effects from the urges, I'd never go after an angel. They're not my type, even with my mating lust goggles on."

"What are mating lust goggles?" I said.

Forzi shrugged. "Like beer goggles but worse."

I smirked, and Zandra chuckled. Cythera and Bertoli didn't look happy that not everyone found their radiant beauty impressive.

"It's all the blonde hair, isn't it?" I said. "And those feathers get everywhere. They always tickle my nose."

Bertoli tutted at me.

"I have no issue with angels. And I don't want trouble. I'd really just like to leave," Forzi said.

"Unless anyone can confirm where you were at the time of the murder, for now, you remain in Crimson Cove with us," Cythera said. "And I trust you'll consent to have a bite cast taken."

His mouth drooped at the corners. "What for?"

"To see if the marks on Thomasina are a match to your bite." Bertoli's tone was testy.

Forzi slumped in his seat. "If I say no, you'll think I'm guilty."

"It would go against you," Cythera said.

He was quiet for a moment as he twirled his thumbs around each other some more. "Sure. I'll do it. I'm hiding nothing."

"I'll have an angel arrange for the bite cast to be taken immediately. Bertoli, make it so," Cythera said.

He scurried away and returned a moment later with another angel, who led Forzi out of the room.

"This is positive news to share with the higher angels," Cythera said.

I waited for a thank you for our contribution, but it didn't materialize.

"I still think a ghoul was involved in Thomasina's murder," Bertoli said.

"What about Forzi? He's your lurker! He most likely attacked my witch recently in the woods. His teeth are enormous and blunt. And he's in mate mode. You have your man. Why waste any more time on a fictitious ghoul?" I tensed. Bertoli was determined to find himself a ghoul to blame.

"Ghouls are unstable. And all those bites on Thomasina." He shuddered. "It was a frenzied attack. Much more like a ghoul would inflict than any other magical being."

"Or a love struck yeti who doesn't know how to handle his lustful urges," I said.

"Not every ghoul is bad," Zandra said.

Bertoli grimaced. "Every ghoul needs destroying."

"I'm surprised an angel shows such prejudice." I decided to jab him where it hurt. "Aren't you supposed to be kind and loving to all?"

Bertoli opened his mouth to argue, but Cythera raised a hand, and he stopped.

"The angels are all about fairness," Cythera said. "Bertoli, you have my permission to continue searching for the ghoul. We need to cover all bases."

"It would be my pleasure." Bertoli shot a viperous smile at us before leaving the room.

"Now, if you'll excuse me, I have a meeting with a forest guardian about some damaged trees." Cythera stood and pushed back her chair.

"Just a minute," Zandra said. "Where's Finn? I thought he was involved in this case."

"Not anymore. I've suspended him from duty."

Chapter 14

Bakery bites

I leaped onto the table. "Why suspend Finn? He's an excellent angel. The most effective I've ever dealt with, and I've been around plenty of angels over the years. Their skills usually linger on the wrong side of competent."

Cythera pursed her lips. "Finn was reported for using his demon power while on duty. He knows that's forbidden. It's in his employment contract. I really must go. Lateness is a sign of disrespect." She strode out of the interview room.

We were hot on her heels.

"Maybe Finn had no choice but to use his demon power," I said. "Cannibal Bill was a hideously unpleasant person to deal with. And he shot Finn with a crossbow bolt. He had a right to be angry."

"Did you witness the use of his demon power?" Cythera continued walking.

"We did. He had a tiny lapse in judgment because of being wounded. It could happen to anyone. Even you."

"Impossible. All my angels are vulnerable to being injured while in the line of duty, yet you don't see them unfairly using their powers to get the upper hand." Cythera paused to gather some paperwork.

I jumped on top of the paperwork and pressed down with my paws. "Let's see what you do when you've got a crossbow bolt lodged in your shoulder and a cannibal wanting to take a bite out of you and add your butchered remains to his cold store."

Cythera shot me a glare as she yanked the papers free. "I'm aware of what I'd do. I'd keep control and apprehend my attacker."

"Cannibal Bill took us by surprise," Zandra said. "How was Finn to know he wouldn't keep firing bolts at us? Or attack me and Juno? Finn was doing his job by defending us."

"And all the trapped creatures Cannibal Bill had in his shed. That shows he's unstable. Anyone who does that to poor, innocent fluffies..." I shuddered.

"Then Finn should have used his angel ability. Cannibal Bill reported an entire shed and its valuable contents were destroyed."

"Carcasses! The shed was full of illegally hunted animals," I said.

Cythera grimaced as she tucked away her papers and headed to the door. "Be that as it may, Cannibal Bill has been nothing but cooperative while in our care."

"You mean, he gave you information in exchange for getting away with being a disgusting brute?" Zandra said.

Cythera wheeled on Zandra and loomed over her, her wings fluttering. "The criminal world is immersed in shadows. Sometimes, we step into the gloom to ensure righteousness is achieved."

"Simply put, you're letting one criminal go to catch another," I said. "How is that fair? If you'd seen all the bodies in that shed and the ones in the cages awaiting the same fate, you'd feel differently."

Cythera huffed out a breath. "I understand how close to home this would have hit for you. You could easily have found yourself inside one of Cannibal Bill's cages."

"That would never happen," I growled out. "If he'd come at me, I'd have torn his head from his body and used it as a plaything, before mounting it on a stake and setting fire to it as a symbol to warn anyone thinking about caging an animal."

"Juno, take it down a notch or two," Zandra muttered.

I drew in a steadying breath, allowing my anger to subside. "My apologies, but you weren't there to witness the gruesome scene."

"It could have been another fairy massacre on Mossy Mount, but I'd have ensured I didn't overstep when using my powers. Finn knew what would happen if he lost control."

"Wait!" Zandra caught hold of Cythera's elbow as she walked away. "Finn is an asset to Angel Force. You can't afford to lose him."

Cythera kept walking, dragging Zandra behind her. "I must think about what is best for my team and Angel Force. Now, unhand me before I take flight. I'm never late for a meeting, and you have delayed me for too long."

Zandra clung on for another few seconds until we were out of the main door before letting go. Half a second later, Cythera was a blur in the sky.

I jumped on Zandra's shoulder and nuzzled her ear. "The angels never liked Finn. They've been looking for an excuse to get rid of him."

"We should go see how he's doing," Zandra said. "He must feel lousy after getting suspended. It's so unfair. This is the thanks he gets for doing his job."

"It is unkind, but he has strong demon power. Even I was alarmed when dealing with him in the woods. For a moment, I didn't think he'd regain control."

"He wasn't that bad, was he?"

"You didn't see the whites of his eyes. Or rather, the red. I wonder if Finn is more demon than angel."

"He's never said he struggles, although he rarely uses his angel energy. Maybe he's more comfortable using demon power." Zandra looked over her shoulder. "We'll visit him later. With Thomasina's killer in custody, we need to focus on finding Adrienne."

"Then we should visit Gingerbread Bakery," I said. "It's reopened, and since Adrienne is visiting her old haunts, she may return to her former place of work."

"That makes sense. And she liked that job."

"Let's chat to her employer and enjoy a few savory pastries while we're there."

"Trust you always to think about food," Zandra said.

"We left our breakfast muffins inside, so what else am I supposed to do?"

"Oh! They'll be long gone by now. We know what angels are like with free food. Gingerbread's it is."

We made the short walk along the main shopping street. The bakery was located close to Vorana's bookstore, and when we passed it, I looked inside to see if I could spot her, but all I saw were piles of books.

Since it was early, there were only a few people waiting to be served when we got inside the bakery, so we didn't have to wait long. There was just enough time for me to examine the enticing glass-fronted display case full of tempting treats and inhale warm bread, cheesy croissants, and the enticing tang of freshly carved meat.

"I'll have the smoked salmon and cream cheese bagel." I was perched on Zandra's shoulder as we waited to see the bakery owner, Tia Starbow.

Zandra nodded. "Sounds good."

"Hey, what will it be?" Tia turned her attention to us as her last customer walked out. She was tall and lean with a runner's physique and had close-cropped pale hair and startling green eyes.

"Hi. I'm not sure if you remember me," Zandra said.

"Sure do. You're friends with Adrienne, right?"

"More than friends. She's my mother."

Her eyes widened, and confusion licked across her face. "Oh! You're Zandra?"

It was an expression I'd seen many times before when people learned of their relationship. Adrienne was technically too young to have such a grown-up daughter, but thanks to a huge hit of magic in the form of an age-up spell, Zandra had skipped a few awkward teenage years and gotten a super young parent as a result.

"That's right," Zandra said. "And this is Juno."

"Greetings," I said. "You have a fine establishment. We're intrigued by the smoked salmon and cream cheese bagels."

Tia grinned as she wiped her hands on a cloth. "Thanks. Can I get you one?"

"We'll take two," Zandra said. "And answers to some questions if you've got a moment."

Tia glanced behind us. "It's your lucky day. The breakfast rush has yet to begin. What do you need?"

Zandra drew in a breath. "There's been sightings of a ghoul in town."

She nodded as she lifted out our order. "I've heard. People like to chat when they're waiting for their food. What about it?"

"It's possible that ghoul is Adrienne."

Tia's eyebrows flashed up, and the tongs she held froze midair. "For real? Adrienne's been turned?"

"We believe so," I said. "And we'd appreciate your discretion in this matter."

She set down the tongs and leaned against the counter. "This is crazy. How did it happen? I mean, I heard about the Shadow gang's shady business in their warehouse. Adrienne got messed up in that?"

"It's more than likely," Zandra said.

"You're absolutely sure?"

"I've seen her," I said. "We don't think she's a risk to anyone, and we're not sure how she's doing it, but she's remained stable. Adrienne's not attacking at random."

Tia whistled out a breath. "Even so, she needs to be found."

"We also believe she's feeding herself," I said. "And my encounter with her led me to believe she still has some presence of mind."

Tia straightened and crossed her arms over her chest. "I'm stunned. Adrienne is so full of life. I mean, was. I'm struggling with this. Ghouls are sort of alive, aren't they? And you say she's on the loose in Crimson Cove?"

"Yes, but please, don't spread that information around," Zandra said. "We need to find her. We have to protect her."

"You're sure she's safe?"

"As safe as a lone ghoul can be. It's the reason we're here. It's possible she's visiting places she remembers. Adrienne came to Vorana's house. That's where I'm living."

"No way! She's looking for you? She really remembers you?"

"As we've mentioned, Adrienne is a unique ghoul. We believe she can be saved, but to do that, we must find her," I said.

Tia scrubbed her chin. "I've not had much to do with ghouls, but from the way you're talking about her, she seems different. A ghoul who's not attacking, remembers her old life, and who has the presence of mind not to get caught. Astonishing."

"If Adrienne's visiting the places she remembers, it's most likely she'll return here. She talked fondly about working for you. She said she'd never had a nicer boss." Zandra said.

Tia grinned, and a light flush rose up her cheeks. "Adrienne was fun to work with. She always got the customers smiling. She wasn't perfect, though. Her timekeeping was terrible. And I once made the mistake of getting her to balance the cash register. It took me four hours to sort out the mess she'd left behind. I never had the heart to tell her, though."

"For all her faults, she has a way of making people like her," Zandra said somewhat reluctantly.

"Adrienne must have had you really young." Tia's steady gaze ran over Zandra.

"That's a story for another time," I said. "Have you been experiencing anything strange in the bakery?"

Tia pursed her lips. "What sort of strange are you talking about?"

"Noises late at night or someone attempting to break in."

She finally finished bagging our order, which I'd been staring at wistfully and trying not to drool over. "You mean the trash attacks? I've got an alleyway out back where I put the waste for collection. It's stored in big metal containers so the vermin don't get it. But a few nights ago, the lids had been raised and the bags sorted through."

"Someone's been eating from your waste?" Zandra said.

"Yeah, but only the meat. They leave the bread, the cakes, and the fruit. They've been taking out the fish and meat slices. It's all gone. It's happened three times."

"That could be Adrienne," I said.

Tia grunted. "Incredible. She always was an amazing woman."

Someone had a girl crush.

"Could you keep a look out for her?" Zandra said. "Any sighting could be valuable. We work at animal control and are staying with Vorana if you need to find us."

"Sure. Of course, always happy to help. I just wish I had... well, I used to have this great familiar. She'd always look out for trouble or problems. She'd sniff out your ghoul and bring her home safe."

"You lost your familiar?" I said.

"It was so weird, but she just disappeared one day. It happened three months ago. I came down to find the back door broken, and she was gone." Tia sniffed and glanced at a large, empty dog bed tucked in one corner. "I miss that big old furball. I looked for her for weeks, but it was like she vanished. I still go out most nights and call for her. I keep hoping... well, it's dumb. Whatever happened to her, she's long gone."

"I'm sorry for your loss." I bowed my head for a second. "Can you still feel your bond?"

"I feel something, but it's weirdly distorted. If she's still alive, she's in a terrible place. I've tried finding her, but my magic won't cooperate. It keeps kicking up weird results and false data. I miss her every day." Tia turned her back on us.

"What's her name?"

She took a second to compose herself then turned to face us, her green eyes hazy with tears. "Binx. Really, it's Binky, but I always shorten it to Binx."

"We're sorry you're going through that," Zandra said. "I don't know what I'd do without Juno."

"Yeah, our familiars are incredible." Tia pushed the bag of food our way. "These are on the house. I hope you get things figured out with Adrienne. If she's still okay, I'll have to visit her. I'd love to have her back here, but a ghoul serving customers would be a huge health violation."

"Understandably. Ghouls shed body parts, and you don't want a customer finding a gray finger in their bap. Thanks for the food," I said.

We left the bakery and got to work on our smoked salmon and cream cheese bagels.

"Where to now?" Zandra said.

"Let's try the woods. Since it's daytime, Adrienne will be keeping her head down."

"Save some of your bagel. We could use it to tempt her home."

"You save some of yours! She's your mother." I yanked out a piece of salmon and gobbled it down.

Zandra smirked at me. "Do I need to remind you how annoyed I am that you hid important information about Adrienne? Surely, a couple of small strips of salmon won't be a problem."

"That's emotional blackmail. And it's cruel to deprive a cat of her fishy treats." I pulled out some of my beloved salmon and tossed it at her.

Zandra caught it in the bag and chuckled.

We were soon in the woods, walking along a worn path and looking for signs of a ghoul having recently fed or trampled through the undergrowth.

"Uh-oh. Non-magical alert," Zandra muttered.

Bentley was up ahead of us, rooting around in the trees then peering up and taking pictures with a huge camera he wore on a strap around his neck.

We diverted to avoid him.

"He'll soon get the hint Crimson Cove isn't for him," I said. "The magic will drive him out eventually."

"It's weird he's got such a high tolerance for it," Zandra said. "Most non-magicals would have abandoned the place by now. He should be experiencing headaches, poor sleep, and even nausea. All the usual symptoms to keep the non-magicals away or drive them out if they stumble across this place and get curious."

I hopped off Zandra's shoulder as a set of big cat prints appeared in front of us.

"What have you got there?" She crouched beside me.

"These are fresh. Last night, when we were watching Cannibal Bill, we found prints just like this. And there was a large cat watching us."

"It didn't cause you any trouble?"

"No, it was just observing. I wondered if it was a familiar who'd lost its bonded magic user and was hiding out here."

"Another animal needing our help," Zandra said. "It never ends."

The woods were illuminated with a blast of white magic, which was followed by a heart clenching scream.

Zandra shot to her feet and looked around.

"This way." I raced through the woods in the direction the scream had come from.

Sounds of a tussle and growling reached my ears. I puffed my fur and prepared my magic, ready to face whatever was in the woods.

"Slow down, Juno." Zandra raced along behind me.

There was another scream so laced with terror that it made my breath catch. I couldn't afford to slow.

I blasted through the trees and discovered Cythera on the ground being mauled by a huge, pale brown cougar with a black stripe up its nose.

Zandra caught up with me. "Cythera!"

Cythera was on the ground, not fighting back. Were we too late? Was she already dead?

"She needs help." I flared a spell, planning on slamming it into the cougar. Before I thrust out my magic, a bolt of lightning slammed into the ground, almost frying the cougar and Cythera.

The matted-furred cougar snarled and leaped away as the bolt of power cracked across the ground.

"Where did that come from?" Zandra was looking around the woods while I raced over to Cythera.

I sniffed around her, grateful her chest moved up and down, although her eyes were open and not blinking. She must be in shock.

"Hey! Stop right there." Zandra marched along the path, magic blazing on her fingers.

I looked up to see a gorgeous guy with black hair and piercing blue eyes stagger into view. "Sorry. I don't mean any harm. You weren't hurt by my lightning, were you?"

"Stop moving. Who are you? What are you doing here?" Zandra raised her arms.

"I... I saw the attack, and... Excuse me. I'm about to..." He collapsed into the dirt in a dead faint.

Chapter 15

A wounded angel

"Watch Cythera. She's alive but isn't moving." I raced across the clearing.

"What about this guy?" Zandra pointed at the slumped, handsome dude who was face down in the dirt.

"He only fainted. I'm more worried about the frozen angel and why she's not moving." I kept running.

"Where are you going?"

"I'm bringing down that cougar."

"Juno. Wait!"

But I was already racing away. That creature was dangerous, had brought down an angel, and was a threat to my witch. It had to be stopped.

I jumped over fallen trees and dodged bushes in my pursuit. The cougar had left a clear trail of broken branches and footprints as it bounded away, not doing anything to hide its escape route.

The creature must be half out of its mind to attempt to destroy an angel.

I rounded the corner, ducking half a second before a huge paw swatted at my head. After skidding to a halt, I wheeled around. The cougar had concealed itself behind a tree and waited for me. Clever kitty.

It snarled at me and ran off.

"No, you don't. I have questions. And you need to be somewhere you can't hurt anyone." I'd yet to try the boundaries of my recently acquired magic, but now felt like the perfect opportunity.

As I raced after the cougar, I dug into the ancient well of power inside me. It willingly stirred to life, which was a new experience. But it was a risk, trying this magic when I was so uncertain about it. Needs must, since this cougar wasn't playing nice.

I thrust out a knockdown spell. The magic wavered through the air and skimmed the cougar's head.

The scrawny beast roared its outrage and sped up.

I increased my speed and thrust out another spell. This one hit home, but the magic had felt unstable as it left my paws, so I had no idea if it would do damage.

But I got the result I needed, and the cougar tumbled head over tail before stopping at the base of a solid fur tree.

Without hesitating, I leaped on the creature's back and buried my fangs into its ruff. I held the monster as it struggled beneath me, my restraining magic pouring over the ragged creature. After a brief struggle, it slumped onto its belly and huffed out a breath.

I slowly detached my teeth from the animal's ruff but remained planted on its back in case it attempted to escape again.

Now the pursuit was over, I was shocked to see its terrible condition. Fresh scars covered its body, its fur was matted, and the unpleasant smell of grease, sweat, and dirt suggested it had been many weeks since this beast had attended to its bathing needs.

"Let me go," it growled out.

"I can't do that. You're too much of a risk."

"Need to destroy. It's my mission."

"Before we talk missions, let's start at the beginning. Greetings, I'm Juno. I'm bonded with the most powerful witch you'll ever have the privilege of being close to. And you are..."

"Death and destruction. That's my purpose."

"Your name. You must have one."

"Devastation."

I huffed out a breath, smiling to myself. Some of these creatures took on the most pretentious names to appear more intimidating. "Let's call you Dougie. That's close enough."

Dougie growled. "I'm female."

"Okay. Deirdre? No, too old-fashioned. Daphne? Daffodil? I've always thought the name Daisy was adorable. I'll call you Daisy until you decide to let me know who you really are."

The newly named Daisy simply grumbled.

"Now we've established the polite and appropriate introductions, you need to answer for what you've done. Why attack an angel?"

"Mission."

"A mission you planned?"

"Must destroy."

"Very good. We've established that. Are you working alone?"

"Do you see anyone else here?"

I looked around. There was a tree rat watching us, which I ignored, but other than that unpleasant menace, we were alone. "You've been attacking and killing angels for fun?"

"Not fun."

"Then why?"

"Must. Need them to be sorry."

"What for?"

"Pain. Sadness. Loss."

"Who did you lose? Someone you cared for?"

Daisy growled.

"Do you have a magic user you're bonded to?"

"Yes! No. I don't remember. There's someone, I think. No, there isn't. I don't know them. I feel too much anger to concentrate."

I shuffled into a more comfortable position to avoid Daisy's spine digging into my ribs. "We never forget those we bond with. Do you feel a connection with someone?"

She didn't answer.

"If your bond has failed, there are plenty of kind, decent magic users who'd respect you." My gaze traveled over the many new scars littering this poor animal's skin. Daisy could do with a month of good meals to get some meat on the bones that jutted out.

"No choice," she whispered.

"Everyone has a choice."

"I must fulfil my mission."

"You've yet to tell me why you hate the angels so much."

"Ruination is my only purpose."

Poor, half-mad creature. "Perhaps you think it is, but from the way you're talking, you've been tainted with a terrible darkness to want to do this. Has your bonded magic user always treated you so poorly?"

"Never! Not my bond."

"I don't understand. Are you working with someone else?" I risked hopping off her back and circled around to her head. Her large amber eyes were dull, and there was a deep, oozing slash across her nose.

She looked away. "I must complete my mission."

"And your mission was to kill Cythera?"

Daisy didn't reply.

"Show me your teeth." I'd seen a disturbing sight when Daisy had snarled at me, but everything had moved so quickly during the pursuit, I wasn't certain my eyes had been truthful. I was hoping they weren't.

She glared at me.

"I'll show you mine." I bared my teeth at her. "They're magnificent. But I have a feeling yours aren't so splendid."

After a minute of grumbling and shuffling about in the dirt, Daisy opened her mouth to reveal blunt teeth. Even her fine fangs were blunted.

My stomach roiled, and I swished my tail. "Did your bonded magic user do this to you? He took away your beautiful sharp teeth?"

"I don't remember. No, I do. Not them."

"Someone else?"

She remained mute.

"And your claws. Have they also been blunted?"

Daisy splayed a paw, exposing miserably blunt claws that would do nothing if she needed to defend herself.

"If this is the work of the person who is supposed to care for you, you must break your bond. What's been done to you is the worst kind of cruelty. How can you defend yourself when your weapons have been taken?"

"No need for claws and fangs."

"We always need the things nature has bestowed upon us." I pressed a paw on her nose and pulsed out healing and calming magic.

Daisy winced and hissed at me, but I kept my paw in place.

"Calm yourself. I mean you no harm. I suspect it has been a long time since anyone has shown you kindness. But it's out there." I left my paw in place, hoping my magic would heal a small piece of this broken creature. "You must come with me. Angel Force will require answers since you attacked their leader."

"I have nothing to tell them."

"Did you also attack Thomasina?" I said.

Her glare slid my way. "The angels must be destroyed."

"Is that what you desire?" I shook my head. "I must know if you're working alone, or if there are others we need to stop. I cannot have any threats remaining in Crimson Cove. My witch must always feel safe."

Daisy launched at me. Her blunt teeth caught me, and I was shaken, but I was ready with a knockback spell. I slammed it into her stomach, and she slumped to the ground. Her eyes fluttered closed, and she heaved out another breath, relieved the fighting was over.

I touched my booping snooter to hers. "Rest while we figure this out. You're sick and hurting, and I intend to find out why anyone considered it acceptable to treat you this way." I briefly considered dragging Daisy back to Zandra. I'd used a serious amount of magic in a short space of time to defeat her, but it would take too long, and I was eager to get back to my witch and make sure no harm had come to her in my absence.

With a little effort, I cast a floating spell. Daisy lifted off the ground so I could push her back to the scene of the crime.

When I arrived, the place was overwhelmed with flapping, panicked, sweating angels. Some stood around Cythera, others ran around looking like they were hunting for something, and the others talked in small groups. All of them looked worried.

Zandra stood back from the chaos, taking in the scene, her arms folded and her mouth twisted in a half-snarl.

I circled the chaos and approached Zandra from behind, with Daisy in tow to avoid drawing any attention to us.

"I see you called in backup." I deposited the slumbering cougar on the ground, behind a bush so as not to alarm the already panicked angels. When they learned it was Daisy who'd savaged their boss, she wouldn't get a second of peace. And this animal had seen little of that.

"No choice." She eyed the cougar, concern flooding across her face. "Oh, that poor creature. And look at all those injuries. Did she fight you?"

"There was a small tussle, but she's exhausted and making little sense. I've named her Daisy. She kept talking about her mission to destroy and obliterate."

"The angels?" Zandra was crouched and examining the cougar. "There are some poorly healed bones here. She must be in pain."

"I suspect she is. She's also tainted with dark magic. And someone blunted her teeth and claws." I hissed at the gross tragedy.

Zandra looked over at Cythera. "Cythera has the same bite marks on her as Thomasina. You think the cougar attacked them both?"

"It seems likely. I'd ruled out a wild animal attack, but with her blunt teeth, it makes sense. How's Cythera doing?"

"She's alive but not saying much."

"What about the fainting guy with the magic? What's his involvement in this?"

"He's still unconscious. I reckon the lightning blast wiped him out."

"It happens. It always surprises those inexperienced with weather magic just how powerful the elements are. But you can't expect to control the skies and not pay a price." I peered at the fallen man, who'd been laid on his back a short distance away from where we stood. "I don't know him. He's not a local."

"Neither do I. We'll have to wait till he wakes to figure out what he's doing here." Zandra ran her hands over Daisy several times, pulsing out her warm, comforting healing magic.

Daisy's breathing evened out after a few minutes, but she remained asleep.

"The angels will want to talk to Daisy about the attacks," I said.

Zandra nodded, her expression tight. "She's in trouble."

"Before she gets interrogated, she needs downtime and healing. And I expect she'd welcome a break from the monster who messed with her claws and teeth. Perhaps time away from her tormentor will help her heal, and she'll be more willing to talk."

"What have you got in mind?"

"You stay here and keep an eye on the angels. Make sure they aren't messing up. I'll translocate Daisy to Finn's sanctuary. He's taken in injured animals before, when they've been involved in investigations. Daisy can recuperate before the angels get to her."

"Good idea. And with Cythera out of action, I'm worried Bertoli will take over. If he gets his way, he'll destroy Daisy before even talking to her."

"Bertoli would make the worst leader. I'll see you back at Angel Force in a couple of hours. Hopefully, the chaos will have died down by then, and we can ensure sense is knocked into the angels."

"Knowing how these panicked feathers like to operate, I doubt that'll happen. I'll keep them in line."

We briefly pressed foreheads together, then I touched Daisy and translocated us to Finn's animal sanctuary.

We arrived, and I looked around. There were the usual bleating and roaring noises coming from the barns but no sign of Finn. I checked Daisy was still asleep then headed around the side of the barns in search of him.

Finn stood with an axe in his hand, staring at a pile of wood. He looked up as I drew near. "Hey, Juno. I wasn't expecting to see you here."

"Greetings. I have good news. Well, good and bad news."

"You're here to help me deal with all this wood?"

"No, but we've solved Thomasina's murder. I've brought our new prime suspect to you."

His usually sunny expression was absent as he set down his axe and wandered over. "I'm guessing it's an animal since you came to me."

"A rogue familiar. I've named her Daisy. She's in desperate need of recuperation before she has to face her punishment."

"What's the bad news?"

"Daisy was caught attempting to kill Cythera."

His eyebrows flashed up. "She failed?"

"Of course. We were there to stop things from getting out of control."

Finn walked around the barn with me, sucking in a breath as he saw Daisy. "Some people don't deserve to live. This amazing creature must have gone through hell." He crouched and gently examined several of the scars on her body.

"It would seem so. And if you check her teeth and claws, you'll see they're blunt."

He sat back on his heels and shook his head. "Someone turned her into a weapon to kill the angels? She wouldn't do this to herself, would she?"

"I don't think Daisy's working alone, but she wouldn't admit to being involved with anyone. I think she has a familiar bond, but withdrew and attacked me when I pressed her on it."

"Why would she go after the angels for no reason?" Finn pulled clumps of dirt out of her fur while I sniffed around her. "Hey! Watch out, Juno. Her eyes are flickering."

"Then I suggest we get Daisy somewhere secure. She's prone to attack with little provocation. And we need to get a bite cast taken to see if she attacked Thomasina as well as Cythera."

"I've got some work stuff in a storage shed. I can find something to make an impression of her teeth. Then I'll send it to Angel Force. They can run the checks they need."

It hadn't escaped my attention that Finn wasn't mentioning his suspension. Perhaps he felt ashamed or humiliated. I wouldn't press him.

Before Daisy had a chance to rouse fully, we placed her in a secure barn surrounded by magic wards. Finn found a kit to get the impressions of her teeth, and once he'd whizzed them to the angels with a nifty spell, we locked the barn door and stood on the other side as Daisy slowly lifted her head.

I was perched on Finn's broad shoulder, so I had a good view. "Daisy, you have nothing to fear. I've brought you to an animal sanctuary. It's run by an excellent angel."

She swung her head toward me and growled. "All angels are bad."

"If it's any comfort, I'm only part angel. I've got a lot of demon in me, too." Finn raised a hand and smiled at her.

Daisy bared her teeth at him. "Still angel. Toxic sludge in society. Must be ruined. Made to pay."

"She's says things like that a lot."

"Does that mean you want to destroy me?" Finn said.

"Of course," Daisy growled out.

"Why?"

"Orders."

"Not yours? Is someone telling you to kill the angels? Does this someone have a name?" I said.

Daisy staggered to her feet. She paced the barn on wobbly legs, testing the door and trying to find a way out.

"What about your bonded magic user? You said you have a connection with someone. Do they live in Crimson Cove?" I said.

"I don't know." Daisy kept pacing and snarling, her head down and sliding from side to side as she moved.

"How long have you been bonded? A year, five years, ten years? You must remember. My memory of joining with Zandra is happily burned clear and bright in my memory. It was the happiest day of my cat life."

Finn gave me the side eye. "Not your other lives?"

I shrugged. He didn't need to know my full history.

"No memories. Just feelings. Rage and hatred and a desire to destroy."

Finn glanced at me, worry in his eyes. "Have you always felt like this?"

"I already said I don't remember. No memories. Just live to fulfil my mission."

"Could Daisy have had her memory wiped?" I whispered to Finn. "I clearly remember the day I bonded with Zandra. You don't forget when you join with your perfect magic user."

"It's possible," Finn said. "Or it could be this familiar has gone bad, and she's lost control. It happens. More than I care to think about."

"Must get back," Daisy hissed out. "Work to do."

"How did you get all those injuries?" Finn said.

"I deserved them."

"No one deserves to be hurt like that," I said. "Was it your bonded magic user? Or did you get them when you were attacking the angels?"

Daisy spun around and raced toward the door, her blunt teeth exposed and a madness in her eyes I was worried would never be extinguished.

I shot out a sedation spell before she could reach us, and Daisy crashed to the floor.

Finn whistled out a breath. "It breaks my heart to see an animal so broken. If I get my hands on the monster who did this..." He clenched his fists together and then yanked them apart.

"I may join you in that revenge mission." I studied Daisy for a few seconds. "At least the case is closed. And since you've been so helpful by taking Daisy in,

Cythera will reinstate you back at Angel Force in no time."

He slid me a glare, his eyes cold. "You heard about my suspension?"

"We did. We argued the case against it, but Cythera dug in her heels. She won't be able to do that now. You're helping keep the angel killer away from everyone. You're a hero."

Finn shrugged, his face turning gloomy again. "She won't want me back."

"You'll be shuffling papers across a desk and fighting with Bertoli for the last muffin before you know it."

He shook his head. "Nope. I have no plans to go back. I'm done with Angel Force."

Chapter 16

Change is in the air

I hopped off Finn's shoulder and stared up at him. "Why aren't you going back to work? You make the place great. You help the other angels avoid making too many mistakes. The place will be in chaos if you leave."

"That's hardly a ringing endorsement for Angel Force. That's why I want out." He kicked a stone across the barn and then turned and walked away. "It was a dumb plan to change things from the inside. The other angels hate me because of what I am, and I was only recruited because they had to fulfil a quota so they wouldn't look prejudiced. They don't want me there."

I hurried along and caught up with him. "Finn, you're smart, capable, and hard-working. Your desire to help injured animals is your most remarkable trait, and you're funny and easy on the eye. It's a perfect combination."

His grin was short-lived. "And while I appreciate those compliments, I'm done with the angels. I figured they'd be more accepting, and I've worked hard to prove myself to them. It was a waste of time. I've always got someone watching my back and waiting for me to make a mistake. And you know what? I just did. I almost tore Cannibal Bill apart. When I saw what he'd done to those animals..."

"If it's any comfort, I felt the same. Anyone would. You can't be blamed for that."

Finn turned to me and shoved his hands into his pockets. "But you didn't act on those feelings. You felt them, but you controlled yourself. I let my demon out. I didn't try to fight it. I'm not sure I could have done. And of course, the other angels learned what I did."

"Because Cannibal Bill is a troublemaker, and he was sore because you chargrilled his disgusting feast."

"They were right to suspend me. I'm not safe to be around."

I walked forward and stamped on his foot. "Listen to me. Those who want to change things for the better will never have an easy ride. People will mock them, fight them, and discredit them."

"I can put a tick in the box to all that happening to me. So why bother?"

I pressed harder on his foot. "Those who fight to make things better for others are remembered. They make a difference. They change things for the better for those who come after them. Perhaps you won't get an easy ride, and there'll be many times like this when you wish to give up."

"I'm not wishing. I am giving up. I have better things to do that give me less hassle." Finn gestured at the barns.

"You won't give up, because you're better than that. You see a world that can be better for other half-angels. Half-anythings! A world where you aren't seen as different or wrong because you don't quite fit in anywhere."

Finn tipped back his head and sighed. "That's what it feels like. The angels won't accept me, and the demons think I'm too angel to help them. I'm not bad enough or chaotic enough to join them."

My ears twitched. "Have you tried?"

Finn ducked his head, looking shamefaced. "I was at a low point not so long ago and couldn't find a path to follow. One that felt right. I reached out to Angel Force and a few local demons to see if any of them would be interested in having me around. I got a lucky break with the angels because of the new recruitment rules. They'd started their drive for inclusivity, and I fit the mold."

"What did the demons say about your interest in embracing your less angelic side?"

"They ignored me. I heard nothing from them. That silence told me everything I needed. So, I joined Angel Force. But it wasn't long before I realized it was a front. The angels stick with their own kind. They don't want half-breeds muddying the water."

"You're a magnificent half-breed. And diversity makes this world such a wonderful place. Finn, you must keep fighting. You make a difference."

"But I can't see an end. And always fighting and defending yourself is exhausting. Why should it be me that has to do this?"

"Because of creatures like Daisy. You fight for the underdogs. And you never pass judgment until you have all the facts." I stepped back and fixed him with a steady gaze. "I remember when we first met."

He nodded. "Sure. You'd found Osorin with his head missing."

"And Bertoli instantly wanted to arrest Zandra and charge her with murder. What did you do?"

"Got him to see sense." He blew out a breath. "It's hard work."

"You gave us a chance. You gathered information, collected evidence, and looked at the facts. You were fair. That's important."

"But I'll never be accepted for who I truly am while I work at Angel Force."

I sighed gently. "You remind me of the amazing beings I've ruled over. If I were in a different form, you'd have been an excellent fit for my establishment."

"Huh! Your establishment? And what other form are you talking about?"

I wrinkled my booping snooter. I'd said too much in my effort to comfort Finn. "I simply meant, if I could rule over an incredible society, it would be full of diverse and wonderful individuals such as you. I'd embrace your difference and nurture it. You'd receive nothing but love and support."

Finn's eyes narrowed. "This is in theory, right?"

I swished my tail. "Naturally."

"Uh-huh. You've never had another form or been a powerful ruler of some bizarre establishment I'm trying to get my head around." Finn crossed his arms over his chest and arched an eyebrow.

I narrowed my gaze. "There's something about you that gets me talking. That's a dangerous quality you possess. I'm not certain I like it."

"It's only dangerous if there are things you don't want to talk about. And I have a feeling there's a lot in your past you keep hidden."

"If I do, it's only for the benefit of others."

"Does Zandra know?"

"About what?" Finn was a little too good at digging into my past for comfort.

"That you're different, too. You're as unique as I am. You have qualities and abilities that don't fit anywhere."

"They fit with Zandra." I twitched my whiskers. "She has an inkling. That's all she needs for now. I suggest we visit Angel Force and discuss the next steps with Daisy. They'll be eager to close the case."

He smirked. "Just as eager as you are to change the subject. Getting too close to home, am I?"

"I can't imagine what you're referring to. And I almost forgot, an unknown hero emerged from the woods when Daisy was attacking Cythera."

"Who was it?"

"No idea. But we need to speak to him and then check on your boss. She received multiple bites. And she'd been immobilized, so there's powerful magic at work. Since Daisy is sleeping, we should go now."

Finn stepped back. "I don't want to go to Angel Force."

"Of course you don't, but you will because you have your own mission to tackle. It's much greater than your worries and despondency." I looked up at him again. "You have the makings of an outstanding leader, Finn. Don't let the other angels beat that out of you with their feathers and foolish assumptions."

"You reckon I can become the Head of Angel Force, do you?" He chuckled, but it sounded forced.

"You could do so much more than that. Shall we fly, or shall I translocate us?"

"How about we drive? I'm kind of done with magic for now."

"That's an acceptable form of transport, so long as you have a comfortable passenger seat." I'd need to watch Finn to ensure he made no swift moves away from Angel Force. He was an ally on the inside, and Zandra relied on him.

"I've got heated seats. Would that be suitable for her royal fluffiness?"

"I always appreciate having warm toe beans. Lead me to your carriage."

Ten minutes later, we were walking through the front door of Angel Force. Finn was tense but, so far, seemed determined to see this through.

Bertoli marched over the second we entered the office. "No, no, no! You're suspended from duty. You can't be here."

"Finn needs to be here," I said. "We have crucial information regarding Cythera's attack."

Bertoli's face went red. "Cythera doesn't want you here. She's seen your true colors."

"And I've seen yours. Bertoli, look at me." I locked eyes with him. "You want Finn and me here. You think we're incredible, and you want to be friends with us. You respect Finn as a colleague and value his input on all cases. You stop being a snide, unpleasant individual and support him in his endeavors to make changes at Angel Force."

"Um... Juno, what are you doing?" Finn whispered.

I was so focused on beguiling Bertoli, I didn't pause to inform Finn of my actions. "You'll never criticize Finn again. You'll always make him a coffee first thing in the morning, and when he wants the last donut, you'll give it to him. He's a valuable colleague."

Bertoli's eyes were glazed as he swayed on his feet. "I like Finn?"

"You want to be his friend. You like and respect him. You may even buy him the occasional gift because you think he's so awesome."

"Hey, don't push this too far, or people will think it's weird if Bertoli suddenly buddies up with me." Finn glanced around, making sure no one was watching my beguilement efforts.

"Bertoli, do we have an understanding? And just so you know, I like firm scratches between my ears, on the back of my neck, and at the base of my tail. But always ask permission before touching me. And a regular supply of fancy fishy treats is always in order. I suggest you make a space in your desk drawer for them. I shall be a regular visitor once you do."

Finn chuckled and shook his head. "You are something else."

I blinked slowly several times, breaking the beguiling link. "I like to think so."

Bertoli staggered away. He stared at me then Finn. A crooked smile licked across his face, and he clapped Finn on the back. "It's good to have you here. There's been so much happening since you've been gone. We need a catch up."

"Juno!" Zandra dashed over and scooped me up. "Everything okay with Daisy?"

"Finn took excellent care of her. She's sleeping it off after we briefly questioned her, but she got overwhelmed and attempted an attack, so I had to knock her out again." My gaze lifted as Forzi was escorted out of the building.

"The angels are letting him go," Zandra said, as she noticed where I was looking. "Since Daisy's been captured, they no longer think he was involved."

I raised a paw as Forzi looked at me and nodded. "I just hope the angels treat Daisy kindly."

"None of them are happy, but Cythera will survive. She's been taken to a specialist medical unit and is in recovery. She should be back in a few days. Maybe sooner. Angels are made of tough stuff."

"Please don't tell me they put Bertoli in charge in her absence."

"Not that I know of." Zandra looked over to where Bertoli and Finn stood. Bertoli had an arm around Finn's shoulders. "What's going on? They seem friendly."

"They're building bridges. Did you find out anything about the guy who fainted?" I didn't want Zandra to pay too much attention to my magical interference. She may not approve.

"He's awake and downing coffee. He seems shaken up. The angels were about to question him."

"Perfect. I'm sure they won't mind us sneaking into the room next door and watching the interview through the glass. After all, we were pivotal in breaking this case wide open and catching the killer."

She grinned at me. "That's what I was thinking. And now Finn's back, it'll make things much easier. I kept getting roadblocked by Bertoli and his sidekicks whenever I asked a question."

I wrinkled my booping snooter. "Finn may not be back for long. We have work to do with our feathered friend. I'll fill you in later."

A few minutes passed while the interview room was set up, so we grabbed refreshments and settled in chairs in the room next door and waited for the questioning to begin.

Bertoli brought in the fainting man and settled him in a seat. He was as handsome as I remembered. Tall, dark, and yummy.

Finn came in a second later. He glanced at the glass and gave us a discreet thumbs-up, although he didn't look happy to be there.

"Thank you for agreeing to speak with us," Bertoli said.

The guy shrugged. "Sure. I mean, I'm glad to be here. It's all been a shock."

Bertoli ran through the usual formalities before starting the interview. "Could you begin by telling us your name?"

"It's Ascal Sarlen."

"Elven?" Finn said.

"Kinda. My family is a mish-mash. My great grandpa had some Elven in him. Ascal was his name."

"What were you doing in Crimson Cove woods today, Ascal?" Bertoli said.

"Taking a walk. I'm on a short break and like to wild camp in new places. Wildlife is my thing. I make sketches and take pictures as a hobby."

"And how long have you been camping here?"

"Two weeks. I hadn't planned on staying so long, but I've seen a few weird things and wanted to investigate."

"What kind of weird things?"

"I was going to visit Angel Force to report it, but I wasn't sure how big the problem was. I didn't want to waste your time if my eyes were playing tricks on me." Ascal shrugged. "I love those fantasy role play games, and my wife is always telling me they make me daydream about fighting orcs."

"What problem are you talking about?" Finn leaned forward in his seat. "You've seen orcs in Crimson Cove causing trouble?"

"No, not orcs. But something else. The first week I was here, I set up camp in a quiet part of the woods, but it felt like I was being watched. I got the real creeps."

"I expect he was camping in Cannibal Bill's territory," I muttered.

Zandra nodded. "Makes sense."

"I was about to move when I saw this woman watching me from a distance. She was far away, but she wore a yellow dress, so she stood out."

I gasped at the same time as Zandra.

"You were concerned about her?" Bertoli said.

"She looked sick. I called out to see if there was anything I could do to help, but she ran off. Then I started seeing her regularly. That's when things got really weird."

This interview had taken a worrying turn, and I wasn't liking where it was going.

"What happened?" Bertoli said.

"She attacked me. I'd just gotten up and was brewing coffee when I was jumped from behind. The woman tried to bite me. That's when I knew what I was dealing with." Ascal gulped. "You have a ghoul living in your woods."

Bertoli sat up straight. "I knew there was a rogue ghoul out there. No one would believe me."

"I didn't believe it myself. I've not met many ghouls before."

"You obviously fought her off without getting bitten." Finn looked as tense as I felt.

"Yeah, not really. I got a lucky break. For a few seconds, she sucked on my neck but suddenly froze and then was gone. Like, she just vanished."

"The ghoul stopped herself from eating you?" Finn glanced at the one-way glass.

"Impossible! They don't do that. When ghouls find prey, they don't change their minds because they're not hungry," Bertoli said.

"Maybe a noise spooked her, or she saw something running and chased it. I'm no ghoul expert, but I believe they have a primal hunt instinct." Ascal chewed on his bottom lip. "Or maybe it was me. I was too stunned to move, so I wasn't interesting prey. Whatever the reason, she left me alone."

"Why didn't you report this straightaway?" Finn said.

"Because I couldn't believe what had happened. So, I tracked her. Ghouls sometimes operate in packs, and I was worried there were more out there, or maybe she'd gone to get friends."

"Ghouls rarely make friends," Finn said. "They often travel together but not for social reasons. They can bring down bigger prey and get more to eat if they work together on a hunt."

"Sorry, that was a stupid thing to say." Ascal raked a hand through his tousled hair. "I'm not feeling myself after what happened to that angel. I can't stop shaking. And I'm so tired."

"He's talking about Adrienne," Zandra whispered. "She attacked him in the woods. She's turned feral."

"Almost. But this is good news. She had a desire to hunt but stopped herself. She's still in control," I said.

"Barely. She almost bit that guy. She could have turned him into a ghoul or torn him apart. We have to find her." Zandra stood from her seat.

"Let's wait a minute. Ascal could have more information for us."

She hesitated, her hands gripping the back of the chair.

I rested a paw on her hand, and after a second, she nodded but remained standing.

"What were you planning on doing once you located the ghoul?" Finn said.

"They have a terrible reputation, which I don't think is always fairly given. Since she didn't harm me, other than spooking me, I wanted to see if I could help."

"Ghouls can't be helped. The best thing to do is destroy them," Bertoli said.

There was a tap on the door, and an angel came in with a tray of drinks. She set them down on the table and smiled at Ascal. "Nice to see you again."

"You know each other?" Bertoli said.

"Ascal is a hero. Didn't you hear what he did for Mrs. Flowerpot the other day?"

Ascal took a fresh mug of coffee, his cheeks glowing pink. "Anyone would have done the same."

"What did he do?" Finn said.

"She fell in the street. Tripped over a loose stone, landed in the road, and hurt her leg. Ascal was there to help her up. He picked up her shopping and walked her home then stayed with her until she felt better. She contacted us to say she wanted to give him a medal."

His flush grew deeper. "It was nothing. I was just in the right place at the right time."

"It was something to Mrs. Flowerpot." The coffee bringing angel smiled and left the room.

There was a moment of quiet as they grabbed drinks, and Bertoli shuffled his paperwork and consulted his notes.

"From the information we've gathered on the attack in the woods, you have powerful weather magic," Bertoli said.

"No! That's the weird thing. I'm an average warlock with a hint of elf. I can do most spells to a limited degree, but I've never tried a lightning bolt. But when I saw the angel being savaged by that cat, I knew I needed something strong, so I just acted. And then... well, I fainted. Kind of embarrassing. Not what a hero would do. And it's not a story I'll share with my wife anytime soon."

"You saved an angel. That makes you a hero in my eyes," Bertoli said.

We listened for several more minutes as Ascal retold his story and discussed helping to find the ghoul. He was an all-round good guy, although I wish he'd kept quiet about seeing Adrienne. He'd just made our lives trickier.

"We should speak to Daisy again," Zandra said. "We need to find out why she's killing angels. But..."

"You need to find your mother. Let's divide and conquer. I've spoken to Daisy before. I doubt she trusts me, but we have a connection. I'll try again with her and see if I can get anything useful."

"Thanks, Juno. Stay safe. I'll find you as soon as I can. I just can't stop thinking about Adrienne." Zandra pressed her forehead against mine then dashed out of the room.

I eavesdropped for another five minutes, but it seemed Ascal was your average Joe who got lucky with his magic. From the way his hands shook, he needed a long lie down and a cold compress on his head to get over using such a powerful spell.

After the angels had finished taking his statement, Ascal was free to go back to his tent.

I hopped down and skipped out of the room. Time was no longer on my side, since Angel Force would now be focused on Daisy. That was good in a way, since they'd be less fanatical about hunting Adrienne, but Daisy was troubled and needed help, not condemnation. I was certain she hadn't told me her full story.

I had no concerns about Finn keeping quiet about where she was, but he wouldn't be able to stay silent for long.

It was time to tackle Daisy again, but I needed a different approach. And I had just the approach in mind.

Chapter 17

Magical mission time

It was later that same day, and I'd returned to Finn's animal sanctuary. I wasn't alone.

I glanced at my companions. I'd summoned Archie, Sammy, and Sage to provide a united front when talking to Daisy. Perhaps if she saw how well we worked together and that being part of an awesome team had benefits, she might be willing to share. Or at least lower her guard and feel calmer knowing she was with animals who'd never harm her.

"She should wake in a few minutes." Finn backed away from the closed door. He'd joined us not long after the interview with Ascal finished. Since he was still suspended from duty, he had no reason to stick around the office. "You want me to stay while you talk to her?"

"Absolutely. She needs to know she can trust you, too," I said. "If Daisy is as damaged as I think she is, she doesn't need jail time. She needs therapy and healing magic. She'll get that here."

"I'll go check on our new arrivals and then come back. Any trouble, just holler."

I gently shooed Finn away with one paw and then hopped onto the ledge by the door so I could peer through the open flap and see Daisy.

Archie rested his front paws on the open hatch and peered in. "It's weird, but I'm sure I know her from somewhere."

"You've seen her in the woods?"

He cocked his head. "Nope. But she looks familiar. The same but different."

Daisy growled, flipped onto her back, and waggled her legs in the air.

Sammy hopped up to join me and peered in. "She's in bad shape. Did she say what happened to her?"

"All Daisy kept talking about was death and destruction. I'm hopeful rest and food will help her open up. When she knows not everyone wishes to hurt her, she might be more open to talking."

Sage floated up, her harness and wheels suspended behind her by magic. "I can't say I know her, but then I don't get out much."

"There'll be plenty more of these kinds of missions in the future if you're interested. You don't have to stay inside."

"I suppose this beats sitting at home and being hand fed like a baby."

"You love the way Vorana takes care of you," I said. "And I expect she did that before you got your harness and wheels."

"Now and again, when I allowed it." Sage's eyes narrowed. "The cougar's staring at us. And she looks mean."

"Daisy! Greetings and welcome back," I said. "Do you remember me?"

"Unfortunately." Daisy staggered to her feet and shook her head. "What prison is this?"

"No prison. You're in Finn's animal sanctuary. He works for Angel Force. He was here earlier."

Daisy snarled, exposing her blunt teeth. "Then he must be destroyed."

"No, he's a good one. He helps injured animals and familiars who have no homes. You can trust him."

"I trust no one. That's why I destroy."

"Do we know each other?" Archie tilted his head to one side. "You look familiar."

"I don't spend my time with mutts."

He growled. "Hey! I'm a fully-fledged hellhound who's bonded with a magnificent vampire. And I go to the grooming parlor three times a week. I even get my claws polished."

Daisy chuffed out a breath of annoyance. "Let me out. I have a job to finish."

"Talk to us about that job," I said. "Why are you so intent on destroying the angels?"

"They deserve it."

"What have they done to make you think that?"

"They interfere. They cause trouble. They're cruel."

"To you?" Archie said. "The angels can be dull, and they love their rules, but I've never known one to be intentionally cruel. They didn't give you all those wounds, did they?"

"My scars prove my endurance and my loyalty."

"To whom?" I said. "Who are you loyal to? Are you working with someone to destroy the angels?"

"Only myself. I trust no one."

"It's not a bad standpoint," Sage said.

I glared at her. "It's a terrible point of view. It means you always expect to be deceived."

She shrugged. "It happens more commonly than not. Daisy trusted the wrong person and look what happened to her."

Daisy bumped the door with her head. "I must get out of here. I can't rest until my mission is completed."

"A mission you came up with?" I said. "We must know if you're working with someone. Are the angels still at risk? Will more of them be attacked, or are they safe now you're in here?"

"I'm the weapon of destruction. My blood is full of hatred, my thoughts rage filled, my—"

I sighed. "We get the point, Daisy. You're a lethal killing machine, but somehow your claws and teeth have been blunted. You wouldn't have done that to yourself. So, who did it to you?"

"The angels must die." Daisy charged the door and head-butted it.

It shook so hard, I was knocked off-balance and landed nimbly on my paws on the floor. Sammy didn't land so elegantly, but he did an impressive belly roll to recover.

Sage floated down to join us, and Archie moved away from the door, concern on his fuzzy face.

"I don't like the look of her," Sage said. "She's full of darkness."

"Archie, are you sure you know her?" I said.

"Not for certain, but there's something about her. I can't put my paw on it. It'll come to me."

"Could she have lived in Crimson Cove?"

"Sure. It's possible. But she's different. Maybe it's a different fur color. I dunno."

Daisy slammed into the door again.

"She's a scraggly, underfed creature that has lost her mind," Sage said. "We'd know her if she lived here."

"Could magic have altered her appearance?" Sammy said. "She's been disguised, so she won't be recognized."

I looked back at the shuddering door. "The more I learn about Daisy, the more I'm convinced she isn't doing this on her own. She's been mistreated, abused with dark magic, and those beautiful fangs and claws have been mutilated."

"Why do that?" Sage said. "A dark magic filled cougar would be an excellent killing machine, but only with her weapons intact."

I shook my head, unable to answer that question. "You think she's too far gone, don't you?" I said to Sage.

She grunted. "I wouldn't know how to fix her damage."

"I never give up on a troubled creature, but the angels will take one look at her and destroy her. They won't see a way to rehabilitate her." Sammy jumped as Daisy rammed the door again. "If she's lost the bond with her magic user, it could be the reason she's so unstable. She needs a new connection. Something to pin her hope to."

"It worked for me," Archie said. "I'd thrown in the towel after losing Osorin. The bond I forged with Juno and Zandra gave me a tiny flicker of light in a pool of inky blackness. It kept me going."

"That's remarkably poetic of you," Sage said.

"Remus has been reading me poetry at night. I don't understand much of it, but some words are pretty."

I smiled. I was still surprised by what an excellent pairing an ancient vampire and an overenthusiastic hellhound with a slight drool issue had turned out to be.

Daisy had stopped smashing her head against the door, so I risked hopping up and peeked in at her. "Hey there, sad kitty. Would you object to forming a temporary bond with me?"

"I bond with no one. I am a lone avenger."

"Not to me. My bond will help get you stable. You'll have clearer thoughts and see reason. You'll stop wanting to kill anything within your line of sight."

"Leave me alone."

"I can't do that. Let's try." Zandra wouldn't mind if I formed a temporary bond with another magical creature. We had more than enough power to let a third individual join us. And it would only be a short-term connection. If Daisy had killed Thomasina and attempted to do the same to Cythera, she wouldn't have long left in this world. The least I could do was give her a few stable days, so she could get her affairs in order.

I closed my eyes and swirled out a spiral of bonding magic.

Daisy reared up on her back legs and batted it away.

"None of that. This is for your benefit."

"Stop interfering."

"Let's try again." I was glad to have the boost from my recently returned magic. It made the bond stronger, and I could pulse it out again with ease.

For a few seconds, it connected to Daisy. I grimaced as her hectic, troubled thoughts flooded through me, and her rage and fear pulsed through my veins and made me pant.

Daisy roared, and the connection snapped.

I looked in at her and shook my head. Was it kinder to accept this magical creature had been too badly damaged? Would she be the one I couldn't save?

"How's it going in here?" Finn strolled in, dusting off his hands.

"We're making little progress." I hopped to the ground and shook out my fur.

"We're making no progress. Daisy's stubborn and has refused our help," Sage said.

"She's a sad kitty," Archie said. "I'll be her friend. Even though she's scary, I'm bigger than her and have better teeth. We could play fight together when she calms down."

"Angel!" Daisy slammed into the door several times.

"She still has a pure hatred for all angels," I said.

"Did Daisy tell you why?" Finn backed up a couple of steps, his attention on the door.

"She just keeps repeating it's her mission to destroy all angels."

Wood splintered, and Daisy smashed through the door, the magic wards warping and then evaporating into white wisps of angel energy. She crouched for a second then lunged at Finn, grabbing his arm in her mouth.

Instead of fighting back, Finn froze and dropped to the ground.

"Team, subdue the cougar. Don't kill her." I fired a knockback spell at Daisy. It whacked into her side, and she staggered but still kept hold of Finn's arm.

Why wasn't he moving? There were no flickers of angel or demon power coming out of him.

Archie landed on Daisy and clamped his mouth onto the back of her neck. Sage whizzed forward on her wheels and blasted dazzling magic into Daisy's eyes. A second later, she was joined by Sammy, who threw out an equally impressive spell that sparkled and fizzed.

I dashed over and landed on Daisy's head to stop her from chewing off Finn's arm. A quick glance at his face showed him motionless and unblinking.

Daisy growled and let go of Finn's arm, so she could shake me off her head. The second she dropped Finn, Archie dragged her away, while Sage and Sammy weakened her with their magic.

"Hold her down," I said. "I'll check on Finn."

"You can't stop me. I'll never be stopped!" Daisy slashed her giant murder mittens through the air.

While Archie pinned Daisy with Sammy's help, I raced back to Finn with Sage.

"He looks dead. Is he dead?" She peered at Finn's face. "His chest isn't moving."

I pressed my paws on his arm. It was like stroking an icicle. "He's frozen but not dead. Daisy must have freeze magic. The second she touched him, he couldn't move."

Sage grimaced. "Freeze magic is nasty. If we don't get him moving, everything will turn frosty and break. His arms, legs, wings, heart. He'll be a goner."

"Not with us here. Summon your biggest fireball. I'll do the same. We need to heat this angel." I stood at Finn's feet while Sage remained by his head. We blasted our fire balls up then hovered them close to him.

The air grew stifling, but we had to get Finn warm quickly. A glance over my shoulder showed Archie and Sammy had control of Daisy. I could barely see her, since she was squashed under Archie's enormous bulk, although I heard her frenzied growls.

Archie caught my eye and wagged his tail. "This fluffy is going nowhere."

Finn gasped in a breath, and a faint hint of color returned to his cheeks.

"Don't move unless you want to be incinerated." I drew back my fireball a few inches, and Sage did the same. "How do you feel?"

Finn took several slow breaths, his teeth chattering. "I'm so cold. What... what happened? Daisy bit me, didn't she?"

"She did. And I now know why Thomasina and Cythera didn't fight when she attacked them. The second Daisy bites anyone, she floods them with freeze magic so they can't move."

He rubbed his hands up and down his arms. "That's one powerfully twisted spell."

I decreased my fireball so Finn could sit without his wings being singed. "Sage, stay with Finn. I need to see what Daisy has to say for herself." I strode over to the cougar. "Archie, ease up a few inches."

Sammy primed magic on his paws and pointed it at Daisy as Archie shifted off her.

Daisy wriggled away a few inches then heaved in a breath and remained on her belly, her eyes closed.

"How do you have such strong freeze magic?" I said.

She slow blinked at me, looking confused. "I don't. My specialty is speed."

"You touched Finn, and he couldn't move. You definitely have freeze magic."

Her eyes narrowed. "No, I don't."

"Archie, you're a tough, powerful hellhound, aren't you?" I said.

"The toughest. The strongest. And the hellhound with the loveliest fur. Remus got me a plaque saying that. And also that I'm the goodest boy. Why?"

"You won't mind if Daisy gives you a tiny nip to test her magic and show her she freezes everything she bites?"

"Oh! I suppose not. Will it hurt?"

"It'll feel a little chilly," I said.

"Why don't you get bitten if it's not so bad?" Sage said.

I considered her point. "I'm more a warm weather creature."

"I don't freeze anyone when I bite. You're making a mistake," Daisy said.

"You need to see this for yourself. Every time you use those blunt teeth on someone, they can't move. Pay attention while you gently–and I mean gently–nip Archie. See what he does."

We were joined by a slow-moving Finn, who still shivered, and a narrowed-eyed Sage.

Daisy looked around the group, shrugged, then caught hold of Archie's front leg in her teeth.

He swayed from side to side then crashed to the ground.

"Now, let him go." I had a knockback spell ready in case she got feisty. But Daisy had no beef with us, so she obeyed me.

She stared at Archie. "I did that?"

"Touch him. He's frozen."

Daisy jabbed Archie with a paw then stared at her foot pads. "How?"

"Heat magic, everyone! Whatever you've got. Let's get Archie back on his paws," I said.

We supplied fire to warm Archie, and a few seconds later, he was waggling his paws, his tail thumping on the ground.

"What did that feel like?" I said to him.

"Super strong but unstable. It's like no magic I've experienced before." Archie shook out his fur and did a full body stretch. "It felt like the joy had gone from life. It was just like when Osorin was killed. I was filled with sadness."

I looked at Daisy. "It's because you've been given a power you shouldn't have. That means you're not working alone. Who is controlling you?"

Daisy's gaze slid from side to side. "I... I don't know. All I know is I've never had freeze magic in my life."

Finn's mobile snow globe buzzed in his pocket, and he pulled it out. "It's Zandra. Hey, what have you got for us?" He slid his finger across the globe so we could all hear.

I moved closer, so I could see my wonderful witch and make sure she was safe.

"I just heard from Angel Force. They got the results from the bite cast impression from Daisy's mouth."

I nosed closer. "And?"

"It's a match. The angels know she's our killer."

Chapter 18

Furry fury

Finn glared at Daisy. "You murdered Thomasina and tried to do the same to Cythera. Why?"

"Wait! This looks terrible for Daisy, but she doesn't know what she's doing." I stood in front of the cougar to shield her from Finn's anger.

He lifted his mobile snow globe. "I can't argue with the evidence. She's the killer we've been searching for."

"She's also under the influence of nasty, twisted magic. Daisy has been used as an unwilling weapon by someone much more devious than her. That's who you should target."

"The angels are insisting she's brought in," Zandra said. "Bertoli found me in the woods and demanded to know where she was." She flicked up her eyebrows. "He wouldn't leave me alone until I promised to make a call. He's demanding you bring Daisy to Angel Force, or they'll send a troop of angels to collect her."

"You didn't tell him where Daisy is, did you?" I said.

"No, but everyone knows where the wounded critters are sent in Crimson Cove. It won't be long until they come to Finn's place."

"Can you buy us more time?" I said. "We're close to a breakthrough."

"Bertoli won't listen to me. Besides, he's gone back to base." Zandra glanced away from the screen. "Hold on a sec. There's someone out here."

"Adrienne? Is she there? You're still in the woods?"

"No, it's something else. Something huge." She yelped. The screen went fuzzy, and the connection died.

Panic flipped my stomach up and down and side to side. I ran one way and then the other. Only Archie standing in my way stopped me from doing it again.

"Zandra's in trouble. I must get to her. She was in the woods. But where? She's in danger." I flung out a translocation spell to take me to the woods, but my magic set fire to a stack of hay.

Finn raced over and flapped his wings to extinguish the flames.

I couldn't get myself centered, but I had to get to Zandra. I forced myself to focus and began to cast again when a sharp pain in my tail made me pause.

Sage was biting me!

"Are you out of your mind? I must get to my witch."

"And burn this place down while doing it," she mumbled around a mouthful of my tail.

"If that's what it takes. I must go to her."

Sage dug in her claws but extracted her teeth from my skin. "You're unfocused. And with magic as weird as yours, that makes you dangerous."

I growled. "Something jumped Zandra. What if it was Adrienne? What if she's gone rogue?" I should have been with my witch. I shouldn't be helping Daisy and the angels. I tried another translocation spell. The ground beneath my feet split apart, tearing a jagged scar through the dirt.

Finn raced over and crouched beside me. "If you don't calm down, you'll destroy this place. I saw what happened to Zandra, and I'm worried too, but Sage is right. You're not focused."

I hissed at him. "You don't understand. We have a bond. Zandra needs me."

"I understand well enough how special your bond is and how much Zandra means to you. She means a lot to me, too. So, let us help."

My frantic gaze cut to my friends, who guarded Daisy, worry clear on their faces.

I drew in a breath, scrambling to get control. Just when I needed my magic to perform, it failed me. My old power tingled through me, but I didn't trust it enough to use it again.

Sage's paw landed on my shoulder. "Let us help. We have enough power to share. What do you need us to do?"

I squeezed my eyes shut for a second, my heart trying to tear out of my chest and my toe beans hot and pulsing. "Finn, we need to get Daisy safely locked away. And expect a visit from some angry angels soon."

"Sure. I'll do what I can to get them to see sense."

"You have to. Daisy's not guilty. She's just been horribly misused. We need to find the power behind that abuse." I looked at my other friends. "Archie and Sammy, you stay with Finn and help with Daisy."

"I want to come with you," Sammy said.

"There's no time to debate this. Sage, we must find Zandra. I need you to translocate me to the woods and then cast a location spell."

"Got it." Sage dabbed her nose against mine, the ground tilted, and a second later, we were in Crimson Cove woods.

Sage backed up, a focused look in her eyes as she cast a location spell. I was impressed with her efficiency. You usually needed a physical item to locate a person or a drop of their blood.

The ground lit up, and a small dot appeared.

"Is that her?" I said.

Sage peered at the light. "I reckon so. I used you as the connection. But she's moving fast. She must be sprinting."

"Zandra doesn't sprint. Something has her and is taking her away from me." Rage and fear flooded through me, fluffing my fur and sending out involuntary sparks of magic.

Sage stamped on a leaf that caught fire. "Calm yourself! This forest is older than you, and I'm not watching these trees burn because you lose control."

I struggled to calm myself but dragged back enough magic so I wasn't flaring my emotions in a mess of glittery fire.

"This way." Sage made off along the path. "We'll catch up with them."

"Not without magic. I would, but... well, I'm all over the place."

"You're pushing the boundaries of this friendship," Sage grumbled, but the gleam of excitement in her eyes suggested she was enjoying herself.

I only wish I was, but I'd find my joy when I saw Zandra and knew she was safe. And I'd destroy the beast who had her. "One more spell, and I'll pay you back with a week's worth of smoked salmon dinners."

Sage chuckled, shot a spell under our paws, and we lifted a few inches off the ground.

For a second, I pedaled in the air then zoomed off so fast the wind stung my eyes. We flew through the woods, dodging trees and bushes, following the small ball of light in front of us that would lead us to Zandra.

My pulse still pounded, and I felt sick at the thought of anything bad happening to her, but we were drawing nearer, thanks to Sage's beautiful magic.

"She'll be okay," Sage said. "Zandra's power may be young, but there's so much of it, I almost can't look at her. Does she have any idea how strong she is?"

"She has an idea. When she's ready to explore that power fully, I'll be there for her."

"With your own weird magic?"

"My weird magic is what'll keep Zandra safe if she oversteps the boundaries while she's learning. We all need a mentor."

"Who's yours?"

I slid her a glare. "Let's focus on finding Zandra."

We sailed through the air for several minutes, drawing ever closer as the location spell guided us.

"This direction takes us out of Crimson Cove," Sage said. "If we keep going straight, we'll hit the boundary in about twenty minutes."

I growled and sped up. No one took my witch away from me.

"They should be up ahead," Sage said. "We'll see them any second."

My heart stuttered with joy as magic flared close by. That was Zandra's power. I'd know it anywhere. My wonderful witch was fighting back.

The path slanted to the left, and as I whizzed around the bend, I caught a flash of pale skin and dark hair. "It's Zandra! I see her. She's being carried." I sped up, and as I gained on Zandra and her mystery abductor, I picked up the scent of musky dog. "That's Forzi! The yeti we questioned over Thomasina's murder. I thought he'd left Crimson Cove."

"It seems he has unfinished business with your witch," Sage said. "Let's get him."

My wheeled friend showed no fear as we flew straight toward the enormous, speeding yeti.

"This'll take a joint effort to bring him down," I said. "You ready?"

"I've dealt with worse than a giant, hairy ape." If Sage had knuckles, she'd have cracked them.

"Zandra," I yelled. "Look out. Incoming!"

She'd been whacking her fists on the yeti's back, but her head shot up when she heard me. "Juno!"

My paws slammed into Forzi's back.

He hollered and staggered forward then righted himself and kept moving. He glanced over his shoulder, bared his teeth, then continued running.

"He's in full mating lust," I said.

"Does that mean he mistook Zandra for a yeti?" Sage smirked. "You need to have a word about her grooming habits."

"My witch's grooming habits are impeccable. Mostly. But yetis have a thing for dark-haired females. He must have met Zandra in the woods and lost control."

We slammed into Forzi's back again. This time, he lost his grip on Zandra. She wriggled off his shoulder, dropped to the ground, and rolled away.

I slowed and wheeled around to check on her. "You good?"

She waved a hand at me. "Just shaken up. And embarrassed. Get Forzi."

Because I'd slowed to speak to Zandra, Sage was way ahead of me. As she continued her pursuit, she flipped around and used her wheels to slam the side of Forzi's head.

He howled and attempted to bat her away with his huge hands.

She opened her mouth, and magic poured out in a beautiful rainbow arc. It hit Forzi in the chest.

He grunted, his arms waving in the air as he tried to keep his balance, but he crashed to the ground.

After a brief nuzzle with Zandra, I raced over to join Sage. She'd planted herself firmly on Forzi's chest and was hissing in his face, her murder mittens hovering over his broad nose.

I added a restraining spell to her magic and stood by Forzi's head. "How dare you take my witch."

The blackness in his eyes receded, and he blinked. "Juno? How did I get here? What's going on? I feel weird. Why is there a cat with wheels squashing me?"

"You need to be neutered." Anger dug into my gut, and magic flared around me.

"Careful, Juno," Sage cautioned. "He seems confused."

"I... I didn't mean to take anyone. I thought she was somebody else."

"Who did you think I was?" Zandra walked over, brushing dirt off her jeans.

His gaze cut to her, and he gulped. "No one. I made a mistake. I didn't mean to say that."

Zandra arched an eyebrow. "Why are you still hanging around Crimson Cove?"

"No reason. I... I just like the place."

I hissed in his face again. "Tell us the truth. You being here for so long isn't a coincidence. And it's clear you're seeking a mate."

He attempted to sit, but Sage hit him with another spell, and he sank to the ground with a groan.

"This'll go easier for you if you cooperate," Zandra said. "These familiars take no prisoners. If you keep hiding what you're up to, it suggests you're guilty of something."

"You're guilty of taking my witch." I slashed a murder mitten close to Forzi's nose, and he cringed away. "What else have you done that you shouldn't?"

"Not murder, if that's what you're thinking," Forzi said. "I never attacked that angel."

"We know," Zandra said. "But tell us what's keeping you in town. We can't let you stay if you're a danger to other women."

His hands went to his colored ruff, and he smoothed the fur. "I'm not. I promise. There's someone I like, but she's not interested. I've asked her out several times, and I even attempted a mating bite to persuade her I was her one and only, but she laughed at me. She said I was pathetic and she could do better."

"That was unkind of her," Zandra said after a short pause. "But when someone makes it clear they're not interested in you, you accept that message and move on."

"I can't. I want to, I really do, but I've fallen for her." Tears filled Forzi's eyes. "She's always in my thoughts, and my desire has grown. Before I knew it, I was following her everywhere."

"Stalking is uncool," Sage said. "It's a surefire way to get yourself a creeper label."

"I know, I know. But this is only the second time I've had full mating lust. I'm still learning how to handle these emotions." His shoulders sagged. "I'm an embarrassment. Maybe I should be neutered. No one will ever love me."

My anger faded as I realized how young and scared this yeti was. Forzi wasn't a threat. He was just lost in a sea of uncontrollable emotions. "What happened the first time your mating fever struck?"

"I hid in my room and tied myself to the bed. The feelings were so intense, and I had nowhere to channel them."

"What about your family? Weren't they around to teach you how to handle these feelings?"

His gaze dipped. "No family. Few friends, either. I was figuring it out as I went along. It's not easy being a lonely yeti when your mating urges kick in."

I exchanged a glance with Zandra, and she gave a gentle shrug.

"I'm sorry you've been struggling, but stalking someone who's not interested in you and then taking my witch is wrong."

He gulped back tears. "I'm so desperate for a mate. And I sometimes lose myself to the urges. This time, they've stayed much longer. I wonder if they're ever going away. I wish they would. I hate them."

"There are dating apps if you're serious about finding someone," Sage said.

"Not for the likes of me."

"Absolutely for the likes of you. There's an app for everything. Vorana is obsessed with them. She's always finding something new to add to her snow globe."

"Really?" A hopeful look entered Forzi's eyes. "I don't need to keep chasing after the mate who rejected me?"

"No, don't do that," I said. "Any female who laughed in your face and said you're pathetic isn't worth wasting time or thoughts on. You're a young, strapping yeti. Someone will desire you. You've yet to find the right someone, that's all."

Zandra held her hand out to Forzi to help him up. He took it, waiting a second to allow Sage to slide off him and not get her wheels tangled in his fur.

"I am sorry," he said to Zandra. "I already feel better after talking to you. And if there's a possibility I could find a mate through an app, I'd love to try it. It feels lousy lurking in the shadows, hoping someone will take pity on me."

"That's because it's creepy," I said. "And you don't strike me as a creep, just a misguided youngster."

"Is the female you like from Crimson Cove?" Zandra said.

"No, but she came here a few weeks ago. She's been visiting friends, and they like to walk in the woods, so I hung around and waited for her. I haven't seen her for a few days, though."

"Perhaps she moved on while you were being questioned by the angels," Zandra said. "You should, too."

He nodded. "I will. I'll head home. Is there anything I can do to make up for grabbing you? I hope I didn't scare you too badly."

"You're good. I knew I wasn't in any real danger." Zandra winked at me. "There is one thing you can do for us, though. We're looking for information about visitors to these woods."

"Sure. I can help with that. Who are you looking for?"

"A female ghoul."

"Ghoul! Are there ghouls here?" Forzi glanced over his shoulder.

"Yes, but she's not a threat. At least, we don't think so. She could be wearing a yellow dress."

"I've seen no ghouls. If I had, I'd be long gone."

"Even though you were lurking about and waiting for the love of your life?" Sage said.

"I'd have been no good to her dead!"

So much for not giving up on true love. The first sign of trouble, and Forzi would have high-tailed it out of here. "We also need to find out more about a cougar. She's skinny, bad teeth and claws, and covered in fresh scars."

"Her! Sure, I've seen her around. I avoided her. She was often hanging around the tent of that nosy non-magical. Have you met him? He's always out and about, taking pictures. He almost got a picture of me. I had to dive into a pile of rotting leaves to avoid getting on camera. Anyone would think he can see our magic the way he keeps snooping and questioning."

"Daisy's been spending time with Bentley?" I looked up at Zandra. "Was she trying to eat him?"

"No, nothing like that. She'd rest near his tent. I even saw him talk to her once. I thought it was weird."

"It's very weird. Our magic should repel him out of here. Do you think there's something special about this guy?" I said, more to Zandra than Forzi.

"There must be," she said. "When I spoke to him, he was really interested in Crimson Cove."

"He could have latent power," Sage said. "It happens. People reject their heritage and move somewhere where magic isn't practiced. Perhaps he had a great grandparent who renounced magic.

It's still there, but he just doesn't know about it. Magic doesn't go away because you ignore it."

"It would explain why he's so comfortable staying here," I said. "Or he could have stumbled on a magic item, and he's misusing it."

"Or using it without being aware of its power," Zandra said. "Magic items can get into the wrong hands, especially when they get sold to the highest bidder. Non-magicals have died because of it."

"I didn't see him using any magic or carrying any special items," Forzi said. "Maybe he just fed the cougar, so she hung around hoping for more food. She looked really sad."

We all nodded, but I had a tingle at the base of my spine that suggested there was more to Bentley than met the eye.

Zandra looked at Forzi. "Thanks for the information."

"Of course. Am I forgiven?"

"You are. Under these conditions. Learn how to keep your mating lust under control, don't tackle anyone else to the ground, sling them over your shoulder, or run off with them. Got it?"

"Unless they want you to do any of that," I said.

He shrugged. "Sorry. I've learned my lesson. Although I'd appreciate it if you could show me the yeti dating apps. I promise, I'll only use those from now on to find my true love."

Zandra's smile was rueful as she pulled out her mobile snow globe. "We'll do some swiping left and right while I walk you to the boundary." She looked down at me. "I'll be back soon. Have a look around and see if you can find where Bentley is camping.

We need to make sure he's not playing with magical fire." She walked away with Forzi, their heads bent over her mobile snow globe.

I turned to Sage. "We need to find that non-magical creep fast."

"And warn him that playing with something he doesn't understand will get him killed."

I nodded. "Exactly. And possibly by me if he doesn't behave himself around my witch."

Chapter 19

A magical non-magical

It took an hour of searching, but we'd located Bentley's campsite and had set ourselves up to watch what he got up to while concealed behind a row of tall bushes in the woods.

"We could compel him to tell us everything," I said.

"We don't use spells on non-magicals. It would send him crazy." Zandra shook her head. "We should stroll over and act like concerned citizens. Tell him there's a dangerous animal on the loose, and he needs to be careful. He should pack up and leave before he gets attacked."

"He didn't listen to your suggestion to move on the first time," I said. "This needs strong-arm tactics, so he reveals what he's playing at. Why would Daisy spend any time with Bentley unless there's magic involved?"

"I say we pin him down, beguile him, mind wipe him, and then burn his stuff and chuck him out of Crimson Cove," Sage said.

If I had eyebrows, I'd raise them. That was a little too strong-armed for my liking. "Or Sage and I could sneak into his tent and poke around while Zandra asks questions. If Bentley accidentally picked up a magical item without knowing what it can do, and it's malfunctioning, he won't be aware of how much danger he's in. And since he's attracting magical creatures, it's only a matter of time before something goes wrong."

"He'll get eaten. Or chopped up by a misbehaving witch and his bones used in her spells," Sage said.

"I was thinking more that his mental health would suffer. Non-magical brains are fragile. But your suggestions have value, too."

"Maybe in a Grimms fairy tale," Zandra said. "What if this isn't accidental? Sometimes, a non-magical will come across an old textbook that hints at what lies behind the magical veil. He could have found one and be searching for the truth."

"Which means we use whatever tactics we need to get answers out of him," Sage said. "I hate it when these non-magicals meddle in stuff that doesn't concern them."

"Have you dealt with many non-magicals?" I said.

"Enough to know I'm not a fan. I stay away from them as much as possible."

"Let's go for a simple approach," Zandra said. "I'll ask him questions, and you look around his tent. I'll take Sage with me."

"I can handle some light interrogation work if you need the backup," Sage said. "I'd use minimal spells if he resists talking."

"No magic. We can get answers without this getting nasty, but I figured he'd be interested in a cat with wheels. It'll hold his attention," Zandra said. "Juno, we'll distract him and get him away from his tent then you sneak in."

"Got it." I remained behind while Zandra and Sage walked slowly toward the tent.

Bentley looked up, and his gaze went to Sage. "Hey! Is that another of your cats?"

"She's a friend of mine. You're still here," Zandra said.

He set down his tin mug and grinned. "I'm hardly going to miss the story of a lifetime."

"What story is that?" Zandra deliberately moved past him, so he had no choice but to turn so he was facing her, putting his back to me.

I tiptoed to Bentley's tent and slid through the zipper opening. I kept an ear on the conversation as I took a second to get my bearings and look around.

"The murder! Everyone's talking about it," Bentley said.

"Everyone's talking to you about it? I'm kind of surprised. Locals are usually shy around strangers."

"Well, let's just say I'm asking lots of questions. I may not be getting many answers. It only makes me more intrigued. What's the big secret about Crimson Cove?"

"No secret. It's your average place. Have you bought any trinkets or memorabilia while you've been here?" Zandra's tone was falsely breezy.

"I travel light. I don't buy stuff when I'm on the move."

While they chatted about the different stores he'd visited, I snooped around his tent. It was small, only made for two people. There was a single blowup mattress with a sleeping bag on top, basic items for making food, and a single paperback book. There was also a small pile of clothing in one corner and a bag of toiletries.

I inspected everything and came up with nothing.

It wasn't until I lifted the air bed that I struck gold. There were neat piles of notes and photographs, all showing Crimson Cove. There were pictures of most of the residents, and as I flipped the photographs, there were notes on the back. *Possibly a shapeshifter? Did I see her cast a spell? If vampires are real, this guy would be one.*

The notes and pictures went on. Bentley had been thorough in his investigation and worryingly accurate in his description of the individuals he'd been watching. Whoever this guy was, he must be gathering information to expose Crimson Cove to the world. But how could he know about our magic? He shouldn't be able to see these things or when magic was used around him.

I looked through several of the notebooks. Bentley had been out at all hours, watching residents and looking for strange behavior. And he'd noted down plenty. For whatever reason, he was seeing Crimson Cove for what it really was.

And that terrified me. Magic was kept secret for a reason. If everyone knew about it, we'd be overwhelmed with demands from the non-magicals to fix their problems, but our magic didn't work right on them. It was dangerous. Most of the spells were toxic to them, and if it didn't kill them, it changed them forever.

I placed the blowup mattress over the notes and pictures. There was no sign of any artefacts that would enable Bentley to see magic in this town or talk to Daisy. Maybe Sage had a point. He could have an ancestor who'd had magic, and it had passed onto to him and was making an appearance.

I shoved my head out of the tent and caught Zandra's eye. I shook my head slowly, so she knew I'd found no magic, then crept away, waiting a few seconds before making my grand entrance.

"There's your other cat!" Bentley held his hand out to me. "Here kitty. You're pretty."

Although I didn't want to be touched by a non-magical, it could be useful. I'd be able to detect if he had anything special about him. I allowed him to pet me for exactly three seconds before hissing and backing away. There was nothing special about this guy.

Bentley was smiling and shaking his head as he watched me. "Cats are weird. One second, they're all over you, and the next, they treat you like you're the enemy."

"At least they're honest about their feelings," Zandra said. "They hide nothing."

"True. Although at least people don't scratch or bite you if they're in a bad mood."

I resisted the urge to make a sarcastic comment.

"Have you seen a big cat in the woods? It's a cougar," Zandra said. "I thought I'd better come over and warn you about her."

"Sure. She's been hanging about, but I haven't seen her today. I figured she may have turned up her paws and given up. She was a sorry-looking thing."

"You didn't feel under threat from her?" Zandra said.

"Never. She seemed sick. Her breathing was labored, and she was panting. I threw her food and left out a bowl of water, but I couldn't think what else to do. After all, she's a wild animal and wouldn't have liked it if I'd taken her temperature and given her a pain pill. I figured she was old, and it was just her time to go."

"She hasn't died," Zandra said.

"Oh! Well, that's good. I didn't see her last night, so I assumed the worst. I left a small fire outside for her, but I don't think she came back."

"Even so, you should move on," Zandra said. "If the cougar is injured, she'll get desperate. She could attack you because she's starving."

Bentley's relaxed expression faded. "There's not a chance of me leaving. Besides, this is public land. I've got a right to be here."

"You must be bored with the place by now."

"I've only explored a fraction of Crimson Cove. Everyone here is so freaky, and I need to find out all about them. What about you? You didn't tell me your name the last time we met. What secrets are you hiding?"

I hopped onto Zandra's shoulder and pretended to lick her ear. "He's got pictures of Crimson Cove. He can see our magic."

Zandra remained calm as she petted my side. "Are you a journalist, trying to get some imaginary scoop on this place?"

Bentley grinned. "I'm surprised you don't recognize my voice."

"What's so special about your voice?"

"I've got over a million subscribers who tune in to my weekly podcast to learn about the dark underbelly of cute little places like this."

"We don't have a dark underbelly to expose. At best, it's a light beige," Zandra said. "You're wasting your time investigating Crimson Cove."

"I'll have to disagree with you. And since there's been a murder in town, it's more evidence there's something special about the place. I also heard there was another near miss not so far from here. Someone else got attacked. What do you know about that?"

"Nothing. And a tragic murder is evidence misfortune happens everywhere. It's not something you should pull apart on your podcast."

"Why not? People love dissecting murder. I heard the victim was bitten to death. Is that true?"

"Who told you that?"

I was as surprised as Zandra to learn residents had been talking to Bentley. They'd have been able to identify him as a non-magical, and that automatically meant the conversation stayed short and light-hearted.

"I don't remember. I've talked to a lot of people. So, is it true?"

"You should be careful," Zandra said. "If you keep poking around in a murder, you could become a suspect. Maybe I should check your alibi."

He laughed. "I have nothing to hide. I got chatting with this old boy in town just before it happened, and he made some joke about being a wizard. He said he'd show me magic tricks if I bought him a drink."

"And did you?"

"Of course. He did some cheap card tricks. I kept pressing him to show me the real stuff."

"What do you consider real magic?"

"That's something I think this place will show me if I stay long enough. It's just not ready yet." Bentley's gaze went around the woods. "Something is building. Things are changing, and I plan to witness what they are."

"You have an overactive imagination," Zandra said. "There's no such thing as magic."

"There is." He waggled his eyebrows. "And there's something special about you, too. Every now and again, I get a shiver down my spine when I look at you, but then it's gone. And you may think this is crazy, but you have an aura."

"Yeah, that is crazy. People don't have auras." She pressed a hand against my side.

This was getting worrying. This guy really could see our magic.

Sage stood abruptly and shook out her fur. "I've heard enough."

Bentley jerked back. "Did... did you just talk?"

"No! Sage just meows in a very talky-like way." Zandra glared down at Sage.

"It's no use hiding it. This guy senses the magic. He's onto us, and I'm not letting him expose our secrets and put Vorana at risk. We need to silence him."

Bentley raised his hands, his eyes wide. "This is the best day ever. I knew it! I knew this place was special."

I gently cleared my throat. Since Sage had let the literal magical talking cat out of the bag, I no longer had to keep silent. "Greetings, I'm Juno, this is Zandra Crypt, and chatty wheels down there is Sage. You've guessed correctly. Magic is real, and we're in possession of extensive, ancient, incredibly powerful magic. If you had any sense, you'd bow before us and grovel at our feet."

"Um... what are you doing? This wasn't in the plan," Zandra said to me.

"Making Bentley's dreams come true. Then destroying them," I said. "His tent is full of evidence about us. We can't let him keep that. And we can't let him keep any of the memories he has about his time in Crimson Cove."

"Wait, now! We can come to some arrangement." Bentley stood slowly, his hands still held out. "I spent weeks gathering that information. It'll change my life. I'll double my fans. And I've been chasing a book deal. Maybe even a TV show. With this expose, everything will change."

"We like things how they are," Sage said. "And we hate people poking around here when it's none of their business. You have no right to reveal our happy little lives to the world."

"Everyone has a right to know how incredible this place is. You should share your knowledge. Change lives. Use your magic for good."

"We'd end up killing people and becoming hunted and feared," Zandra said. "If you know your history, you'll have read about the witch trials and witch hunts that used to happen. They're the blunt reality for magic users back then, when we tried to share and be benevolent. Magic isn't for everyone. It's why we have places like Crimson Cove. We live in blissful isolation and have no negative effect on other people."

Bentley tilted his head. "People like me, you mean? Those who don't have magic?"

"Exactly. We don't hide our magic because we don't want to share. We hide it because if we share, you die. And we don't want that," I said. "It never ends well for those who have no power to be around those who have too much."

"Just enough in my case," Sage said. "I vote we blow up his tent and obliterate him."

"You're taking a page out of my book," I said.

"No obliteration," Zandra said.

"Definitely no obliteration," Bentley said. "But I owe this to my fans and myself. I'm a pursuer of the truth."

"What you are is an ungrateful busybody, and we don't want you here." Sage lifted a paw and slammed a spell into the tent. It exploded, sending up a plume of flames and incinerating everything inside.

Bentley yelped and leaped out of the way of the flaming tent. "That's my stuff! All my work. Why did you do that?"

"To keep my witch safe," Sage said.

"Witch! You're admitting there are witches in this town?"

"Now we'll definitely have to mind wipe him," I said. "I didn't know you had such a big mouth, Sage."

"I have a low tolerance level when I discover a threat to Vorana. Bentley's evidence is gone. We'll clear his memory and get rid of him. Job done."

He backed away, waving a finger in the air. "I have rights. You can't do that. You'd be breaking the law."

Zandra shrugged. "Unfortunately, we would. But the Magic Council will understand we had to do this for the greater good."

"Magic Council? Are they your law enforcers?"

"Nope. That would be the angels," I said.

"Angels! You have angels, too?"

"Yep. And you can't remember anything about them."

Bentley kept moving back. "What will you do to stop me? Kill me?"

Zandra twirled her fingers in the air and then held her hands up with her palms facing Bentley. Magic plumed out and coiled around him.

He tried to move, but his legs refused to cooperate. "Stop! I don't want to die. I'll keep quiet. I promise."

"I'm not killing you. I'm bringing you closer, so I can get rid of all those puzzling thoughts that have had you so confused." When Bentley was within touching distance, Zandra placed her hands on either side of his head. "Forget about Crimson Cove. Forget talking to anyone here. You have no memory of this place, and you have no interest in exposing Crimson Cove's secrets. Do you understand?"

Bentley squirmed in her grip for several seconds before his shoulders slumped and his arms hung loosely by his sides. "I understand."

Zandra stepped back and drew in her magic. She winked at me. "Sorry about your tent. Those propane portable gas heaters are lethal. I've heard of several exploding recently."

Bentley blinked several times and then turned and stared at his tent. "Yeah, no kidding. I guess it saves me the tedious job of packing my stuff. I actually can't wait to get home. This trip has been a bust. I've never been to such a dull town."

"It's the worst. You must be looking forward to a decent night of sleep in a real bed. If you head along this path for five miles, you'll be at the border. Where are you headed after you leave town?" Zandra walked along with Bentley, while I sat on her shoulder and Sage trundled behind us, not looking happy that no non-magical obliterating took place.

"I'm not sure. I'm gonna spend some time at home and figure things out. It was nice to meet you and your cats." Bentley headed off, glancing back at his tent several times and shaking his head.

Zandra blew out a breath. "I'm glad his brain didn't explode. I hate using magic on non-magicals. You never know if it'll take, or they'll go ka-blam and make a mess."

"I never doubted you for a second," I said.

Sage cocked her head. "Is that someone shouting?"

My ears pricked, and my eyes widened. "That sounds like Cannibal Bill. We're not too far from his home."

"What's he yelling about?" Zandra said. "I can't make it out."

It took me a few seconds to believe what I was hearing. "I think he's calling for Adrienne."

Chapter 20

The family reunited

My heart was racing at twice its normal speed, so I knew Zandra would feel even more panicked as we followed Cannibal Bill's voice as he continued to call for Adrienne.

"If he's got her," Zandra muttered, "if he's hurt her or done anything to her, I'll destroy him. And I'll take my time doing it. It would be just like this piece of scum to taunt a ghoul and use her as hunt fodder for his own amusement."

"And I'll help you," I said.

Zandra had always struggled with the relationship with her mother. They had a complicated bond and didn't always like each other, but Zandra would always protect Adrienne, no matter what she said or what she became.

"Me, too." There was no wobble in Sage's voice, and I appreciated her show of support, given Adrienne had almost bitten Vorana.

"How does Cannibal Bill know she's in the woods?" Zandra shoved past some bushes.

"He must have found her hideout."

She looked at me, her eyes a little too wide and her face pale. "You don't think he'd eat her, do you?"

Sage's booping snooter wrinkled. "Would he be that gross?"

"Cannibal Bill may have a creepily unhealthy obsession with all things flesh related, but even he's not crazy enough to eat a ghoul. If he did, he'd turn into one."

"Cannibal Bill is unhinged. What if he thinks he's found an easy meal in Adrienne?"

"He won't get a chance to hurt her. We're getting close. I can smell him." I lifted my head and breathed in deeply. There was the unpleasant aroma of ketones in the air, providing a slightly sweet rotten smell to track. I noticed it the first time we encountered Cannibal Bill.

"I see movement up ahead." Zandra broke into a run.

I joined her, Sage close behind, her wheels not slowing her down. "Careful. We don't know what we're dealing with. If Adrienne is close by, you don't want to startle her."

"I want to startle Cannibal Bill. That guy gives me the serious creeps." Zandra shivered. "And I can sense we're back in what he believes is his territory. The paranoia magic is creeping over me like an army of anxious ants."

"There are storage sheds up ahead. And there's Cannibal Bill. He's heading straight toward them," I said.

We slowed as Cannibal Bill strode toward a shed with a bucket in his hand. We crept closer, keeping ourselves concealed behind a tree as he pulled open the shed door.

Zandra's fingers dug into the tree bark so hard it splintered. "It's Adrienne! He's got her."

I blinked. There she was. After weeks of searching, Adrienne stood less than twenty feet away from us. She was dressed in a large checked shirt, which would fit an average-sized man. She also had on plain black slacks. Her feet were bare.

For a ghoul, she didn't look in poor condition. She was missing a toe on her right foot, but she had all her fingers, her limbs were intact, and there were no head wounds. It was remarkable, considering she'd been a ghoul for some time.

I jumped onto Zandra's shoulder, and her panic tickled my toe beans. "She's not trying to get away from him."

"Of course not. She's a mindless ghoul." Zandra exhaled through her nose. "Although she's also not attacking Cannibal Bill. Are they having a conversation?"

I clung to Zandra as she broke cover. Sage sped along beside us. Cannibal Bill had his back to us, so he didn't see us coming. But Adrienne did. Her head jerked up, and her eyes widened. She made a grunting noise that sounded like a bee buzzing.

"There's no need to worry. I've got everything you want in here." Cannibal Bill lifted the bucket. "I told you you'd never go hungry if you stayed with me."

"Hey! What are you doing with my mother?"

Cannibal Bill whirled around, and some of the bucket contents spilled out and splatted onto the dirt. It was a hunk of bloody meat. He attempted to shield our view by holding out his arms. "This is private land. You shouldn't be here. You're not welcome."

"And you shouldn't be holding my mother captive." Magic sparked on Zandra's fingers. It tasted of rage and hurt. "Have you had her here this whole time?"

His forehead wrinkled. "Did you call this ghoul your mother?"

"Answer the question. Why are you holding her? Do you intend to eat her, you sick son of a gun?"

"No! I wouldn't eat her. Go on. Get out of here."

Adrienne made another buzzing bee noise and shifted from foot to foot.

"It's okay. We're getting you out of here," Zandra said to her. "Has he hurt you? Can you understand me? Do you know who I am?"

I was surprised when Adrienne nodded and attempted to smile.

A breath whooshed out of Zandra. "That's good. Adrienne, you must know, Angel Force is looking for you. They're worried you could have something to do with the dead angel. Do you know about that?"

Adrienne immediately shook her head.

"She's not involved in that." Cannibal Bill made a 'move along now' gesture. "You need to leave."

Zandra ignored him. "We must get you out of here. You have to hide until the case is closed and the angels stop thinking a ghoul was involved."

"She can't leave. She's fine here." Cannibal Bill stupidly still blocked our way.

Zandra grabbed the front of his T-shirt. Her magic blazed in an impressive show of strength. I also flickered warning magic across my fur, but Zandra had everything under control, as evidenced by the look of terror on Cannibal Bill's face.

"You say the word, and I'll whack him." A blaze of beautiful rainbow magic shimmered around Sage.

Cannibal Bill dropped his bucket of bloody meat, and it spilled on the ground. Adrienne made a move toward it, peeling her lips back from her teeth, but then stopped and her ashamed gaze shot to Zandra. She hid her hands behind her back and lowered her head.

"You're making a mistake," Cannibal Bill said. "I didn't take Adrienne. She's not trapped here. She can go any time she likes."

"Why was she locked in your shed?" Zandra shook him.

"Adrienne found me! She wants to live with me."

"Even before my mother was a ghoul, she wouldn't make such a terrible life choice."

I tilted my head from side to side. I wasn't so certain about that. Adrienne had always had terrible taste in men. She'd consider dating a hunting, flesh eating paranoid if he made her laugh and showed her a good time.

"I don't believe you," Zandra said. "You're planning on doing something awful to her. Send her out in the woods so you could hunt her."

"No! I wouldn't do that."

"You do it to just about every other animal," I said. "Why is Adrienne different?"

"Stop!"

I was so stunned Adrienne had spoken, I almost fell off Zandra's shoulder. Only a thorough application of claws into cloth stopped me from toppling.

Zandra let go of Cannibal Bill and stepped around him. "You can talk?"

Adrienne nodded. "Basic. Hard to think. Better when practice."

"And you understand us, too." I peered closely at Adrienne. Most ghouls never regained the power of speech, and the ones who did needed months of training. We weren't dealing with your average ghoul.

She nodded. "Feel different. I'm a ghoul but have control. Not easy."

"The Shadow gang turned you, didn't they?" Zandra said.

"Fought with Anan. He's a bad man."

"He's also in jail, and he's never getting out. The Shadow gang's rule is over." Zandra raised a hand but then lowered it. "I'm sorry you got tangled in their mess."

"My fault. Heart ruled head. Dumb."

"She's impressive, isn't she?" Cannibal Bill had backed up a few steps. "When we first met in the woods, I almost shot her, but then she talked, and I couldn't believe it."

Zandra glared at him. "Go on."

He shrugged and looked away. "I didn't know you were related, or I'd have told you she was here when you invaded my home. Adrienne struggles to remember names, but she often talks of a daughter. That's really you?"

Zandra nodded, her gaze on the spilled bucket of meat and entrails. "I don't understand why you're looking after her. What's in it for you?"

Cannibal Bill shuffled his feet through the dirt. "She reminds me of my sister. Erin died years ago. She was sweet and pretty, like Adrienne."

"What happened to your sister?" I said.

He drew in a slow breath. "She ate a poisonous plant. It was a horrible death. We thought magic had saved her, but that poison had a hold on her. She lived for a week, but then her heart gave out."

I tilted back my head. That was the real reason Cannibal Bill couldn't stand to eat anything green. "You blame plants for your sister's death?"

"Vegetables murdered the only family I had." He scowled at me. "For a few seconds, when I found Adrienne, I thought I was seeing a ghost and Erin was back. Then I realized what she was."

"Yet you kept her alive," Zandra said.

"Sure. It's not as if Adrienne has difficult needs. I gave her some clean clothes, and she has somewhere dry to live and regular buckets of food. She's due for a feed now. She needs feeding three times a day, or she struggles to control her urges. I don't mind sharing what I hunt."

Zandra's gaze was fixed on Adrienne. "There has to be more to it than that."

He drew a line in the dirt with his foot. "Maybe I like the company. I never thought I'd hear myself say that, but I enjoy having others here. Even ghouls. And she's no trouble."

Cannibal Bill was a flawed individual, but he'd done good when he could have obliterated

Adrienne. I was conflicted over my feelings in this matter. I hated Cannibal Bill because of his hunting, but he'd been kind to Zandra's mother.

I nuzzled Zandra's ear. "What do you want to do about this?"

She shrugged slightly. I could understand her conflict. Zandra had spent her life looking after her wild, live-in-the-moment mother, attempting to keep her safe and out of harm, but she couldn't protect her from this. Adrienne was a ghoul, and there was no turning back. But she was a different kind of ghoul. She had intellect, she could talk, and she clearly knew right from wrong. Perhaps there was hope for her. Hope they could have a relationship.

"Adrienne is welcome to stay here," Cannibal Bill said. "I'd like her to."

"We can do better than a shed as her home," I said.

Adrienne shook her head. "Nice here. Like it."

"You don't get cold?" Zandra said.

"No. Don't feel cold or hot. Always the same." She plucked at her shirt. "Would like a nice dress, though."

Cannibal Bill's cheeks flushed. "I only had shirts and pants. I donated my sister's things to Goodwill. Never figured I'd have need of them."

A smile flickered across Zandra's face. "I'm sure we can arrange that. Maybe a bath and some shoes, too?"

Adrienne nodded and smiled. She'd lost a few teeth, but she still had a pretty smile.

"You want to leave?" Cannibal Bill said to her.

A pensive look crossed Adrienne's face. "Think about it. Need time with family. But happy here, too."

"You said ghouls," I said to Cannibal Bill. "You said you enjoy having others here. Even ghouls. Are there more ghouls in the woods you're feeding?"

Adrienne's eyes widened a fraction. She looked at Cannibal Bill for a silent second and then nodded as if giving him permission to speak.

"I didn't like to say because it ain't my place, but your mother has a friend," he said.

Zandra glanced at me. "Who?"

Adrienne gestured behind her and held out a hand. A large, well-muscled male zombie shambled out and caught hold of her waiting hand.

"You are unbelievable!" Zandra shook her head, although there was a smile on her face. "After everything you've gone through, you've found a ghoul boyfriend."

I chuckled as I studied the new arrival, and even Cannibal Bill cracked a smile.

Adrienne giggled and wiggled her hips. "This is Joel."

"I don't recognize you," I said to him. "Did you get caught up in the Shadow gang business, too? Was that where you were turned?"

"It was. Joel doesn't talk much," Adrienne said. "Like it that way. No one to complain at me."

"That's how you found each other?" Zandra said.

She nodded. "He was there. Got in trouble with gang, so they punished him."

"What brought you to the Shadow gang's attention?" Zandra stiffened, and a scowl crossed her face.

Joel kept his gaze down and rumbled out a noise.

"He's not a bad guy. Quiet. Keeps to himself," Cannibal Bill said.

"I'm waiting for an answer," Zandra said. "Did you trade with them? Work for them? Did you kill for them?"

"Why does it matter?" Adrienne clutched Joel's hand and drew him closer. "Friend now."

"Why were you hiding him from me if he's such a good friend? What's he not telling us?"

"Worried what you'd think."

"Or Joel has something he doesn't want other people to find out about," Zandra said.

"Where are you going with this?" I whispered.

She glanced at me. "The dead angel covered in bites."

Joel lifted his head and glared at Zandra. It looked like he understood every word being spoken.

"Daisy killed Thomasina," I said.

"She wasn't working alone, though," Zandra said. "How do we know my mother's new boyfriend didn't help to kill Thomasina?"

Joel growled, and I hissed a warning to back down, unless he wanted a taste of my murder mittens.

"No! Joel is kind." Adrienne tried to tug him away, but he wouldn't move, and he'd begun to snarl and flex his substantial arm muscles.

"Maybe when he's with you, but we have one dead angel and a messed up cougar who was used by someone with twisted magic. Joel, what do you know about that?" Zandra squared her stance, her focus on Joel. "What magic runs through you? How dark is it?"

"Keep it calm. Ghouls get angry fast," I said.

My warning was too late. Joel bared his teeth and lunged at Zandra.

Chapter 21

Unmasking the villain

I sprang at the ghoul at the same time as Sage. We smashed into Joel's chest, but it was like hitting a rock. He was all muscle. He swatted us aside, intent on getting to Zandra.

I rolled onto my paws and flipped Sage's wheels upright. "We need something stronger to deal with this ghoul. You ready for this?"

She nodded.

We blasted Joel with powerful knockdown spells, sending him staggering to his knees before he could sink his teeth into Zandra.

She'd backed away, her magic blazing on her fingers, but she'd yet to strike.

Adrienne ran to Joel, hovering around him as he shook his head and grunted, while we blasted him with magic to keep him subdued.

"I've never seen Joel behave like this. He doesn't like you." Cannibal Bill had backed away from the fight.

"He's reacting this way because he has something to hide," Zandra said. "We knew Daisy had an accomplice. Did you mess with her before you were turned into a ghoul? Is that why her behavior is so erratic? She's got no one controlling her anymore."

"No! Joel's sensitive and gentle. Would never kill or hurt another." Adrienne crouched an inch from Joel, who continued to snarl, but he sounded less rage-fueled as she petted his head and cooed at him.

"You barely know him," Zandra said. "You do this with all the guys you date. You think the best of them and overlook their staggeringly bad flaws, thinking you'll change them. Then they take advantage, break your heart, and leave."

"No need to change Joel. He's a good man. Looks after me." Adrienne kept stroking his hair.

"He's not safe to be around," I said. "And he almost attacked my witch. Joel must be obliterated."

Adrienne dropped to her knees and put her hands in a prayer position. "Please, no. He loves me. I love him. We're together. Can't lose him."

Zandra rolled her eyes. "This has always been your problem. Turning in to a ghoul has done nothing to fix your issues. You can't be in love with someone after only knowing him for a few weeks."

"Can and do." Adrienne lifted her chin and glared at us.

"These ghouls had nothing to do with what happened to that angel." Cannibal Bill was edging closer to the confrontation.

"Is that because you were involved with the angel slaying?" I kept my steely gaze on Joel. One false move and I was roasting him. "You cursed Daisy and turned her into a killing machine?"

"You know I'm innocent. And I don't know a Daisy."

"You're not innocent." I'd never forgive Cannibal Bill for trapping those animals.

"Why do you think they aren't involved?" Zandra was glaring at her mother.

"Because they're always together. They never leave each other's side. Most of the time, they're happy to stay in the shed. I even lock the door at night so they're safe and nothing can get at them, but I let them out in the mornings. They sometimes take a walk or eat breakfast outside, but I got the shed set up nice." Cannibal Bill gestured at the open door. "There are camp beds and chairs. I even put books in there, though I'm not sure they can read. It's their home. And they know they'll always get fed, so they have no need to search for food and get in trouble."

"It's true," Adrienne said. "Bill is kind. Given us a home. We keep to ourselves. Want no trouble. Had enough of that."

Zandra crouched, so she was eye level with her mother. "Cannibal Bill is a bad person. He's been hunting and trapping animals."

Confusion crossed her face. "His food?"

"He may eat what he kills, but there's always room for compassion," I said.

Cannibal Bill cleared his throat. "I could have done better. And having hung out with Adrienne and Joel, I get that all creatures deserve respect."

"Don't tell me you're thinking about turning vegetarian," I said.

He grimaced. "Never. But I have enough land here, so I'm thinking about setting up a smallholding and raising my food properly. Making sure the animals have good lives and don't suffer when the time comes for them to go on my griddle."

I shared a stunned look with Zandra. Had Cannibal Bill's time with Adrienne and Joel really changed him that much?

"I'm not a perfect guy, and I went off the rails because of what happened to my sister. I spent a long time being angry and blaming other things, but she was the one who picked that dumb plant. She cooked it and served it to herself. Erin should have been more careful. And maybe I should have done a better job of looking out for her."

My anger toward Cannibal Bill faded a fraction. "Unless you're a plant expert, it's easy to mistake something that looks harmless for something poisonous. Your sister simply made a mistake."

"Yeah, you shouldn't beat yourself up because of it," Zandra said.

"Bill flawed but good. Like all of us." Adrienne rested a hand on Joel's shoulder.

For a ghoul, she showed a remarkable amount of intelligence.

Cannibal Bill blushed again. "I've been doing some thinking since meeting your mother. She's kind, and it's been a long time since I've had kindness in my life."

"Happy to be here." Adrienne shuffled forward and reached for Zandra's hand. After a second of hesitation, Zandra caught hold of it. "And happy here. Happy with Joel. He didn't kill the angel."

Tears filled Zandra's eyes as she hugged her mother.

I kept an eye on Joel, but his anger had died, and instead, he watched Adrienne and Zandra embrace with a tender look on his face. Maybe Joel had the makings of a decent step-parent, so long as he could get a handle on that quick temper.

"Come home with us." Zandra pulled back from the embrace. "You know I'm living with Vorana. She rented me her basement. There's room for you, too."

Adrienne looked away. "Sorry for scaring Vorana. Does she hate me?"

"No! We understand why you reacted that way," I said. "There are no hard feelings. I'm sure she'd welcome you into her home."

Sage grumbled something I didn't quite catch. It didn't sound friendly.

"I want them to stay here," Cannibal Bill said. "I'd miss them if they left."

Zandra exhaled slowly. "If you're looking for company, Sorcha holds a social night for singles at her café. Or you could get a new hobby, one that doesn't involve killing anything."

He pursed his lips. "Maybe once Angel Force is done with me, I'll give that a go."

"I'd advise brushing up on your social skills before you look for a woman," I said.

Cannibal Bill puffed out his sparrow chest. "There must be fine ladies out there who like hunting, shooting, and fishing."

Zandra, Adrienne, and I wrinkled our booping snooters while Joel chuffed out a laugh.

"Maybe not." Cannibal Bill scratched the back of his head. "I like making homebrew. And barbecuing. Would those hobbies be more appealing to a single lady?"

"Keep working on the list," I said.

He pushed his hands into his pockets. "There's a home here for Adrienne and Joel for as long as they want it." His gaze flashed to the two ghouls. "Do you want it?"

Adrienne looked at Joel, and it seemed as if they were having a silent conversation. Joel kept nodding as Adrienne mumbled quietly.

"Would like to stay," Adrienne said. "But also spend time with my daughter. Go with her now."

"But you will come back?" Cannibal Bill said.

"Soon. Come back soon." Adrienne reached over and gave his hand a gentle squeeze.

"Do you need to collect any of your things?" Zandra said. "We can go straight away."

"No, won't be away for long." Adrienne hugged Cannibal Bill, then Joel shook his hand.

While they said their goodbyes, I hopped onto Zandra's shoulder and twirled my tail around her neck. "Where will you put them?"

"Not in the house," Sage said. "I see these ghouls aren't mindless chompers, but I won't have Vorana put at risk."

"I was thinking about the sheds. We could clear one, and they could stay in there." Zandra pressed a hand against my side. "Juno, I can't believe we found her. And she seems good. Stable. I was so worried we'd have to put her down."

"Adrienne's always had a way of getting through the tough times and coming out the other side smiling." I studied the ghouls. I was uncertain about having them in my witch's life. Ghouls could be unpredictable, as Joel had demonstrated, but if this made Zandra happy, I'd accommodate it. But like Sage, I'd be on my guard around them.

Once the goodbyes were finished, we walked slowly through the woods, letting Adrienne and Joel set the pace, since they were barefoot and their joints seemed stiff.

I walked behind them with Sage, while Zandra stayed behind us at my insistence.

"Those ghouls shocked me," Sage said. "I figured they'd be after our brains."

"As Elijah has shown us, not all ghouls are bad."

"He still has his moments of being a jerk, but he's better than he was. We have you to thank for that. Are you planning on using that same magic on Adrienne and Joel to fix them up?"

"They're too far gone for that. Maybe there's magic we could use to stabilize their mood swings, but we'll have to work with what we've got for now."

"You're sure they're safe?"

"Safeish."

"You're happy for them to be so close to your witch?"

"Not really, but Zandra won't abandon her mother."

She huffed out a breath, her shoulders bunching.

We walked in silence, only the ghouls shuffling, bird song, and the slight squeak of Sage's wheels disturbing the peace.

"How will this work?" Sage said. "You've often said Zandra had a complicated relationship with her mother."

"It's about to get more complicated. Time will tell." I slowed as the scent of charred paper filled my booping snooter. "This is where Bentley had his campsite."

Sage glanced around. "Yep. Near to here. Just through those trees."

I checked everything was okay with the ghouls and Zandra then stepped off the path and looked at the burned remains.

Sage followed me. "I'm glad he's gone. Being around non-magicals makes me uneasy."

"I hear you." I sniffed around. There'd been something different about Bentley. He'd known too much about our magic, and I couldn't figure out why or how that was. I never liked not knowing the answer to a puzzle.

"There are a few photographs here that didn't get completely incinerated. You want me to do the honors?" Sage was also sniffing the ground.

I headed over and inspected them. There were a couple of selfies Bentley had taken of himself standing outside different stores in Crimson Cove.

"Juno, look at this one." Sage's whiskers were stiff.

I joined her and stared at a partially charred picture. It showed Ascal and Daisy together. "He's got his hand pressed against her side." I narrowed my eyes as I studied the picture.

"You think they know each other?" Sage said.

My cat instincts tingled. "They must. If Ascal is involved with Daisy, he's been hiding that from us. We need to find out why."

❦

I was stretched out on a wonderfully soft part of our bed in Vorana's basement. Zandra was at the window, peering out as dawn arched a pink glow across the sky.

"I haven't heard any movement for a while. You think they're sleeping? Do ghouls sleep? There's so much I need to figure out about them."

"You're the one who needs sleep." I rolled over and exposed my belly for a tickle.

"I can't rest. I have to know Adrienne is still okay. And I want to keep an eye on Joel. I didn't even know ghouls dated. This is so strange. It's like discovering I was adopted and having to find my family all over again." She looked at me, the tiredness clear beneath her eyes.

I rolled upright, wandered over, and hopped onto her shoulder, snuggling close into her neck. "You've got time to figure things out. The most important thing is you got Adrienne back, and Angel Force didn't trap her and interrogate her. Even though we know she's not guilty of killing Thomasina, they'd still want her restrained and monitored. We won. Victory is ours."

Zandra rested her hands against the glass. "Maybe that's what should happen. I'm out of my depth here. What if she changes?"

"We all change. Even ghouls. It's never comfortable."

"I wish they didn't. I want life simple. You, me, animal control, and the weekly dinners with Vorana, Sorcha, and the guys. A ghoul parent throws it all in the air."

"We'll make it work. And Adrienne and Joel were happy to stay in Vorana's shed. They seemed to like it. And it's what they're used to. One step at a time."

Her breath steamed the glass. "I'm just glad Vorana didn't freak out when we brought them here."

"She let Sage do that." As we'd inched closer to home, Sage had become less friendly and more concerned about the ghouls. Even though Vorana had been happy to accommodate them, Sage was tense and unsettled, and nothing I said convinced her they were suitable house guests.

"Sage is only watching out for her witch. You'd do the same if the roles were reversed."

I booped her cheek. "I would. But be positive. There's hope. We got your mother back."

"Yeah, but she's so different."

I gave Zandra a few seconds to mull things over. "Is that so bad? You weren't happy with how she used to be. Maybe having a ghoul mother will be an improvement."

She slid me a glare. "That's not a compliment to Adrienne."

"And you've got a stepdad, too. Two ghouls for the price of one. Bonus!"

"I'm not calling him dad." Zandra groaned. "This is too much. I should go out there again and see if they need anything. The silence worries me."

"Stop pestering them. It's the weekend, so we've officially got time off. You need to chill, get some rest, and then visit your changed family. Get to know each other again."

Zandra stifled a yawn. "I am exhausted. What will you do, though? You've been dead to the world for hours, so you can't want more rest. I expect you want an early breakfast."

"No, I'm good. I planned to hang out with Sammy. Now, you get in bed."

After staring out the window for another few seconds, Zandra did as I instructed. I stayed with her until her eyes closed before sneaking out of the basement.

I'd put a plan in place after discovering the charred picture of Ascal with Daisy. And I had a meeting to get to with my wonderful magical misfits.

Archie, Sammy, and Elijah were waiting for me outside Sorcha's café as I'd requested.

I nodded a greeting. "Did Sage inform you all of our new mission?"

"She did. It's exciting," Archie said. "Watch me turn almost invisible so I can help with the stealthy observation you need." He dropped to the ground and slunk around, looking no less invisible, given he was the size of an average black bear just before going into hibernation.

"Good work, Archie," I said.

"Isn't Sage joining us on this mission?" Elijah said.

"No, she's staying in with Vorana today."

"Sage always complains, but she loves these missions," Archie said. "She should come with us."

I nodded, not yet certain how to explain the ghouls in Vorana's shed and Sage's natural caution about the new tenants. "She'll join us the next time. Now, focus. Ascal is hiding something. He knows Daisy, but he didn't mention it during his interview at Angel Force. We need to get him talking, so he reveals his true colors and we can discover how he's connected to Daisy."

Sammy nodded. "That picture Sage showed us looked dodgy."

"What's the plan?" Elijah said.

"Simple. We sniff out Ascal, rattle his bars, and see what darkness slithers out."

Chapter 22

Never trust a nice guy

It took us hours and lots of going around in circles in Crimson Cove as daylight filtered through the dawn and the town stirred to life, but we finally discovered Ascal's scent at the Serpent Inn, run by Virgil Goodbody.

We'd watched Ascal grab food and come and go several times already, and it wasn't even eight o'clock in the morning. This wasn't a guy who sat idly and twiddled his thumbs. He was always on the move. He also didn't seem to be camping in the woods anymore. Had that been another lie?

"Are you sure this guy has been messing with Daisy? He doesn't look like a super villain to me." Elijah had his paws tucked underneath him, his eyes half-closed, as we watched from an alleyway close to the inn.

"Daisy has been designed for ultimate destruction. It's all she can focus on. And I have a feeling Ascal is the reason for that. We just need the proof." I was also settled in a comfortable position, resting beside Sammy. Archie was snoring behind us. My gang wasn't adapted for long periods of covert surveillance. Archie snores occasionally rattled the nearby windows.

"He could just be a nice guy who was trying to help a troubled familiar," Sammy said. "We do exist."

I gently nuzzled his ear. "You do, and you're wonderful. But there's something too pure about Ascal. He's only been in the area for five minutes, and the angels are fawning over him as if he's the ultimate hero. And the alibi he has for the time of Thomasina's murder is so obvious. He staged it."

"You think old lady Flowerpot lied to the angels?" Elijah said.

"No, but maybe Ascal scared her into lying. Or used magic on her to make her believe that's what happened."

"People saw him help her up, though."

I sniffed. "Or did Ascal push her over and then make a show of helping to ensure maximum attention?"

"He's on the move again," Elijah said.

I had to nudge Archie several times to get him to wake, but then we were on our way, tracking Ascal as he headed out of the inn and onto the main shopping street.

"He's going to the bakery," Sammy said, as we trotted along behind Ascal.

"I'm starved," Elijah said. "Did anyone bring any snacks?"

"Go hunt rodents if you're that hungry," I said.

"Too much like hard work."

I glanced at him. "Moving in with Sorcha has made you soft."

He didn't protest. "She makes amazing food, and she's always generous with the portions."

"I see that from your ever-expanding gut."

Elijah sucked in his belly, which was entirely visible because of his lack of fur. "Hey! No body shaming. It's mainly muscle. Or it will be once I've worked out a few times."

We concealed ourselves close to the bakery as Ascal went inside. He stopped at the counter and chatted with Tia for a few moments.

"Seems friendly enough," Sammy said.

Elijah shuffled forward. "We should go in and order something. Then we can listen in to their conversation."

I stopped Elijah from exposing our mission by stamping on his tail. "We watch. We don't want Ascal to know we're on to him. We can always go in and ask Tia if he was behaving oddly."

Elijah grumbled to himself but settled on the ground.

Ascal glanced over his shoulder, turned back to Tia, lifted his hand, and zapped a spell into her face.

"Whoa! That wasn't cool," Archie said. "What did he do that for? Everyone loves Tia."

I shook my head as I watched Tia's reaction. She stood in one spot, not moving a muscle. Ascal strolled around the counter, filled two large brown paper bags with breakfast treats, nodded at Tia, who still wasn't moving, and left the bakery.

"Archie, you keep tracking Ascal. If you get in any trouble with him, give us a signal."

"What kind of signal?"

"A jet of flame should do it," I said. "We'll see that. Everyone else, follow me." I dashed into the bakery with Elijah and Sammy.

Tia stood behind the counter, slowly blinking. She shook her head and looked around in confusion.

"Hey, are you okay?" I said.

She looked around some more, not seeming certain where I was.

"Down here. Do you need help?"

Tia's gaze drifted down, and her eyes widened. "How long have you three been here?"

"Only a few seconds. Did your last customer do something to you?"

"My last customer?"

"Ascal. We saw him use magic on you."

"Err... nope. That didn't happen. Why would he do that?" Tia shook her head again. "I need more coffee. I'm suddenly so drowsy. You think I'd be used to getting up early to make sure the fresh bread was ready to sell."

"It's most likely an aftereffect from the magic you've just been whacked with." I followed Tia along the other side of the counter as she grabbed a mug and filled it. "You do remember Ascal coming in, don't you?"

"This morning? No, he hasn't been in."

I exchanged a glance with my companions. "You know who I'm talking about?"

"Sure. Ascal is a great guy. He comes by most days, and I enjoy chatting with him." She grinned. "He's a huge flirt. Cute, too."

"What do you talk about?"

"This and that."

"He was literally just here," Elijah said. "And you let him come around the counter and take food. Did he pay you for it?"

Tia shook her head. "He wasn't here."

"Where are all your cherry croissants?" I said. "It's early. You can't have had a breakfast rush yet."

Tia stared at the almost empty tray and scratched her head. "Maybe I haven't put them out. Like I said, I'm not properly caffeinated."

Sammy sniffed the floor. "There's water down here. Have you got a leak?"

Tia grabbed a cloth and hurried around the counter. "Huh! Not that I know of. There aren't any pipes under here."

I touched the water and found it was icy cold. I shook my paw. "This came from Ascal. It's not the first time I've found water after he inflicted a spell on someone. Thomasina and Cythera had icy water around them after they'd been attacked." I pressed a paw against Tia's arm and found it chilled. "It's a side effect of his magic."

"That must have been why Tia stopped moving," Sammy said.

Tia's expression grew puzzled as she mopped up the water. "I don't know what you furballs are on about, but I'm fine. No one has cast any spells on me this morning. I'd know if they did."

"Ascal's victims don't know what's happening to them," I said. "He's got strong magic."

"It wasn't Ascal," Tia said. "Besides, there's no reason he'd use magic on me."

"There is if he has something to conceal from you or something he doesn't want you to learn, remember, or reveal," I said. "How long have you known Ascal?"

She sat back on her heels and dropped the cloth. "Not long. He's only been in Crimson Cove for a couple of weeks. Listen, I appreciate your concern, but I'm good. Can I get you anything while you're here?"

"Yes," Elijah said.

"We'll eat later. We must focus on Ascal," I said. "He's up to something. Something bad."

Elijah jabbed a paw at the glass cabinet. "Tia has sausage and bacon rolls."

"Later!" It was rare I resisted delicious food, but this situation was serious.

We dashed outside and looked around for Archie. He was some distance away, lurking behind a row of box planters, close to the Angel Force office.

Ascal stood outside the building with his bags of stolen treats. He was staring at the main doors from the other side of the road.

We dashed over and joined Archie.

"What's he been doing?" I said.

"Nothing. I followed him, and he stopped here. He's been standing outside the building for several minutes muttering to himself."

"Ascal is working up the courage to attack another angel," I said. "And he didn't get those treats for himself. Everyone knows angels can't resist sweet food. Those croissants are angel bait."

"What will he do, bribe them with croissants and then freeze them?" Elijah said.

"No, but he can get inside Angel Force with the promise of a free breakfast. The angels won't think it's odd he's here. They already believe he's a hero after helping Mrs. Flowerpot."

"And then what?" Sammy said. "Ascal can't take on all the angels and destroy them. No one is that powerful."

"Whatever freeze magic he has could be powerful enough to slow them down. Even if it doesn't stop them, it would mean they couldn't defend themselves properly. That makes them vulnerable to whatever he has planned."

"You think he'll bite them all to death?" Elijah shook his head. "That's impossible."

There was a whoosh of warm air over our heads, and a second later, Finn swooped down and landed outside the building. He looked more rumpled than usual, and his hair was messy. He was about to go inside Angel Force but turned when Ascal called out to him.

Finn stepped back then strode over to Ascal, his hands clenched and his shoulders set.

We were too far away to hear their conversation, but it didn't look pleasant, despite Ascal's too good to be true smile remaining in place.

Finn's wings expanded, and faint flickers of red traced across them.

"Uh-oh. Finn's pulling out his demon card," I said.

Before Finn could make a move, Ascal's right hand shot out and slammed into Finn's chest.

Finn staggered back, his wings sagged, and he collapsed on the ground.

Ascal looked around, dropped his bags of treats, and dragged Finn into the nearest alleyway.

My magic thrummed to life, ready to be unleashed as I raced over to help, my friends close behind. Finn was part of my family. No one hurt him and got away with it.

There was a flash of magic. It shot out of the alleyway and slammed into the side of the Angel Force building, scorching the wall and slashing a jagged black line across the pristine paint.

"What the heck was that?" Elijah had plastered himself to the ground, his ears flattened.

"Keep moving. We have to help Finn." I was almost at the alleyway when the doors to Angel Force blasted open, and Daisy appeared. She was a blur of movement as she sped closer.

Angel Force must have found her at Finn's sanctuary and brought her here.

My gaze flicked to the alleyway. If I'd had any doubts about Ascal, I didn't now. "He's controlling Daisy! Ascal's behind all of this. Archie, you head Daisy off. Sammy and Elijah, you're with me."

Archie's normally cheerful, mildly gormless expression hardened, and he growled, his hackles raised. "I'll make sure she doesn't hurt you." He bounded off and slammed headfirst into Daisy, driving her sideways like he was a huge, furry plow, and preventing her from getting into the alleyway and killing Finn.

With Elijah and Sammy beside me, I ran into the alleyway.

Finn was on his back, his arms and legs splayed. His eyes were fixed open, and his chest wasn't moving. A thin film of frost encased him. Ascal stood over him, his hands raised and his teeth bared.

"Stop! He's done nothing wrong to you," I yelled.

"Stay out of this, kitty," Ascal snarled, his focus remaining on Finn. "You don't know who you're dealing with."

"Neither do you." I stalked toward him with Elijah and Sammy flanking me on either side. "Finn is part of my family. And I always protect my family."

Ascal's eyes were rimmed with red as he flicked his gaze my way. "Leave now, if you wish to live."

"Oh, I'll live. I plan on living a long, happy life, and it doesn't involve you being in it. Step away from the angel. We know you're the killer. You've got nowhere to hide."

Ascal's gaze latched onto me, and a shudder ran down my spine. There was nothing kind in that gaze. All I saw was a desire to destroy. "You had your chance to escape."

"Now!" I yelled.

We blasted Ascal with everything we had, sending him sprawling back and slamming into the wall.

He gasped, appearing stunned for a few seconds, then a carpet of frost trickled out of him, heading toward us.

"Avoid his magic! Once it touches you, you won't be able to move," I said. "I'll help Finn. You two stop Ascal from getting to us."

Snarling and growling behind me revealed Archie was doing an excellent job of keeping Daisy occupied, but I wasn't certain how long he'd be able to keep it up. The last thing we needed was an angry, messed up cougar with a kill quotient in the mix.

While Elijah and Sammy dodged the spreading ice magic, I made a heroic leap and landed on Finn's chest. I spread myself flat across him and poured magic into him, willing him back to life. My newly acquired powers worked perfectly, and rather than jerking out of me, they flowed calmly into Finn.

His eyes moved a fraction, and he grew in a shaky breath. "It's him. From the trial."

"Don't speak. Focus on remembering how to breathe."

"Important! Juno, I remember who Ascal is. His wife. She's dead."

"Don't mention her," Ascal snapped out between harsh intakes of breath. "Don't even think about her."

Sammy and Elijah were perched on a huge dumpster. They fired magic repeatedly at Ascal to keep him pinned to the wall, but every time they shot out a spell, he batted it away and inched closer to me and Finn.

"You knew he couldn't be trusted?" I said to Finn.

"Not at first. But I recognized him from somewhere. I just couldn't remember where." Finn tried to sit, but the ice magic inflicted on him meant he could barely lift a finger, despite the healing, life giving magic I flooded into him.

"Ascal is here because of his dead wife?" I said. "In his interview, he talked about her as if she was alive."

Finn gave a tiny nod. "He's here for revenge. Against Angel Force."

I was still missing information, but I had enough to know Ascal was dangerous and had to be stopped. I kept pumping magic into Finn to keep him alive then turned to face Ascal, resting my fluffy butt on Finn's chin. "You're doing this because you think Angel Force let you down? Your wife died because of them?"

Ascal's face contorted into a broken grimace as he slammed away Elijah's magic.

There was a roar, followed by a whimper, which made my heart lurch. Archie had been hurt.

A few seconds later, Daisy blasted into the alleyway. She was bloody, and there were chunks of fur missing. Her gaze went to Ascal then to me, and she snarled.

Ascal held out a hand to her. "Protect me. My life is in danger because of these creatures. You're mine to obey. Destroy them."

Daisy shuddered under his power drenched words.

"Don't listen to him," I said. "Daisy, you know me. I'm helping you get free of this monster."

Daisy snapped her blunt teeth then groaned and dropped to her belly. One second, her eyes were black, the next, they'd turned tawny and were full of fear.

"I control you. Do as I say." Ascal shot a spell at Daisy, but his aim was off, and it skimmed her head.

"Daisy, he's a bad guy. Don't trust him. Whatever magic he's using to keep you trapped and compelled to do his bidding, we can get rid of it. And we can get rid of him. You won't have to see him anymore or do anything he tells you."

"Stop talking!" Ascal directed his anger at me and shot a spell my way.

I deflected it, but it shuddered off me, revealing how strong Ascal was. His magic was laced with a horrible darkness that would chew on your bones until they were dust.

"I don't know what to do." Daisy whimpered. "I have to protect Ascal, but all this killing..."

"Is wrong. And you know better. Ascal is making you do this. You don't want to kill angels. You don't want to take another life," I said.

"Ignore the cat. You do. It's what you were born to do," Ascal yelled.

"If that's true, why blunt her weapons and inflict your poisonous magic on her? You took Daisy's fangs and claws and created a monster."

Sammy and Elijah kept whacking Ascal with spells, but they were tiring and wouldn't be able to keep it up for much longer. When they were drained, Ascal would be on me and Finn in seconds.

"Get out of here," Finn whispered through my tail fur. "He's too strong."

"I'm not leaving you," I said. "You're one of us. You're a magical misfit, and that means we'll protect you until the end."

"It's too dangerous. Zandra is your priority."

"Always. But I can have other priorities, too." I drew back my magic a little. I had to focus on destroying Ascal but couldn't do that while I used my magical mojo to keep Finn alive. "Can you survive without me for a short time?"

"You do what you have to do. I'm good."

The second I stopped pumping healing magic into Finn, his breath caught in his throat.

Archie dragged himself into the alleyway. His ears were torn, his head down, and he limped badly on one leg.

I looked from him to Sammy and Elijah. "We need to use everything we have to stop Ascal. This won't feel good. Don't get caught in his magic."

Elijah shrugged. "When does hanging out with you ever feel good?"

Sammy nodded. "We've got your back. Whatever it takes."

Archie grunted out a breath of agreement. "My vampire will patch me up. I'll get a whole spa day because of this."

"You won't destroy me. I demand my revenge. It's my right. What these angels did..." Ascal paused and drew in a ragged breath.

"What did they do? You blame them for something that happened to your wife?" I primed my magic, testing its boundaries, uncertain it would hold.

Ascal growled out a response then flung his arms wide and shot out a spell that covered us.

My legs froze, and my heart stuttered. His ice magic had pierced me, and I could barely move. My pulse slowed, and my lungs forgot to work.

I fought against it. I thought about everything I could lose. My newfound family in Crimson Cove, my sweet relationship with Sammy, my home, and most of all, Zandra Crypt. My wonderful, perfect witch. The witch who'd shown me how amazing the world could be when you were in it with the right person. I wouldn't lose that.

But I couldn't move a muscle. And Ascal was advancing on me, a feral look in his eyes and his hands loose, ready with more magic.

"Time to pay for your meddling," he said.

"Juno! Where are you?"

My failing heart leaped. It was Zandra.

There was a flash of white in the entrance to the alleyway, and a sea of white feathers appeared. It was a newly recovered Cythera and Bertoli. And behind them was Zandra.

"What's going on?" Bertoli's fingers were splayed across his chest as he took in the scene. "Ascal, are these familiars troubling you?"

He snarled at Bertoli and slammed a spell into his chest.

Bertoli dropped to the ground and flapped around like a beached merman.

Cythera's wings flared, her gaze flashing around as she tried to work out who the bad guy was.

Zandra's magic flared a pale green aura around her as she glared at Ascal. She stepped past Cythera. "Hey, jerk. You touch a single fur on my familiar's head, or any of her friends, and I'll take you apart."

Ascal growled, while Cythera still looked confused, although even she could sense there was deadly trouble in front of her. Her wings were out as she lowered into a crouch.

"I demand an explanation for what is going on here," she said.

Ascal chuckled, morphing from wannabe familiar killer to charming nice guy in the blink of an eye.

"Jeez! I'm so sorry about Bertoli. I thought he was another rogue familiar about to attack me."

"Another?" Cythera's gaze shifted around the alley again. "These creatures are attacking you?"

Couldn't she see what was going on? I tried to move, but my iced paws refused to budge, and there was little air left in my lungs to shout a warning.

"They sure are. Something bad has gotten into them. They chased me. I figured I was a goner until you showed up. Let me help Bertoli."

Zandra shook her head and placed a foot on Bertoli's chest. "He's fine. Stay back. What are you doing?"

Ascal faked a look of bewilderment. "I just explained. I got jumped by these crazed familiars then panicked when the angels arrived. I thought they were reinforcements."

"You don't mistake an angel for a cat, bozo." Magic flickered on Zandra's fingers. "Why isn't Juno moving? What did you do to her?"

Ascal's adam's apple bobbed. "I used a tiny freeze spell to stop her from killing me. I'm stunned it worked so well."

"You're freezing all these creatures?" Cythera stared open-mouthed at us.

Ascal looked down at his hands. "Yeah. I'm shocked, too. My magic is so average. It'll wear off any second. It must be the good vibes in Crimson Cove keeping me safe."

Zandra's gaze was on me. "Juno. Can you hear me? Tell me what's going on."

"I already told you. Why don't you believe me?" The fake nice version of Ascal almost vanished, but he held a bared-toothed smile in place.

"Let me past so I can make sure Juno is fine." Zandra raised her hands, flaring her magic.

I used the last of the air in my lungs to reveal the truth. "Ascal is the angel killer."

Chapter 23

Why I never work alone

Zandra shot out a spell of such dazzling beauty that I could only stare, as her incredible magic blasted Ascal against the wall.

Cythera was almost as effective. She swooped over the ice magic, lifted Finn, and pulsed out a radiant white light around him. Within seconds, his eyes were open, and he was breathing unaided.

I managed a brief waggle of one paw, but that was the extent of my mobility. I wouldn't mind some of that angel magic, so I could throw myself into the fight and protect my witch.

Finn obliged. He lifted me off the ground and ran his hands over me. His magic had a distinctly warm feel to it and tasted nothing like angel magic, but I wouldn't tell if he didn't.

He winked at me. "Feeling better?"

"I feel invigorated. How about you?"

"I had a few seconds of my life flashing past my eyes, but thanks to you, I'm still flapping my wings."

I was lifted from Finn's arms and wrapped in Zandra's tight embrace.

"I knew something was wrong. I got this horrible feeling in the pit of my stomach, and I had to find you. It almost made me sick. You should have told me what you were doing. I'd have helped." She buried her face in my thick fur.

"I needed to confirm my suspicions before putting you at risk. And I had my crew with me. This mission was only meant to gather information, but when Ascal blasted Tia with magic and attacked Finn, we had to act." I luxuriated in her perfect embrace then looked at Ascal, glad to see him being restrained by Cythera.

"I'm still uncertain what's going on," Zandra said. "You really believe he's the angel killer?"

"I know he is. Give me a minute." I licked her cheek then struggled to get down. Ascal's ice magic had dispersed, so it was safe to walk around. I headed over to Archie and gave him a quick dose of healing magic.

He wagged his tail and slowly got to his feet. "Daisy sure is strong. She held her own in that fight."

I looked around and discovered Daisy cowering behind a dumpster. Her eyes were wide and her tail tucked underneath her, while her body shook.

"Attend to my fallen angel," Cythera gritted out through clenched teeth as she pinned Ascal to the wall. "Bertoli isn't moving."

"I have my crew to deal with first." I inspected a scar running the length of Daisy's side.

"I cannot restrain this individual and save Bertoli. You must help him." Cythera's gaze flicked over me. "Please, Juno."

I nodded. That was all I needed, simple common courtesy. I trotted over to Bertoli, thumped myself down on his chest, and pulsed out revival magic and a few healing spells.

He gasped, and his eyes widened as he saw me on top of him. Disgust crossed his face. "What are you doing?"

"Saving your miserable life. You can thank me later. I accept all types of fishy gifts. Catnip is also welcome." I jumped off him before he could continue protesting and headed back to the dumpster. I looked up at Elijah and Sammy. "All good?"

"Getting unfrozen now Ascal's magic is fading," Sammy said. "You?"

"Tying up the loose ends." I slid around the dumpster again and stood in front of Daisy. "You're safe. I know you had no control over your actions when you attacked those angels. It was all Ascal."

She hid her head and shivered.

I inched forward and rested my paw on the tip of her straggly tail. "You need time to heal, but you can heal. And I'm here to help, along with my friends. We never leave a wounded animal behind."

She lifted her head a fraction. "When the angels took me from the sanctuary and brought me in for questioning, it was unbearable. I kept wanting to destroy them, but then different thoughts came into my head. I got glimpses of how I used to be."

"That was because you were away from Ascal," I said. "He must have been forcing a twisted bond upon you. When he could no longer reach you, his hold weakened, and what you really believe emerged. You're a good creature."

"But I killed that angel. And the others."

"We demand an explanation." Bertoli was sitting up, his back against the wall. His skin was the color of sun warmed milk. "What is going on?"

"We could all do with some clarity," Zandra said. "Juno, you up to it?"

I pulsed a jolt of calming magic into Daisy. "Stay here if you need to, but you'll want to hear this, since it involves you. It'll help you realize you aren't responsible for any of this."

Daisy shivered and looked away.

"Keep an eye on her," I said to Sammy and Elijah. They nodded.

I slid around the dumpster and sat in front of the angels. "Ascal is a wolf in sheep's clothing. He's not a good guy who helps little old ladies. He has dangerous magic. He's here for revenge. And he's been using Daisy as a vehicle to do that."

"The cougar?" Bertoli said. "But she bit Thomasina and killed her. And she attacked Cythera."

"She did, but Daisy had no control over her actions. This was all Ascal." I stood and paced in front of Ascal while he squirmed in Cythera's grip. "This murder mystery has led us a merry dance. Not helped by the angels focusing on an imaginary ghoul as the prime suspect."

Bertoli crossed his arms over his chest. "I suppose you're about to show us where we went wrong?"

"As always, I'm happy to oblige." I ignored his snort of derision. "To begin with, Cannibal Bill looked guilty. He had opportunity and means."

"And he's a serious jerk," Elijah muttered.

"You pointed us toward Cannibal Bill," Bertoli said. "This mess is your fault."

Again, I ignored Bertoli. My motives for distracting the angels had nothing to do with letting a killer go free. My witch's needs had to come first, second, and third. It wasn't something I always achieved, but I was trying.

"Upon investigating Cannibal Bill, he showed a side to us that isn't so heinously twisted." I glanced at Zandra, and she snitched her nose.

"I'm still certain a ghoul is involved," Bertoli said. "And Ascal is a decent guy. There's no reason for him to kill angels."

"He just tried to kill you!"

"That was an accident, wasn't it?" Bertoli stared at Ascal.

Ascal was too busy death-glaring at Cythera to respond.

"Ascal has an excellent reason to want you all dead," I said. "And let's not forget, he misdirected us toward a ghoul attack so we wouldn't look at him. That attack never happened, did it?"

"It happened." Ascal sounded remarkably calm, considering he was being pinned by a three-hundred pound angel who could snap his arm with one wing. "I'm innocent. This is all a misunderstanding. Sorry for hitting you with magic, Bertoli, but I panicked. I was under attack and defended myself. I should never have injured you. I'll take whatever punishment you see fit."

Bertoli rubbed his chest, confusion in his eyes.

"All this time, we've been looking in the wrong place. When Forzi was discovered in the woods, we assumed the worst because he was in mating lust, when in fact, he was just a misguided yeti with no training," I said.

Bertoli sniffed, while Finn smiled encouragingly, and Cythera's face remained impassive as she took in the information. Zandra gave me a thumbs-up.

"I still think it was a ghoul," Bertoli muttered.

"It wasn't," Finn said. "I figured out who Ascal really is. His name is Itrix Stormforce. And he's after the angels because he blames us for his wife's death."

"Itrix Stormforce. Where do I know that name from?" Cythera said.

"That's not my name," Ascal said. "You know me. Everyone around here knows me."

I glanced over my shoulder and discovered a small crowd had appeared at the entrance to the alleyway. The magic attacks blasting out had drawn interest.

"You were playing the role of nice guy and getting everyone to fall for your charms, so they wouldn't believe you had anything to do with these terrible crimes. Go on, Finn," I said.

Finn leaned against the wall. "I figured I'd give things one more shot at Angel Force, despite being unfairly suspended."

"Although I always stick up for my friends, you broke the rules," Bertoli said.

"You'll get another whack with a painful spell if you keep interrupting Finn," I said.

The corners of Finn's mouth twitched, but he held back a smile. "I knew I'd seen Ascal somewhere before, and I remembered an old case I'd studied during my training." He glanced at me. "We get a dozen case files to review with the verdicts taken out to see what judgments we'd make based on the evidence. I got a case about a witch who got messed up in seriously dark magic. Her name was Heather Stormforce."

"Ascal's wife," I said. "Or rather, Itrix's wife."

"I'm not that person." Ascal's cheeks were flushed, and his jaw muscles clenched. He was no longer struggling in Cythera's grip, his fury focused on me and Finn.

"It took me a while to find my old notes. I still had some paperwork and photographs I'd copied when studying," Finn said.

"Which is another rule break," Cythera said. "All files and paperwork must be returned at the end of your training."

"I agree with those rules, but Finn should get a second chance," Bertoli said. "He did a bad thing but not out of malice. Isn't that right, buddy?"

Finn's eyebrows rose slowly. "Err... sure. I had no plans to do anything with the information. I meant to shred it but forgot."

Cythera stared at Bertoli like he'd just swallowed a live frog. It must be weird to hear him being so supportive of Finn. Even I found it odd, and I was the one who'd beguiled him into being nice.

She turned her attention back to Finn. "Proceed."

Finn rubbed the back of his neck. "I checked through the pictures I had, and that's when I saw him. Ascal, or rather, Itrix. He attended every day of his wife's trial and was outraged when she was sentenced to life imprisonment in Gravemore Penitentiary. He fought the court attendants and was dragged out of the trial after the judgment was made."

I looked at the newly uncovered Itrix. He breathed shallowly, a spot of color on each cheek. "So you decided, since the angels took your wife, you'd take their lives."

"No! My wife is fine."

"Heather isn't fine. She's dead," Finn said.

No one spoke. The only sound was harsh breathing coming from Itrix. He knew his deception had been uncovered.

"When you mentioned your wife during your interview at Angel Force," I said, "you spoke about her as if she was alive. You're trapped in the past and intent on revenge."

"This is all lies, and I've had enough," Itrix said. "I've been nothing but kind since I came to Crimson Cove, and this is the thanks I get. I'm leaving."

Cythera fully extended her wings to block his exit. "You're going nowhere. Bertoli, are you fit for duty?"

He struggled to his feet. "Always."

"Go to the office and retrieve the files on Heather Stormforce. Bring them here."

Bertoli's tongue darted across his lips. "It's against protocol to take case files off site."

"It would help me out, buddy." There was a note of caution in Finn's voice.

"Oh, sure. Happy to help." Bertoli dashed out of the alleyway, parting the growing crowd that watched as the killer was revealed.

I hopped onto Zandra's shoulder for a quick nuzzle and a pet while we waited for Bertoli to return.

"I can't believe Mr. Nice Guy is behind this," she whispered.

"My suspicions were raised after discovering a charred picture Bentley had taken of Itrix with Daisy. He had his hands pressed on her side. Of course, most magic doesn't get picked up on camera, but I was certain he was doing something to her. Then we followed him and witnessed him attacking Finn and blasting Tia with a mysterious spell that made her lose her memory. That's when I knew he was our man."

"I've got the file." Bertoli dashed into the alleyway. He went to hand the file to Finn, but Cythera grabbed it off him. She flipped it open and spent several minutes looking through it, nodding, then looking at Itrix.

Itrix shifted his weight from foot to foot. "I have one of those faces. Mr. Average. Maybe the guy you're thinking of looks like me. Please, I just want to leave so I can get on with my life."

"And kill more angels?" I shook my head. "Not happening."

"It could be you in these images," Cythera finally said. "Although there are differences. Obviously, you're older, but your jaw is different. And you have a different shaped nose."

"Magic or surgery could have altered his appearance," I said. "Noses and jaws are easy to change when you need to disguise yourself before you go on a vengeful killing spree."

"You're forgetting something crucial. I was with Mrs. Flowerpot when Thomasina lost her life. I couldn't have been helping her and been in the woods at the same time."

Cythera's forehead furrowed. "I've heard several accounts of your noble deed with Mrs. Flowerpot."

"The timeframe isn't important," I said. "Not when Itrix used an innocent cougar as his weapon. He simply needed attention on him around the time of the murder to ensure people saw him far away from the woods. That way, he wouldn't be associated with what happened to Thomasina."

Itrix was shaking his head before I'd finished speaking. "You're looking at the wrong person."

"Finn, finish sharing your valuable information with everyone." I had to ensure Cythera realized what an asset Finn was, so she'd ask him to stay at Angel Force. "You discovered Itrix's wife had been put away for life. Did she die inside?"

He nodded. "Heather had been in the penitentiary for three years before it happened. I contacted Gravemore, and they said her husband visited weekly. He was devoted to her and refused to give up on her."

"It shows there is some good in you," I said to Itrix. "You loved your wife, no matter what she did."

"I still love her," he growled out.

"Five months ago, Heather got into a fight with another inmate," Finn said. "The governor believes Heather got her hands on illegal magic. She used it against an enemy, and it backfired, killing them both."

"And that tipped Itrix over the edge," I said. "You no longer had a reason to live, so you planned revenge. It must eat you up not to admit who you are and how much you loved Heather. You loved her enough to kill."

"That wasn't me." Itrix's chest heaved. "How could I kill an angel? My magic is on the wrong side of average."

"It's not. Stormforce by name and nature. You have power. And by trapping and abusing a formidable familiar, you were unstoppable. Almost," I said. "Daisy, you can come out. I won't let Itrix anywhere near you."

There was a soft whimper from behind the dumpster, and Daisy crawled out on her belly.

"Daisy attacked the angels but not out of choice. The second I touched her, I sensed a toxic, damaged magic flowing through her. Magic that didn't belong to her. Magic that misfires and makes her sick. It's sending her mad." I leaned against Daisy. "But Itrix was so determined to get his revenge, he didn't care if he destroyed this incredible creature while doing it."

Cythera regarded Daisy with caution in her eyes. "Itrix took you and turned you into a killing machine?"

Daisy looked away, her nose almost touching the dirt. "Since I've been separated from my master, I'm having flashbacks to another time. A time when I was happy and pain free. Are those memories real, or is it me wishing I was somewhere else? Someone else? Not a killer."

"They're real," I said. "And I have a feeling you're from around here. Archie knows you. I believe you were taken from a magic user in Crimson Cove."

"I... I don't belong to him?" Daisy's fear filled gaze flashed to Itrix before she looked away.

"You were never his. He stole you and misused you for his own murderous intentions. This isn't you. You never wanted to kill those angels. You're a kind and benevolent familiar."

"This creature has nothing to do with me," Itrix said. "I don't have the power to control it."

"You ordered her to destroy us," I said. "Your power blasted into Angel Force and summoned her."

Daisy growled softly. "You're cruel. You hurt me."

"Binky?" Tia had shoved her way through the crowd and stood in the entrance to the alleyway. Her wide-eyed gaze was on Daisy. "Is... is that you? Where have you been? What happened to you? You're covered in injuries."

Daisy, or rather Binky, lurched to her feet. Her mouth was open and her whiskers flexed.

"You know this creature?" Cythera said.

"She's my familiar. I was in the bakery when I saw the crowd, but I felt this deep tug in my gut. It told me Binky was close, and she needed help. I've been getting faint impressions of her energy ever since she went missing, but then it would fade." Tia fell to her knees, tears in her eyes. "It's really you. You've come back to me."

Binky growled deep in her chest, coiled like a spring, and threw herself at Tia. The angels tensed as if sensing an attack, but Tia welcomed the huge cougar with open arms and clung to her, crying and laughing at the same time.

Binky squirmed in her arms, licking Tia's face and thumping her tail hard on the ground.

"My baby! You're home." Tia's eyes streamed as she held the huge cat. "You've gotten so thin. And your fur is a different color. Oh, sweetie, where have you been? I've missed you so much."

"It's a long story," I said. "Hold on to her. She's about to have a rocky ride." I had to yank the toxic magic out of Binky fast, and there was no gentle way to do it. I flung a reversal spell through the air and pounded it into Binky.

She arched her spine and howled as a flare of sludge gray magic poured out of her.

I staggered back as my lungs filled with foul smelling smoke, and everyone else was coughing and spluttering as the toxic, damaged magic Itrix had inflicted on Binky swirled around us.

As the magic cleared, I was overjoyed to see Binky licking Tia's face again as she laughed and kissed her. Tia caught my eye and mouthed thank you.

"Binky, I hate to break up the family reunion, but have you got all your memories back now?" I said.

She kept licking and nuzzling Tia for several more seconds before turning to look at me. Gone was the rage, and there was only happiness in her beautiful amber gaze. "I remember everything. My life with

Tia, how happy we were, and then... him." She glared at Itrix. "He stole me. He kept me in a dark cave and filled me with so much unnatural magic I was sick. He kept doing it again and again until I was convinced all angels had to die. That was my purpose. I was made to destroy. And any angel who got in my path would feel my wrath."

Binky turned back to Tia and flopped her huge paws over her shoulders. Tia took her weight with ease and stood, carrying her like an enormous, furry baby.

I looked at Cythera. "There's your proof. Itrix is a monster. He killed Thomasina, and he wanted you dead, too."

Cythera nodded and summoned more angels to make the arrest. As they swooped in, Itrix shot me a murderous look, but there was nothing he could do.

Finn leaned against the wall next to me and Zandra. "Good work, Juno."

I gave him the catlike version of a smile. "I couldn't have done it without my wonderful witch or my friends. Now, who's hungry?"

❧ ❦

"If we move the three dogs into the large pen, we could divide this one and make more room for the cats. And I reckon the rabbits would be okay in here, too." Finn poked his head out of the barn. He was covered in straw and fur and had never looked happier.

I trotted out of the barn I'd been clearing with Zandra, Adrienne, and Joel. It had been a week since we'd had our slightly awkward family reunion, but life was already returning to strangely normal. Adrienne and Joel were behaving themselves. They were also happy to live in Cannibal Bill's shed and make daily visits to see Zandra.

Zandra hadn't been thrilled about their decision to stay with Cannibal Bill, but she didn't protest too much.

And Adrienne was genuinely happy. Provided she had regular feeds and wasn't startled by loud noises or sudden movements, she felt almost safe to be around. Still, I'd keep a close eye on the new ghoul additions to the family, just in case.

Randal Nix came around the corner with a full wheelbarrow of straw. "Where do you want this?"

"End barn." Finn dusted off his hands and stood beside me and Zandra as he watched Randal work. "When you brought him here, I didn't have him pegged as a guy who liked manual labor, but he's a hard worker."

Zandra grinned. "He surprised me, too. He's been doing that a lot."

Finn glanced at her. "You didn't bring him here for a first date, did you?"

Her cheeks flushed. "It's not a date. You said you needed all hands on deck to deal with the animals Cannibal Bill trapped, so I figured I'd ask if he was free. He said yes."

Finn's expression was rueful. "Well, I do need all the help I can get around here."

Cannibal Bill emerged out of the barn he'd been working in opposite us. "I've got the water supply rigged up in here. What's next?"

"Muck out the barn at the end, and then we need the door reinforced."

Cannibal Bill tipped a salute at Finn then headed off to grab a shovel.

"I can't think of a more fitting punishment for him," I said.

"Same here. I'm not saying I agree with what Angel Force did, letting him off those charges, but he had valuable information on a network we've failed to crack for years. It led to a dozen arrests. And he was open to doing his community service here. I figured it was a good way to rehabilitate him and show him animals are more than just food."

"So much more," I said. "We give your lives meaning."

"I've even introduced him to a singles night at Sorcha's café." Finn leaned in close, a wicked smile on his face. "I just didn't tell him the singles night is for those interested in becoming vegetarians while they look for love."

Zandra roared a laugh while I chuckled.

"You've got to push the boundaries, or we'll never change anything, isn't that right, Juno?" Finn winked at me.

"I couldn't agree more. Push hard when that change is important."

Just as Adrienne and Joel ambled off for their afternoon feed, Tia and Binky arrived. At least, I thought it was Binky. She looked larger, sleeker, and her scars were almost gone. They stood at the gate and looked around, uncertain where to go.

I bounded over to meet them. "Greetings! It's good to see you out and about," I said to Binky. "You look incredible."

Binky raised her chin and opened her mouth to reveal a fine set of restored teeth. "Tia paid for me to have my injuries healed and the transformation magic reversed. She used all her savings."

"It was worth every penny." Tia grinned as she roughly scratched between Binky's ears.

"How are you feeling now you're home?" I asked.

"Perfect. Tia insisted I rest for a couple of days, but as soon as I was strong enough, I had to see you." Binky crouched, so her head was close to the ground. "I owe you my life. If you hadn't figured out Itrix had taken and misused me, the angels would have destroyed me. I was unable to stop my urges, and all I desired was to kill. I'll never forgive myself for that."

Tia rested a hand on Binky's head. "You have nothing to feel bad about. Itrix misused you. But I plan on spending the rest of our time together making that right."

I allowed them a moment of gentleness together before speaking. "I'm always happy to help another familiar, especially one so badly treated. Finn gave us an update on the case this morning. Itrix has confessed to everything. He was driven mad by his wife's tragic death, and all he could think about was getting revenge. He'll never be free, so will never hurt another animal or angel. You have nothing to fear."

"I don't. Not now I'm back with Tia." Binky purred and leaned against her magic user.

Tia threw an arm over Binky's shoulders. "Same here."

"If ever you wish to hang out with me and my magical misfits, you're welcome," I said. "We're an interesting crew. I have a hellhound, a variety of powerful cats, and a honey badger who drops by now and again. There'll always be room for a fabulous cougar."

She nodded. "I might do that. Thanks, Juno. For everything."

Finn and Zandra wandered over and joined us, and they exchanged greetings.

"I'm closing the bakery for a week, and we're heading to Moon Rise. We could both use some relaxation time after everything Binky's been through," Tia said.

"That's a great idea," Zandra said. "Maybe we could do the same, Juno?" Her gaze cut to the path her ghoul mother and Joel had recently trodden.

"Sounds good." My witch had been through troubling times, so I fully supported her self-care.

As they chatted and caught up, my gaze went to a group of people standing by the gates and looking around as if lost.

I took a few steps toward them and inhaled deeply. Non-magicals! What were they doing in Crimson Cove? I crept closer and watched as they studied maps, scratched their heads, and then ambled off. How strange. When I had a moment, I'd see who was in charge of the magical wards around Crimson Cove and make sure there were no problems. We couldn't have large groups of non-magicals wandering in and out freely.

This was a place for magic users. We needed our haven, so we didn't need to hide our powers, and everyone remained safe. And the wards weren't there to keep the non-magicals out. They were there to keep them alive. Magic was powerful, and as Itrix had demonstrated, in the wrong hands, deadly.

"Juno, is something wrong?" Zandra called out to me. "We're going inside for coffee and cake."

I inspected the spot where the non-magicals had stood for a few more seconds then turned away. "So long as there's something fishy, I'm in."

She grinned. "You know I'd never let you down on the treats."

Of course, she never would. I returned to my wonderful witch and my old and new friends. Maybe there were a few loose ends to tie up in Crimson Cove, but I'd deal with them another day.

The angel killer had been stopped, Zandra had her mother back, and my magic was working again.

Life was wickedly good.

About Author

K.E. O'Connor (Karen) is a mystery author living in the beautiful British countryside. She loves all things mystery, animals, and cake.

If you want to practice spells, solve a few murders, and spend time with amazing witches and their talking familiars, join her weekly newsletter.

Sign up today.

Newsletter:
https://BookHip.com/GXDVFRA
Website:
www.keoconnor.com/writing
Facebook:
www.facebook.com/keoconnorauthor

Also By

Witch Haven: Welcome to Witch Haven, where nothing is what it seems. Meet four fabulous witches as they struggle with their destinies, deal with misfiring magic, murder, and the irksome Magic Council.

Crypt Witches: Meet Tempest Crypt, a witch who swallows demons, and Wiggles, her talking hellhound, while you enjoy magical murder and intrigue.

Lorna Shadow: A cozy mystery series set in the fun world of a personal assistant who sees ghosts. Meet Lorna, her ditzy sidekick, Helen, and Flipper, the dog who senses ghosts, as they solve crimes and save the day.

Holly Holmes: An adorable cozy culinary mystery series set in the beautiful English village of Audley St. Mary. Each book is full of treats, murder, and twists. Join Holly and Meatball, her clue-hunting dog, as they solve murders and eat cake.